A perfectly witty satire with a loud all the way through and th trip."

M000115409

—Renee Carlino, *USA Today* Bestselling Author

"There is no doubt about it: Skolnick has a profound ability to transport the reader into her stories. You might laugh until tears run down your cheeks; then you might cry over the injustice of the universe, only to find her narrative weave its way to a denouement that both surprises and enlightens. Each story she tells is a joy to travel."

—C.J. Valles, author of *The Ever Series*

"Corie Skolnick is magic - pure, absolute, gorgeous magic. Her book, *America's Most Eligible*, is brilliant, funny - truly, laugh-out-loud funny - and superbly written, a stunning satire. She can string a few words together, and turn them into perfect gems so effortlessly. Her characters - each and every one - are filled with so much life, so much wit, so much truth. I can promise you, you will both cringe, and nod in agreement with what falls so effortlessly on to the page. Corie is a grand, stupendous writer."

—Amy Ferris, author of *Marrying George Clooney*

America's Most Eligible is a story everyone can relate to. Through wit and authenticity, Corie Skolnick gets to the heart of, "Don't take yourself so seriously." I laughed and cried; was touched and surprised. I loved it and didn't want the book to end."

—Amy Wise, author of *Believe in Yourself ~ Inspire Others ~ Spread Joy!*

Skolnick's sophomore novel, *America's Most Eligible*, is just as touching and enjoyable as *ORFAN*, the author's debut *tour de force*. With jaunty prose, plenty of plot twists, and myriad cultural references that will keep even the most "culturally relevant" readers on their toes, *AME* gives new meaning to the notion that every family has its secrets and skeletons.

Rule #101 (for writers *and* readers everywhere): Read *AME*. Relish. Repeat.

—Laura Dennis, author *Adopted Reality, A Memoir.*

Corie Skolnick's writing is so wonderfully unique, I honesty can't imagine not liking this book, no matter your genre preference. Written through the eyes of Athena Cervantes, the snarky, intelligent journalist and would-be novelist, Skolnick breaks many of the so-called rules writers are warned to heed and proves that if you have a way with words, which this author inarguably does, the "rules" don't apply. Each time I put this book down, I couldn't wait to pick it up again and that's not something I say often, even about books I enjoy. With a plot that gets a little twisty toward the end, *America's Most Eligible* will definitely make you laugh. Entertaining, funny, and smart!

—*Shelly Hickman, author of Vegas to Varanasi*

Other works of fiction by Corie Skolnick:

Orfan

Non-fiction contributions appear in these anthologies:

Adoption Reunion in the Social Media Age
Edited by Laura Dennis

*Adoption Therapy – Perspectives from Clients and Clinicians on
Processing and Healing Post-Adoption Issues*
Edited by Laura Dennis

To Livia [handwritten]

America's
Most
Eligible

a novel by Corie Skolnick

Thank you [handwritten]

for being in my favorite [handwritten]

india street press
a literary imprint of *book club.* [handwritten]

MANNEQUIN VANITY RECORDS
SAN DIEGO, CALIFORNIA
WWW.MANNEQUINVANITYRECORDS.COM

Corie Skolnick [handwritten signature]

This is a work of fiction. Names, characters, places, and incidents are products of the author's imagination or are used fictitiously and are not to be construed as real. Any resemblance to actual events, locales, business establishments, organizations, or persons, living or dead, is entirely coincidental and/or used as public domain in the interest of providing fictional context for time or place.

india street press is an imprint of MANNEQUIN VANITY RECORDS, San Diego, CA.

Copyright © 2015 by Corie Skolnick

india street press
MANNEQUIN VANITY RECORDS trade paperback edition (2015):
ISBN 978-0-9831544-5-7

eBook edition:
ISBN 978-0-9831544-6-4

All rights reserved. No part of this book may be used or reproduced in any manner whatsoever without written permission, except in the case of brief quotations embodied in critical articles and reviews. For information address india street press mannequinvanityrecords@gmail.com

PRINTED IN THE UNITED STATES OF AMERICA

MANNEQUIN VANITY RECORDS is a registered trademark.
Visit india street press at mannequinvanityrecords.com;
facebook.com/mannequinvanityrecords

eBook version published by india street press, May 23, 2015
ISBN 978-0-9831544-6-4

Cover design by
Book design and cover art by Judy Campbell-Smith, india street press.

ACKNOWLEDGEMENTS

Grateful acknowledgment is made to Jane Smiley, the Pulitzer Prize winning author of *A THOUSAND ACRES* and many more fine books of fiction and non-fiction. Ms. Smiley's epic work, *13 WAYS OF LOOKING AT THE NOVEL* provided both inspiration and information to *America's Most Eligible*. Many of the rules in this manuscript are adaptations of Ms. Smiley's work. Other sources include *The Elements of Style* by William Strunk Jr. and E.B. White, *Put One Word After Another: Neil Gaiman's Eight Rules of Writing* by Neil Gaiman, *Writing Rules* by Hilary Mantel and other writers who have had their way with the rules.

Early readers of *America's Most Eligible* provided important feedback and great support. Patty Albright, Tommie Hannigan, Leslie Paonessa, Ellie Hutner, Dr. Jean Phillips, Holly Babe, Lynne Shaw, Andrea Zinder, and of course the generous writers who appear on the back cover of this book, C.J. Valles, Amy Ferris, Amy Wise, Laura Dennis, Shelly Hickman, Bridget Sampson and Renee Carlino. Thanks to Tracey and Robb Navrides for expert consultation for all things Greek.

Judy Campbell-Smith at india street press, Mannequin Vanity Records edited this manuscript, formatted both versions and gently steered some vital changes to the original book to make it much better. Any mistakes are mine alone and probably exist only because I did not take her advice where it would have been better to do so.

Finally, thank you to Pablo who makes this writing life possible and life in general so much better in so many ways.

For Cat and Jake

America's Most Eligible

ONE

"I am a writer."

Rule #27: Begin at the beginning. As you write your first word you are embracing the novel's greatest tradition, that of obscure beginnings. No other art is so simple or so cheap to engage in as literature.
- From *99 Awesome Rules to Follow When Writing Your First Great Novel*
by Patricia Olivia Orloff

Twenty minutes west of Sacramento via U.S. Interstate Highway 80, smack dab in the middle of California, the not-so-little college town of Davis is nothing but an inescapable inferno throughout the month of August. It is not widely known, but it is spectacular when it happens, that on the hottest of those dog days, mature live oak trees have been known to spontaneously combust into frightening, unpredictable, two-story, street-side torches on the University of California, Davis campus.

One such shimmering day, in the earliest part of the first decade of the new millennium, the newly-appointed chair of the English Department's prestigious Creative Writing Program, Professor Patricia Olivia Orloff, strode obliviously right past the arboreal conflagration on Shields Avenue, bounded purposefully up the stairs of Mrak Hall, and breezed into her assigned classroom at the very top of the hour. Professor Orloff would become famous, among other qualities, for her punctuality. She was never late, but neither was she ever early. Patty Orloff was aggressively ON TIME – for class and all other appointments. It was a *thing*.

I was in that classroom that day as it was the very first day of graduate school for me along with seventeen other eager co-horts, each one of us handpicked by the new chair herself in the early wake of her third novel's Pulitzer Prize win. The excellent reputation of the U.C. Davis Creative Writing Program was well established, but make no mistake, every one of the eighteen people in the room that hot August day were all at Davis for just one reason: Patricia Olivia Orloff.

Already an ascending and shining star in the literary world at large, on UCD's campus, Patty Orloff was destined to become not only a bona fide celebrity but also a true and undeniable *character*. The kind of character you want to know if you aspire to be one yourself, and the kind of person who can open certain doors for aspiring writers. We were there early and eager to be schooled. For the most part.

Picture it. It is the inaugural day of the writing program under Patty Orloff, and all save one of our full complement have been anxiously assembled around the room's ridiculously large round table for nearly thirty minutes before the emergency vehicle sirens herald the arrival of the city's volunteer fire department on the street below. Upstairs on the third floor of Mrak Hall the sirens announce the opening of the classroom door. *Weeeeahhhhh, weeeeahhhh* – then suddenly - *WEEEEEEAAAHHHHH!* Patty Orloff appears as if institutionally framed by the doorway, shod in a pair of hot pink, highly polished and ornately tooled cowboy boots, her tall, slender frame garbed in flowing, filmy garments of questionable taste. She is waving a short stack of syllabi (printed on paper that matches – exactly – the color of her boots). She enters the classroom extravagantly and allows the door to click closed behind her before she steps forward and draws back one of only two unoccupied seats. Seats which, in preparation for this exact moment, she had herself in the earliest morning hours carefully counted, name-labeled, and obsessively arranged and re-arranged around the table.

Now, she pauses for a very long moment–long enough to make significant eye contact with each one of us and to stare unhappily at the only empty chair. Diametrically opposed to the seat that she will eventually take herself, the empty one mocks. The continuing sweep of her eyes is an unmistakable accusation. Finally she drops the pink pages onto the tabletop and leans over them; she places her well-ornamented, beautiful, big hands opened wide, palm down – protectively – on either side of the neat, bright fan of paper. If you are counting (I was), you count no fewer than eight rings adorning her hands, all semi-precious stones in crappy settings.

We begin to squirm uncomfortably when Patty Orloff pauses again to stare for some time at the empty chair. A troubled expression mars her pretty face. Someone has failed to show. *Someone* has failed to show.

How the rest of that first day went:

Or, what I learned on my first day of graduate school:

I learned first that the kind of heat that can cause a tree to spontaneously combust in the open air makes the application of mascara nothing more than a regrettable joke about personal vanity. Also, I learned that higher education can be uncomfortable, even painful. For instance, Mrak Hall's notoriously inadequate AC system huffed and whined loudly but did nothing to cool the classroom even slightly. While my fellows and I grew slick with perspiration, we struggled to give our professor the kind of attention we each thought worthy of the Pulitzer Prize. In a room full of writers,

5

that kind of attention translates into the kind that only a world-class mime on Lincoln Center's stage commands. It is effort that smells of reverence.

Professor Orloff nodded an acknowledgment of our efforts, sighed deliberately, and straightened to her full height, pulling her hands together into a gaudy prayer. Her bejeweled index fingers gently tapped her chin. Notably, *her* thick application of mascara was not running. Once she was absolutely certain that all eyes in the room were upon her, she growled an incantation in a Scotch-soaked voice. The very first words most of us heard from her rust-colored lips:

"I…am…a…writer."

She took another lengthy pause and another deep, deep breath. One more time, her deliberate and inscrutable gaze slowly swept the entire circle of sweating, nervous faces, stopping again at the empty seat. Her azure eyes were unblinking and just then, no hint of any kind of smile played upon her polished lips. It seemed as though the empty chair and its missing occupant caused her to feel some feeling in excess of distress. Something more like genuine physical pain. She sighed before she spoke again.

"If *you* have not already done so, you should start thinking of yourself as a *writer,* and calling yourself a *writer – today!* Nothing else. You have no other identity. You're nobody's daughter. You're nobody's son. You're nobody's spouse. You're nobody's friend or lover. You are not really even a graduate student at the University of California. You are certainly not a part-time barista at Starbucks, even if you *are* a barista at Starbucks. As of today, my dear friends, writing is your complete and only identity and your sole occupation. You are writers."

Suddenly, her lovely face tilted up toward the stained ceiling tile overhead. It was as if, just then, that an inaudible celestial voice called to her; her body swayed, and then ever so slowly she lowered her head and let her trembling hands hover over the syllabi, looking for all the world like a shaman performing a divination ritual. Her lips parted.

"Over the next two years you *will* write for me five good and publishable short stories and by the end of next year I want forty good, *great* pages – no less – of a goddamn novel." She paused. "If today you have any doubts about being capable of this, I want you to have the *cojones* to get up right now. And please. Leave us."

In the split second that Patty turned toward the exit, extending a rigid arm indicating the direction that we should depart should we suddenly determine on second thought that we weren't up to snuff, the classroom door banged open and a boyish looking and disheveled man pitched himself forward into the room. He caught his balance and hitched a ratty backpack higher onto his hunched shoulder. Patty shook her head in a pantomime of disbelief, ran a hand through her long red hair and then blinked at our latecomer with an elaborately uncomprehending look on her face. Hushed, nervous laughter rippled around the table. Patty's head tilted slowly like that of an intelligent canine. It all seemed to me at the time like a tiny piece of amusing theatre.

"May I help you?" Patty drawled at last.

"I'm Burke," the boy/man replied without artifice. No one else in the room dared to even breathe.

"How lovely for you, Mr. Burke," Patty told him. Then, leaning in to the center of the table slightly, with an unmistakable element of menace, she said, "You are very late." Burke nodded, then again hitched the backpack higher on his shoulder.

"Fire," Burke said and shrugged. Patty pursed her lips, shook her head and signaled with a wide arc of her still extended finger that he should claim the empty chair. While he did so she gathered up the pink pages of the syllabi and pressed them to her chest possessively.

7

I may have been the only one then to see how the briefest flash of mirth seemed to play in her eyes because I believe that the men in the room were all busy watching the women who were all taking their first heartsick glances at Burke. Within a second, that rarest shard of Patty's revealed emotion had instantly been re-assembled into an expression on her face of one hundred percent enigma. I found myself wondering, what *was* she thinking?! It would not be the last time I wondered.

Later on, once we were all made well aware of Patty Orloff's unbending rules, (Patty had rules for everything), we would marvel that she hadn't thrown the tardy Burke out on his unapologetic ass right then and there. Inexplicably, she hadn't. She had only nodded and allowed him to open his backpack and withdraw a fresh yellow legal pad and a stubby #2 pencil before she succumbed to her own seat (and the heat, too), little beads of perspiration finally sparkling on her meticulously waxed upper lip. When Burke was settled and the room was again silent, Patty finally distributed the neon pink syllabi.

Rule #59: You are courting trouble if you write a first person narrative. But, if you must, don't chat up your reader like the "two" of you are sharing a beer. That worked only once really well and, need I remind you? You are not J.D. Salinger.

How's that, dear reader, for a dramatic opening scene? Does it immediately *pull you in*? It is all true, every last word. I swear it, and, *thank you, Oprah*, I have at least one million little reasons for telling nothing but the truth (now).

I fell in love with Burke of course. And I mean madly, insanely, incurably. I would soon learn that almost everyone does. You, of course, saw that coming. But, I'm getting ahead of myself. I will get to Burke's part in this story presently.

First, Patricia Olivia Orloff.

More about her:

As the bulk of this story transpires in California and as such things are of great importance to Californians, begin again, dear reader, by conjuring a picture of Patty's principle mode of transportation: a 1973 BMW, the boxy model in the Crayola Crayon color honestly called by the manufacturer "yellow-orange". It was a color generally (except for that particular vehicle) seen only on city taxicabs. For an automobile as old as it was, and it was just shy of thirty years old by the time I entered the writing program at Davis, it was one damn minty vehicle. And, like its owner, it was unique at UCD. Somehow, when Patty stooped to unlock the driver's side door of that Beemer you could imagine the ungainly young woman she had certainly been as a teenager when she acquired it: almost six-feet tall and ridiculously slender, with prodigious quantities of unruly, red hair cascading down her back, and sapphire blue eyes rimmed in kohl. Except for a few delicate laugh lines around her eyes, and one small dent on the front passenger side bumper, Patty and her car had both aged with exceeding grace.

Let's just say, in terms of appearance alone (never-minding her significant literary accomplishments), Patricia Olivia Orloff stood out at UC Davis. Regarding her looks, sometimes Patty herself would be heard saying to people, "I'm nothing to look at," but most everyone agreed that this was downright disingenuous of her. Almost forty by the time she got the Pulitzer, Patty was still quite the looker, if also, as already duly established, outrageously flamboyant in her sartorial efforts.

While the good professor was more than circumspect about her actual origins, (nobody I knew knew from whence she came), it was her shockingly grandiose lifestyle that promoted a lot of speculation about a mysterious, untraceable inheritance, perhaps one generated by a great literary legacy, some speculated. A few purported, for instance, that she was somehow an heiress to the Hemingway fortunes while others claimed that she was the illegitimate great grand-daughter of William Faulkner. Patty Orloff herself was unforthcoming whenever the subject arose. Wherever from her fortunes actually did originate, it was in part the unorthodox attire she favored that supported an amusing supplemental theory about her that almost certainly included the inherited closet contents of an old, hippie era drag-queen. Undeniably, in some way or another she had scored an impressive collection of the worst garments known to mankind from every post mid-century decade: part Elton as Liberace, and part pre-fatty Elvis (circa Viva Las Vegas days) with a healthy dash of Prince, or maybe it was Michael Jackson sans glove, thrown into the mix. I should think that the Smithsonian will one day be interested in acquiring Patty Orloff's apparel. Not everyone at Davis, few in fact, especially most of those among the bad-tweed-set in the English Department, truly appreciated her dedicated non-conformity. Nevertheless, Patty wore every outlandish garment with *élan* and always, no matter the weather outside, with one pair or another from her rainbow collection of hand-tooled cowboy boots and an unambiguous fuck off if you don't like it attitude. I loved her instantly for all of that.

Just a bit more about Patty's dubious lifestyle:

It included the hosting of weekly Friday night salons in a big, old, rented, ramshackle house in Marin. Inside the party the conversation was literate and heady. Good label booze flowed generously until it ran out or the sun came up, and outside under the eaves of a portico, the smokers congregated like so many disenfranchised KGB confederates and the sweet smell of high-quality weed permeated the neighborhood air like night-blooming jasmine. An eclectic bunch braved the shittiest weather to attend each week. A very strict hierarchy of intimacy existed among them that may or may not have established itself *after the Prize,* and you could detect who was who in the various circles of ever-shifting personnel around Patty by the simple way they addressed her.

The inner circle had more students in it than you might have thought it should – past and current – and we were instructed to just call her Patty, but there were also some pretty weighty "bigs" in the word-world whose work dominated the credible literary journals at the time and who often drove up from the city to rub elbows, drink free hard liquor, and roll Patty's dandy pot into fatty spliffs. Acting like they were slumming when they were around her students, that contingent tended to call Patty by her last name, or they called her POO, a nickname we were told she had come by at an east coast private boarding school during her mysterious childhood years.

The Davis crowd were of like mind in maintaining that those writer-ly jerks were, to a (wo)man, unlikable sycophants and posers and we often vowed to each other to never be as creepily elitist as they were, and to never let them forget that we were breathing down their crêpe-y necks with our youth and our fearsome, indefatigable and superior writing talents. (Sadly, as time wore on, we were, if anything, proven even more competitive and even less kind toward one another.)

Rule #5: Do not begin a story (short or long) with a secondary or peripheral character.

Almost immediately, the U.C. Davis writing program, with its demanding figurehead and unforgiving peer criticism, washed out thirty-three percent of the people who'd been sitting around that big round table. Six of our cohorts were gone before the end of our first semester...who knows where? Vanished completely and never to be heard from again, in print or anywhere else. The rest of us simply spread out to claim more inches around the circumference of the table and never did we discuss (at any time) the awful attrition rate among us. After graduation, we willfully forgot the names of the deserters before we had even framed our sparkly new MFAs and hung them up on our rented walls.

Within six years after graduation, another third of the original group (note: not the best writers among us by far, and not me or Burke) did, in fact, publish their short stories in various literary journals, and those same five did, also, publish the novels they had begun under Patty Orloff's aegis. A couple of them even had brief – very brief I have to say – episodes on the *New York Times* bestseller list joining the ranks of the writers we had, as students, once loved to loathe. I can only assume that they returned to the big house in Marin on a regular basis. I did not. Nor did the others who also let their short stories and their first good, *great* pages grow moldy with apathy. (It turns out, when it comes to publishing novels, that there is plenty of enmity and jealousy to go around.)

So, what *had* become of the rest of us? The bitter, envious final 33% who, like myself, were presumably all still slaving away on what had become of our original forty good, *great* pages because we just wouldn't (or couldn't) give up on Patty Orloff's injunction. In part, that is the substance of this manuscript. At least in terms of my own professional trajectory. I can report that (according to near daily random Google searches) the lucky among this subset (like me) did find employment at day jobs reasonably related to writing, hope and ambition surviving weakly beside each other for lo, those half dozen years. I assume that we were tracking each other's lack of progress or success on social media. (I certainly was.) Only Burke among that group remained completely incommunicado and somehow off the internet. Rumor held that he was teaching at some mid-country college, but nobody knew which one.

I hadn't even tried to publish my five shorts. (I knew others had because they sometimes confessed in late night, alcohol saturated monologues the perils of literary rejection.) The original forty pages of my good, *great* novel had grown slowly and steadily like a stubborn fungus on the same ancient hard drive to an unwieldy twelve-hundred page manuscript utterly devoid of cohesion. I was perpetually promising myself an upgrade in technology, but not until I finished my novel. A new laptop was to be my reward. Meanwhile I worked at my horrible-paying day job writing feature articles for the *Oakland Tribune* just to cover the incidental Cup 'O Noodles, and I shamefully let the rent on my basement apartment in Berkeley be subsidized by my generous stepfather. My only redemption was that I didn't have a blog and I never published anything on *Huffington Post.*

Fate would kindly never cause me to accidentally bump into anyone from the Davis program even once in vivo. I did sometimes receive strange, subtly-insulting emails from a wide variety of them.

"Fuck, Athena! Are you still working at the Trib?!!! I'm on a book tour now for (insert NYT best selling title here). Let's grab a drink when I get to SF."

And, *"Hey, nice feature on the black bag lady with the harelip!"*

One time, a mysterious text from an unknown number quoting from a recent feature I'd done, arrived anonymously in my messages:

"So, Athena! u R still aliv. had heard u were ded. R u riting anything...besides this shit?"

And more stuff like that.

I didn't ever bother, not once, to respond to any of those emails or text messages. I might have responded to only two people from Davis, but I hadn't received even one word from neither

Burke, nor Patty Orloff. Not until – and this is where my story really begins – I wrote a feature article for the Tribune's Sunday Supplement about the first Latina Fremont Rodeo Queen.

That story changed everything.

In accompaniment, the paper ran the queen's spectacular, front-page, full color picture. It was a great photo. A prizewinning photo. It perfectly captured the ineffable emotions of the only girl-child of a migrant, Mexican field worker to reign over Fremont's rodeo. Her regal image in awesomely garish rodeo queen regalia froze her stern countenance atop a beautiful, be-ribboned Arabian stallion. On the day the story ran, without a single word exchanged between us since my Davis days, Patty Orloff emailed me.

"Nice boots.   - Best personal regards, P.O.O."

Rule #13: The beginning of your novel is the most important part. By the end of the first paragraph, your reader should have a good idea what the story is going to be about. This is critical.

By the time that the good people of Fremont, California had seen fit to choose Lucy Consuela Rojillo Molina as their first ever non-Caucasian Rodeo Queen, and my editor, one Howard R. Falkenhorst had assigned her story to me, I did not know myself anymore what the silly novel languishing on my old laptop was really about.

Lucy's story created a hullabaloo at the Trib. My features were upgraded to the status of a column, I got a by-line, and more than two hundred papers all across the U.S. asked for syndication. Regarding my novel, I suddenly understood the meaning of the expression, "a come-to-Jesus moment". I had stockpiled more than a hundred and fifty versions of *Wooden Nickels'* first chapter. Like Joseph Grand, I started over and over and over, never satisfied with my beginning. My "good, *great* novel" was foundering on the shoals of dubious uncompleted manuscripts.

The Lucy story gave me a tiny little taste of what recognition might be like. I liked it. I liked it a lot. These new developments at the day job gave me pause. A genuine identity crisis. Was I really a writer? Meaning, a novelist. Or, was I a journalist?

Was a journalist after all a real *writer?* I knew how the Davis people would answer that question. I knew what Burke would say. I knew what Patty Orloff would say, too.

Rule #44: Avoid clunky inter-textuality! Nobody cares that you've read all the right books.

Alright, scratch the reference to Monsieur Grand. And, forget that I even mentioned *Catcher In The Rye.* Also, who reads Camus any more anyway besides the Comparative Lit nerds? French majors and Philosophy undergraduates? You? Whatever. The point is, too many years had elapsed since the day of the burning tree before I met Queen Lucy. My professional life was definitely in crisis. I had suffered the indignity of watching my peers reap success (and in some cases wealth) as fiction writers while I harbored insane jealousy in my heart and a trove of un-publishable crap on my ancient old Dell. (Incidentally, I was not alone. I happen to know that every other so-called writer at the Trib secretly stored manuscripts unseen by human beings.)

My personal life? What personal life? I was fast approaching the age when an unmarried woman begins to at least occasionally contemplate the viability of her eggs.

Rule #21: Backstory is the bane of plot. If the stuff in your backstory is crucial to your plot, it should be in the story. Ditch the backstory and rewrite it in the story.

On certain days we wrote flash fiction in Patty Orloff's seminars. She often used writing prompts to get us started, to get the juices flowing. Sometimes silly, (Describe a day in your life from your dog's point of view), and sometimes ridiculous, (Write from beyond the grave about the person responsible for your untimely demise). But once in while she courted the realm of real life, relational darkness, (Develop a fictional character based on a family member who has betrayed your affection and your devotion. Describe them in detail and just let the story happen around them).

Rule #1: Write what you know you give a fuck about. Get to know about it, and write what you know. Don't try to be right. Be clear.

About William Byrne-McGuire, the artist formerly known as my father. (Note, dear reader: for the most part this factual matter has been lifted intact from the pages of *Wooden Nickels* - my first good, *great* (unpublished) novel.)

If you asked the man himself, Billy's earliest years were an admirably open book. Throughout my childhood he loved to entertain all comers with long rambling tales featuring himself as a sympathetic or amusingly likable character. He often included in such stories other colorful Byrne-McGuire extended family members, all of whom, (the ones still living anyway), live in various cities on the eastern seaboard. Above all, Billy was a raconteur.

In the early part of the nineteenth century, the Byrnes were an Irish Catholic construction clan from upstate New York and the McGuires were somehow in possession of a granite quarry. Through dint of their mutual hard labor, more than a little luck, and a common streak of sociopathy, the Byrne-McGuires had managed together to work their way into wealth and influence building New York City skyscrapers.

A few short generations later, Billy's cohort of Byrnes and McGuires were an inbred Celtic collection of the idle wealthy, spending the bulk of their time in one or another Long Island community country-club clubhouse after nailing down Ivy League educations. Billy's own father, a man ahead of his time and a dedicated black sheep, had reportedly been paid a generous stipend for the whole of his adult life just to be good enough to stay the hell away from the family business, and this he accomplished with a talent that often got him into minor scrapes involving incalculable quantities of alcoholic beverages. Poppy died, inebriated, at the wheel of a brand new Cadillac on the Jersey Turnpike the year before Billy moved to Los Angeles. Every one of my grandfather's progeny, all of my aunts and uncles (the ones not yet in AA by the time I was aware of such things), were likewise all intrepid Irish boozers. But Billy? Billy was their sovereign, whom the family sorely missed when he moved west.

Unashamed that he was a college dropout and unrepentant that he had also scammed his draft board and gotten himself a bogus 4F deferment to avoid going to Viet Nam, Billy liked to say that he'd left the Big Apple in the dead of night one step ahead of the law and another two ahead of a redhead's husband, and neither of these claims seemed at all farfetched to anyone who knew Billy Byrne-McGuire.

Rule #84: Trust me on this one: be not tempted to write about writers. Writers are the most boring people on earth (especially novelists). Who else sits alone day in and day out and does nothing more substantial than make shit up?

I was born into a pack of writers. Billy met my mother, Diana Ward, and the woman who would become her lifelong best friend, Brenda Goldhor in the nineteen seventies at an evening

UCLA extension class that promised to teach the participants how to write a screenplay in just six weeks. *"In Just Six Weeks!"* The girls both had useless liberal arts degrees from public colleges and Billy had worked his way up through the mailroom of a Wilshire Boulevard ad agency to write insipid ad copy for dog food commercials. Though on precious little otherwise throughout their long friendship, regarding their impressions of my father that fateful first night at UCLA, my mother and Brenda agreed: Billy Byrne-McGuire was both exceedingly good looking and endearingly glib, and when he walked into that Westwood classroom, the heart of every single heterosexual woman within skipped a beat.

Billy was to be the only one of the three of them to realize the UCLA promise. The family legend, written and oft repeated by Billy himself, told the tale that he sold the script for *Webster's Peace* in the early part of the same year that I was born, timing which led him to say ever after that he'd fathered twins that year, Oscar and Athena.

Webster's Peace is still regarded by many in cinematic circles as the quintessential anti-war movie. I've been told that Billy Byrne-McGuire is taught as a subject in film schools with whole seminars dedicated to *Webster's Peace*. He still has fans in hard core movie buff circles. But, listen up: Billy Byrne-McGuire never sold another written word. Nothing. Ever. He sold that one script, earned an Academy Award for it, and then he diligently, but with complete futility, pretended to work on his "next project" for more than two decades. An interminable fallow period which, believe you me, haunted me more than just a little bit as time marched on after my Davis days. I worried about a genetic writer's block. (I feared I was my father's child.) The difference between us was that while I quickly started to feel like a fraud when referring to myself as "a writer", Billy had felt no such compunction. In fact, all through my formative years, the years before I knew the truth about him,

Billy continued to call himself a writer long after he'd failed to produce even one single salable sentence. He worked into every conversation lasting longer than five minutes that he was an "Oscar-winning screenwriter". In actuality up there in Malibu he was mostly just carousing with a faithless entourage of bosomy starlets, other screenwriting hacks and movie star wannabes whose careers proceeded to deteriorate apace with Billy's own. I know that now, though for most of my childhood, Billy was a small "g" god to me and I was one of his most devoted disciples. Gods do fall though. And unfortunately for poor Billy, failure in the movie business can be easily tracked these days via the Internet Movie Database. Any fool with access to the internet from anywhere in the whole wide world can look him up and see: Billy's page still sadly reports his one and only film credit.

Meanwhile, you'd be right to ask, if only out of passing curiosity about such things, how did the man survive? And by "survival" I mean in the purest economic sense of the word. That is a very good question and the answer to it is the stuff of Hollywood legend. It turned out that (fortunately in the extreme for Billy) by unlikely prescience, good fortune, and sheer fluke in equal proportions, his agent had negotiated an unprecedented and unheard of deal at the time for a completely unknown screenwriter. The studio heads that produced *Webster's Peace* never expected it to be the classic it became. The negotiations were all in Billy's favor. The points on the back end of his deal gave him the monetary means of one or two grand years of true Hollywood excess following his divorce from my mom, and then, after those scant plum years, enough money trickled in to provide a meager means of survival that has endured, I am supposing, until this very day.

The one smart thing Billy did was take a good chunk of what he'd gotten from the *Webster's* sale and he plunked down cash for the modest bungalow on the beach in the Malibu Colony where he pretty much has just stayed put since. Throughout the years, Billy's faithful, (me included), generally went to Mecca.

Rule #92: Dear Lord, if you have just a shred of decency, avoid cliché. Please!

Hollywood in the seventies was an unkind environment for women who wanted to do anything in the industry other than act. If you were female, the smart thing to do was to marry well and Brenda Goldhor did that almost immediately when an acquaintance introduced her to the fabulously wealthy, Mr. Eddie Fineman. Eddie's money isn't film industry money and none of us really knows where his wealth comes from. It could be blood diamonds or some such scurrilous stuff for all we know. Brenda, to her credit, kept her hand in and continued to write, not willing to rest on Eddie's cash, even after she had baby Rose. She knocked out a few more screenplays, romantic comedies that basically recounted in detail every aspect of her personal life (Before Eddie Fineman) which I shall spare you, but nothing she wrote was ever so much as optioned. Billy always used the word "hack" when mentioning Brenda, if he bothered to talk about her, but my mother was kinder, calling Boo a "very creative story-teller". Eventually, a daytime soap opera hired my Aunt Boo to make dialogue "sparkle", but she flamed out doing that within a year or two. She got pregnant again, had Josh, and eventually an "angel investor" funded her fledgling casting agency, but by now everybody knows that it was Eddie's money, not any kind of real business, that kept the doors to Fineman Creative Artists open.

Ironically, my mom was the only one of the three of them to abandon the idea of writing movie scripts completely. She later called that UCLA class the biggest mistake she ever made, and I still don't know precisely what she meant when she said that. She would not elaborate and I guess I really never wanted clarification since at least one interpretation would have been injurious to my self-esteem for obvious reasons.

When it came to any personal history, compared to Billy and to Boo, my mother was a sphinx. You want to know something of her background? Tough shitzkies. As my mother would have it, she had been an only child of two only children who both died prematurely when she was in her late teens. Period. End of pathetic story. She had worked her way through a public state college, reluctantly she had admitted to Phi Beta Kappa once, and she did not like canned green peas. The short unremarkable history of Diana Ward. She had no baggage.

After divorcing Billy, something she did before I was upright on two feet, my mother did an immediate about-face and went back to grad school to get her PhD in Counseling Psychology. As you will soon learn, her education turned out to be one hell of a "fall back". In the meantime, she and Billy were awarded joint legal custody of me. Naturally, Billy alone was awarded custody of Oscar and he was a devoted father to him as Oscar was maintenance-free. His visitation to me was erratic at best during those earliest years. He was living Malibu life large while my mom and I spent them in a one-bedroom, student-ghetto apartment, kind of barely getting by on student loans. I was the quintessential sad little kid, pining away in the living room window of her shabby, single-mother home every single Friday night for a larger-than-life daddy who, more often than not, just didn't show up. But I never gave up hoping he would. I still remember that hope from those days. I can almost taste it.

Soon after she finished graduate school my mom met and fell in love with Mike, the wonderful, perfect, handsome and accomplished Dr. Miguel Cervantes. She was an intern at a psych clinic in downtown LA and one of her supervisors set them up. She called Mike "Mommy's Special Friend" and had I not been such a clueless little dipshit, I would have known that he was nailing her routinely on the pull out sofa ten minutes after *"Goodnight Moon"* and lights out for little Athena.

Things get a little hazy for me during that period when she was in between marriages. I do remember with some startling clarity a particularly nasty fight my mom had once with Billy. A big one. Billy wanted to take me back to New York for a month in the summer for a gigantic Byrne-McGuire family bacchanal and my mother did not want to let me go. I sided with him because I was an idiot and when my mother drove us to LAX with tears streaming down her cheeks, I didn't know then that there had also been a whole other fight. One between my mother and Dr. Mike. I had actually failed to take note that he hadn't been coming around too much. Well, you know, kids are so self-centered. But, I figured out eventually that Mike and Mom must have made up from their fight while I was in New York, because a month later (a long, miserable, awful, terrible, horrible, no good, very bad month on Fire Island – all credit to Judith Viorst that is due), when I got back to LA from my summer exile with Billy, my mom and Mike were all-of-the-sudden getting married. Mommy's Special Friend, Dr. Cervantes was going to be my new daddy.

A few things from that period are crystal clear in my memory. The dress I wore for the wedding is one: pink and almost long enough to touch my tiny pink patent leather shoes. And the fact that Rosie Fineman got to wear the same dress and I didn't want her to, but she was Aunt Boo's daughter and so that made her kind of like a cousin, so she got to be a flower girl, too. But, I remember hating, just hating, that Rosie got to wear the same beautiful pink dress (my dress).

Also, some things you can never forget, no matter how hard you try. Like how hard it was for my mom to win over Mike's parents. Especially Abuela. People say things in front of quiet kids that they maybe shouldn't say, so I heard stuff in overhead conversations that let me know that the genteel and very Catholic Sr. Cervantes were initially not too keen on their golden boy marrying a divorcée who had a child. I guess they wanted better for him. It was just hard to be burdened with that kind of knowledge. I'm just saying. So, I figured out early on in the way a smart kid can that I was not in any way considered a bonus in the package Mike was getting. The *abuelos* came around. They did. But in the beginning, that was a really hard thing for me to know about the only grandparents I would ever really have.

Right after the wedding we moved with Mike to the house in the Palisades where I grew up. It was just a few convenient miles down Pacific Coast Highway from Billy's place in Malibu, ostensibly making it easier for him to maintain some visitation. It was a straight shot up Sunset Boulevard to Beverly Hills where Boo's family had already grown to four. My mom almost instantly had another child too, Miguel Jr., who was, from the get-go, very much unlike his sulky, shy and brooding sister.

Then, like literary lightning striking, Diana Ward-Cervantes, who had never once in my presence called herself a writer, became an overnight literary sensation with excellent reviews in *Time*, *Newsweek* and *Publishers' Weekly*. And also there was that whole feature once in *People*. The *Los Angeles Times Calendar Magazine* called her "the Paula Abdul of self-help". She had cleverly turned the research for her doctoral dissertation into a best-selling nonfiction trilogy: *Waltzing Alone; Surviving Divorce, Waltzing With Mr. Right; Marriage the Second Time Around* and *Waltzing With Kids; Keeping Your Love Life Vital While Stepping Over Rugrats*. Nothing sells better than recovery from capital D - Divorce in LA. Nobody sells it better than a one-time Hollywood wife turned therapist. You can't shake a stick in that town without pointing at some studio mogul's ex-wife turned shrink.

When the first book came out I was in third grade. I can remember looking forward to her launch because I thought I might learn something personal about my mother from reading her author bio. How sad is that? It wasn't really so much that her personal history was off-limits. There simply was no personal history. (She said.) An author bio was conspicuously missing from all her books. But the critics loved her. She was a really facile writer and she could make even the tragedy of family dissolution quite funny. Throw in that she was smart and a good person to boot and also that she was a MILF before anybody knew what a MILF was – a perfect mother was a painful cross for me to bear.

Even Billy had to admit that my mother's life, and especially her career, looked pretty damn perfect just then. He was beside himself with envy and it caused him to take a sudden interest in me, I suppose as a perverse way to harass my mom. I eventually punished her for her perfection by loving Billy.

It was our splendid little collusion to exclude her. We said mean things about her books. We said she wasn't a *real* writer.

Oh, I guess it would be fair to give me a little bit of credit for, early on, especially right after my mom married Mike and my brother came along, trying to be a mobile Switzerland, shuttling diplomatically back and forth between our perfect house and perfect-looking nuclear family in the Palisades and Billy's seedy existence and decrepit beach house a few miles up the coast highway. But then, as my mom's career and fortunes only continued to improve and the quality of Billy's life only declined, the discrepancies between my disparate worlds were harder and harder to ignore. Something dynamic had to be done. Somewhere in my early teens, I guess it was during that awful period when I started blaming my mother for everything, truly even the most random shit, it was then that I wholly bought into Billy's portrayal as a sensitive and sympathetically woebegone victim of my mother's callous and fickle natures. It made me mean. I'm not proud.

Thus, throughout most of my tortured adolescence, when I was at home in the Palisades, I was a cliché of teenaged angst and rebellion while concurrently, up in Malibu, I had joined the cultish ranks of Billy's worshipful minions; he could do no wrong. While I gave my mom (and Mike) a ton of shit when I was at home, up at the beach, I was Billy's good little Princess. To all concerned parties it looked as if I simply adored my father and forgave him his excesses and his failures alike. I guess I preferred his colorful backstory and his alcohol fueled ebullience to my mother's circumspect, even secretive, origins, and especially her thoughtful sobriety. In contrast to Billy, Diana Ward-Cervantes was, like I told you, a goddamned sainted sphinx. How does any girl live up to that?

Rule #10: Chronology is important! Leaping back and forth on the timeline will confuse your readers and generally annoy reviewers and critics. Avoid using flashbacks!

So, the time has come to reveal the chronicle of Billy Byrne-McGuire's perfidy.

For a very long time, I believed, because of something Aunt Boo once let slip, that Hugh Hefner was primarily responsible for my parent's divorce. This turned out to be not entirely untrue because if Billy hadn't been at the party at the Playboy mansion on the night I was born, let's face it, perhaps my mother would have never discovered what a lying, cheating dog he was. (I now present the tawdry, detailed Quick & Dirty on how that nasty little episode of the perfidious Billy Byrne McGuire coincided with the night of my birth. Again, some details lifted from my everlasting Work In Progress, *Wooden Nickels.*)

The buzz circulating Hollywood about *Webster's Peace* got Billy an invite to the Playmate of the Year party at Hugh Hefner's mansion in Beverly Hills as a product of pure public relations bullshit. Billy, the studio said, was a movie biz up-and-comer – destined for great things. The party was nothing my mother had any interest whatsoever in attending, even if she hadn't been almost nine months pregnant at the time. Anyway, she waved Billy on out the door and ten minutes after he left the house for Hef's, her water broke. She called Boo, who left the infant Rose in the care of her nanny to rush down the hill and ferry my mother in the nick of time to the hospital. From the hospital waiting room, while Mom was delivering me, Boo put in two calls: one to Billy's agent, another to the studio. Long story short, whoever the individual was that found Billy (compromised as he was in that moment by the current, very young Playmate of the Month attached to his penis), that unknown individual turned out to be less than discreet. Word got around oh so fast, and in an unbelievable turn of fate, Mom's lawyer served Billy with divorce papers on the very same day that the headlines in *Variety* announced his Oscar nomination for Best Original Screenplay. (Unlike her first husband, Mama did not fool around.) A kind of sadly trite Hollywood tale this is for sure, but not in any way really Hef's fault.

But, we are talking about Billy Byrne-McGuire here. And, I was not a stupid kid. Over the course of my childhood, I had seen enough of Billy's shenanigans up close and personal to glean that he might not have exactly been husband of the year material. His marital infidelity, though bothersome as it was in retrospect, would not have been such a deal breaker between him and me. No, the perfidy of which I speak was a wholly different kind of betrayal, which was of the most unforgivable sort (just ask any writer).

Rule #33: Beware the hazards of confusing the terms "between" and "among" when describing the actions and emotions shared and experienced within groups of two or more characters.

Ask any three people to describe any shared experience and you will almost certainly get three wildly differing accounts. Add to that simple reality of individual perspective the fact that there were so many vital secrets shared between Billy, Brenda and Diana, and it's almost impossible now to know who among them knew exactly what or when. Oh, they had secrets among them and secrets between them. That one thing I know now to be absolutely true. Big, big secrets. All three of them. In hindsight, it's a small wonder that somebody didn't crack long, long before Brenda did as indeed she did (just a little) the night of Rosie's gala eighteenth birthday party. It was Brenda then, under the influence of several liters of Kendall Jackson (and motivated by the evening's unplanned theme no doubt), who pulled back the curtain to reveal the *real* Billy Byrne-McGuire to me.

Rule #20: Dropdowns will be your undoing.

My engagement to Roger Bernstein (no ring, mind you) and a girlish devotion to Madonna dominated my first year of college. Roger worked at a Blockbuster store on Wilshire Boulevard insisting that he, like my father, was "in the biz". I gave it up to Blockbuster Roger in my USC dorm room right after Easter break while "Material Girl" played on my roommate's boom box. (Don't judge.) At the end of that year, after acing my last final exam and celebrating with my Women In Twentieth Century Spanish Literature *compadres*, I flew down the Santa Monica Freeway to meet up with Roger at Rosie's birthday bash. I was certain that my late arrival was going to upset both Rose and Roger, but my study group had demanded I join them for celebratory drinks. Perhaps my loyalty to my academic chums over my affections for Rose and Roger should have been heeded. Nevertheless I was three hours late when I finally got to the Fineman's house.

A valet took my car at the bottom of the driveway. I bumped into Boo just inside the foyer. She was in a state having nothing at all to do with my tardiness.

"Honey, go find Rose. It's time to cut the cake. I've been looking everywhere," she said. Pleased that I had managed to escape at least Brenda's wrath, (she didn't seem at all miffed that I'd arrived so late to her shindig) I set off to find the birthday girl. Naturally, I was anxious to locate Roger, my love, as well. And I did. Unfortunately for all, after an exhaustive search of the interior dwelling, I located my fiancée and my best friend together in the Fineman's pool house engaged in a rather vigorous and pornographic coupling that at the time defied imagination and would haunt me for years. Upon interruption, Roger did immediately as I suggested and he departed the party, presumably to go somewhere to fuck himself as enjoined. Hysterical, teen girl drama ensued. Rose, the contortionist/felatist, disappeared post haste as well. Excuses were made to the guests, the birthday cake was wrapped in plastic to go, Eddie and Joshie disappeared into the bowels of the house, and Brenda begged me to stay behind urging my family to leave me with her to be consoled.

"It's not your fault, Boo," I repeated several times. Up until that very evening, I'd had precious little experience with both alcohol and prescription drugs, so Boo started me off gently, cutting tiny white pills into infinitesimally small particles of very strong benzodiazepines and having me wolf them down with medium quality wine. ("Why waste the good stuff?" she liked to say.) In the coming years, the administration of this particular drug combo I would come to know as the Brenda Fineman Cure (for a broken heart).

"He isn't much to look at..." she slurred her excuses and leaned toward me to offer a conspiratorial casting suggestion. "I always kind of saw a young Artie Garfunkel in Roger." She sat up and waved the KJ bottle in a perfect circle. "I thought that if you took him out back, hosed him off, cut his hair and put him in something Armani, he'd be alright, you know?" Boo shook her head in apology. The truth was, Roger Bernstein was never going to be a looker no matter what you did with him. And of course, everyone knew that I was ridiculously young to be contemplating marriage anyway. (Steeped as I was my freshman year in the Romantics, I didn't know that.) That night however, I knew that Boo was trying to help, and it seemed unnecessarily mean to point out to her that it had been her own daughter, the birthday girl, who *had* actually taken my fiancé out back and hosed him in her pool house. So I just drank Boo's wine and took her pills and kept my trap shut.

I stared at the starlit night, weeping and listening while she droned on vaguely about insight for what seemed an eternity, and then I allowed her to move on to the weighty topics of love and friendship and loyalty as drunk people often do on consequential evenings. I could have drifted off then, reclining comfortably and aided by the downers, but Boo jerked forward so unexpectedly I let my wine glass slip and cold Chardonnay drenched my nether regions in a not unpleasant but surprisingly bracing way.

"We women need to stick together!" she wailed. "Women need to know the truth, goddamn it!" She punctuated her sentence by slapping my wet thigh with an open palm. Then she squeezed my knee and put her face too close to mine. "Tea, Honey, I wish your mom was here now." I could see streaks in her foundation in the moonlight. *But, Boo, you sent my mom home*, I didn't say. "Oh, god, I wish Diana was here now!" She wailed twice and refilled our glasses.

I think she must have been debating with herself after that what she was about to do. But after just sighing and shaking her head for a good five minutes, all the while incoherently conducting a private whispered debate, she drained her glass and got up unsteadily. She padded into the kitchen barefoot. When she returned she had a third bottle and a corkscrew. With practiced expertise, she extracted cork *numero* three. She leaned toward me to top off my glass still slurring her words and swaying, but not spilling a precious drop.

"Honey, you need to know the truth about your father. It's high time." It certainly was (in every sense of the word).

When the sun came up behind the pool house at dawn, Boo and I were still drunkenly sleeping side by side in two of the many expensive upholstered chaise lounges that circled the Fineman's salt water pool. A half dozen colorful, plush pool towels were draped across our bodies and our wine goblets and empty bottles were miraculously unbroken but strewn around our chairs like small, fragile pool toys.

"I'm sorry, Athena." Everything hurt the way it does when you wake up to your very first hangover. I painfully opened my eyes and blinked at the silhouette that was shaking my shoulder rather roughly.

"I said, I'm sorry." It took a full minute to bring the penitent Rosie Fineman into focus.

"Oh, god," I groaned. "I don't know why but I thought you were Billy!"

"Billy?" Rose repeated. "Your *fa-ther*?" There was something ugly in the way she said it. Something reminiscent of the way she used to taunt me after my mom married Mike. *Miguel is not your REAL father, Athena. Your real fa-ther is Bill-ly.*

Without warning or even lifting my head I rolled over and vomited on the tops of Rosie Fineman's expensively pedicured feet.

Rule #67: Take pains to develop your characters with complexity so that they reflect reality. No one in real life is completely good or utterly bad. Write with some sympathy toward your villains and some contempt for your heroes.

That same day I showed up at Billy's house in Malibu around noon unannounced. The frequency of my visits had declined since the fall semester and I rarely called him because if I did I would surely have to listen to an hour at least of complaints about his crumbling life. He usually managed to let me know that since entering college I had become an untrustworthy deserter in his estimation.

That morning was a hot, still day and my father was alone. Both of these things were unusual; Billy didn't like to be alone and there was almost always an offshore breeze at the beach. He seemed pretty sober, too, and unlike me, not the least bit hung over, another oddity in his regular weekend routine. He was obsessively working the *New York Times* crossword puzzle, another addiction for him, while simultaneously working on his tan. At least in terms of self-amusement Billy was a multi-tasker before the term had become part of the common American lexicon. He didn't look up when I stepped out onto his sunny deck.

"Oh, ho, ho," he said with the false heartiness of a Salvation Army Santa. "It's the very busy Miss College Girl. Long, long time no see. What's a five letter word for *unlucky gambler?*"

"Loser," I said. Billy touched his pencil point to the page and squinted.

"Nope." He scratched his temple with his eraser and rattled the newsprint. *"So-ooooo,"* he asked injecting as much sarcasm as possible into his question. "How are things at USC?"

"Fine," I said.

"How's the boyfriend?"

"We broke up last night." His pencil stopped briefly. Then he finally looked up.

"Oh, so, are you turning into your mother, now?" His smile was crooked. His voice was mean. I bent over and scratched the top of my foot and said nothing.

A seagull swooped down to examine a stale blue-corn tortilla chip on the deck. We both watched the bird reject it and fly off.

"How is she? Your mother? And *el doctór?* And their little shithead wetback offspring?" I looked out at Catalina Island and pointedly ignored the questions again which we both knew weren't really questions at all. I kind of understood his enmity toward my mom and even Mike. Pure jealousy. But I never really got why he hated Miggs so much. From the instant the kid was born it seemed, Billy hated my little brother with a furious, irrational passion.

I stepped around a dirty old beach towel to lean against the railing at the edge of the deck. It needed paint, as did the entire house, inside and out. The wood gave a little under my weight. The Malibu surf was only yards away, slapping softly at a catamaran that the neighbors had beached during low tide.

"You really shouldn't bake like this, Dad. You know it causes skin cancer, right?" Billy hadn't looked up again, even for a second. He pretended not to hear the question so I went over to the plastic-webbed chaise lounge next to his and started to sit down. He reached a sudden hand out to stop me.

"I wouldn't sit there, kiddo."

"Why not?"

Billy tapped the chair with a single finger and it collapsed with an aluminum clatter.

"It's just for show," he said making brief but meaningful eye contact over his shades. He clutched the *Times*. "You want some coffee?"

"Sure." I winced at the thought of putting anything in my roiling stomach but I calculated that moving inside would give me a moment to regroup and consider why I was really there.

"Help yourself and get me a warm up." Billy extended his half-empty coffee cup.

I don't think before that exact moment I could have let myself wholly recognize the persistent decline of Billy's house. It is Malibu waterfront, so worth several million, but, no doubt about it, it was considered both a tear down and a source of more than a little local controversy. All of his neighbors for three houses down on both sides were often vocal about Billy's sloth and noise and a few had threatened lawsuits if Billy didn't do something in the way of maintenance to the property. Billy just told them all at various times that they could fuck off and die. He'd been in Malibu since the seventies, and he was going to outlast them all.

Who knows? Maybe Billy would have done something about maintenance if he had sold anything else after *Webster's Peace,* and if he'd had the disposable cash to do so, but he hadn't. He'd sold nothing. Not a single dollar for a single word. One time, when he was completely tanked, he had called himself the "king of residuals". I was so young at the time I had to ask my mother what he'd meant and she said, "It means that he was really, really lucky, but just that one time."

There was a precarious tower of dirty dishes in Billy's kitchen sink and the Mr. Coffee pot looked ridiculously suspect. I saw a cockroach scurry under a grease-stained pizza box on the table. My stomach lurched. I decided I would wait for coffee until I passed by Starbuck's in the Malibu Center on my way back to the Palisades.

Maybe it was morbid what I did next. I can hardly admit this. I went in to his dusty little living room and studied the sad, disordered state of things in there for several minutes. A sudden anxious fury took me by surprise. Billy's Oscar was perched up on the dusty mantel. I grabbed it. I'd never held it before and the weight of the thing shocked me. I brushed the cobwebs away and, one at a time, wiped my hands on my shorts. Then I went into the bathroom and inserted Oscar headfirst into the toilet where Billy would find it later. If I was lucky, he would only look down after he'd pissed on it. I wiped my eyes with toilet paper and blew my nose, then I went back out on the deck. I stood close to his chair and looked down.

"Dad, why haven't you sold any more scripts? I mean, since *Webster?*"

"Huh?" He allowed the newspaper and his pencil to drop down onto his chest and he knuckled his scratched Foster Grants back up on his nose. His face looked red and greasy. It registered suddenly that he had grown a significant paunch in the year I'd been mostly gone. I stepped backwards. When I leaned against the rickety railing I felt the sodden wood give again dangerously. It felt as if one good push could have destroyed the whole thing. I stood up straight and waited until Billy's shades finally turned up.

"What are you talking about, Athena?" Billy almost never used my real name. There was a dangerous element in his voice, one I'd only heard before on rare occasions when he spoke on the phone to my mother. I had already crossed a line.

"I *know*, Dad." I counted fifteen waves break the shore behind me before Billy said anything.

"What? What do you know?" He removed his shades and looked directly at me for a sustained moment. His mouth was screwed up in a way that made him seem suddenly very, very old. The word "sour" came to mind. In that single second I realized that Brenda had not lied. The story she'd related only the day before hadn't even been exaggerated. I stared back at him, blinking against tears, biting my tongue and counting waves as they hit the shore. I was unable to speak.

Finally, Billy shook the *Times*, punched it, and acknowledged my empty hands, "Where's your coffee?"

I could have nailed him then. I should have. I could have really let him have it. I could have told him straight that I knew that my whole childhood, at least the part of it I had lived in his house on convenient weekends when he had nothing better to do, or whenever he was lonely, or when he had dragged me along as a prop to New York for some Byrne-McGuire family function and then basically ignored me the whole time. All of it, I now knew was a colossal lie. A silly charade. There had never been a brilliant, young screenwriter slash devoted father whose pretty young wife had left him broken-hearted and too devastated by the loss of his family to repeat the magnificent success of his Academy Award winning opus. I could have told him that I knew that he was a complete fraud, that if it hadn't been for the amazing and enduring box office receipts of *Webster's Peace*, a script he had *stolen,* he could very well be homeless down in Venice, or at the very least he'd be back in New York living on what was left of the diminishing Byrne-McGuire family dole. I could have told him that I knew that *Webster's Peace* was my mother's work. Not his. His best work had been the role he'd written for himself and failed repeatedly to perform: the role of a guy that you could rely on. A guy you could trust to tell you the truth.

Instead of saying any of that, I lied too. "You don't have any cream." I whispered it. A tear rolled down my cheek. Billy frowned.

"There's milk. Can't the little Trojan princess use milk, for chrissake?" I stared at him.

"It's spoiled, Dad," I told him. (There was a fifty-fifty chance that it was.)

"Oh, is it? Well, *saw - reeee.*" He lifted the paper and went back to his puzzle erasing furiously.

Twenty-five waves hit the shore behind me.

Thirty.

Forty.

"That's it," I told him.

"What?" he asked me, crumpling the paper to his chest again and letting his annoyance break the surface. "That's *WHAT?*"

"Sorry." I told him. "Your five letter word for an unlucky gambler."

Rule #9: In fiction, what you are aiming for is the willing suspension of disbelief, and the first person who must suspend disbelief is yourself. Some will have more disbelief to suspend than others, but even if your burden of disbelief is heavy, the only way to suspend it is to keep adding sentences to the ones you've already written. Sheer length persuades.

I suppose it strains credulity to imagine that I wrote Billy off just that easily. That I turned on a dime, so to speak, and never again darkened his dilapidated doorway. Sometimes I don't believe it myself. Afterwards, I worried – sometimes - that the ease with which I cut him off illuminated a critical character flaw in me. Then, sometimes I thought, *fuck him. Who is that fraud to me?* Dispatching Roger had been even easier. Maybe that should be even more troubling.

Look here, I completely dispensed with two human beings in under twenty-four hours. Arguably, two *significant* human beings. On the other hand, maybe it was no accident (I now think) that I disposed of both of them within a day. In less than a day. In a strange yet timely quirk of fate I made short shrift of both of them and, as often happens under circumstances like that, the two of them had a brief bonding period. Through Brenda, who heard it from Rose, who got it directly from Roger, I learned that Billy had sought Roger out at the Blockbuster not long after I had expelled them both summarily from my life. Ostensibly, Billy was offering solace to another man who was feeling wronged by me. (A man he had previously no interest in whatsoever I think it's relevant to point out.) Afterward, I heard that for quite some time, in return for free Blockbuster videos, Billy allowed Roger to hang out up in Malibu, no doubt sharing prodigious quantities of inexpensive liquor and "*Bad Athena*" stories long into the star-studded, angry, vengeful nights.

On my own behalf, and alright, I'll admit it, in the interests of procuring just a little sympathy for the narrator here, I would submit the following: My little eighteen-year old heart was broken that weekend. Just crushed to bits. Not only had it been trampled by Roger's poor judgment in cavorting sexually with my best friend (note, NEVER a wise decision), but also remember that a lifetime of idealizing Billy had been rendered idiotic by Brenda Fineman's sudden, ill-timed disclosure that he had stolen *Webster's Peace* from my mother. While it had taken surprisingly scant effort to overlook rumors of Billy's scandalous philandering, what I knew I would never recover from was the knowledge that my father was a fraud and a plagiarist. It was one thing to think of him as a one-hit wonder. Quite another to know he was utterly talentless. And, what was I to make of the sudden revelation that *Webster's Peace* was my mother's work? Oh my. That took me by complete surprise. You're going to expect to hear that I went immediately to demand an explanation from her. I can't really tell you why that did not happen. It. Just. Didn't.

Rule #2: Before you put pen to paper or fingers to keyboard you should know absolutely in your heart why it is you want to write a novel.

One time, it was long after Billy's brief (false) Hollywood heyday, and just prior to the period of his career's indisputable and transparent insidious descent, when Billy was still banging away on his original Apple IIC, an American novelist of great renown, a novelist whose name you would recognize in an instant and whose work you probably admire, but who will not want to be named in these pages (see Patricia Orloff's Rule #11, but also, I don't wish to be sued), anyway, this titan of fiction paid a visit to Malibu.

I was no older than twelve at the time. Old enough to know who the man was, and to be dimly aware of his eminence, though mostly I gleaned how important his pilgrimage to Malibu was by how nervous Billy got. He had actually made some attempt at cleaning up the joint (a pitiful one, but effort that signaled his anxieties about the man's visit), and he had ordered a deli-tray from Mort's in the Village. It was summer, the summer I was reading *Ivanhoe*, and I remember this because when the man walked into the house, he lifted up my paperback without saying even "hello" to me, and said, "Jesus, Billy, what kind of kid this age reads *Ivanhoe* on summer vacation?"

They seemed to share a laugh over that, but when Billy offered refreshments the man cast a glance around the dim room and hovered over Mort's cold cut platter dubiously before he waved him off and asked if they could just go outside on the deck and "get down to brass tacks". There was such a mixture of sorrow and desperate hope on Billy's face as he turned his back on Mort's lunchmeats, I knew without knowing that he already knew it himself: the meeting was doomed. It lasted a grim fifteen minutes. No longer. It was clearly a waste of everyone's time (and good deli, too), because when it came down to it, the guy had an impeccable bullshit detector. What I gleaned later from Billy's tirades against the man was that the guy's latest novel had been optioned by Warner's to be made into a film and somebody there (a great admirer of *Webster's Peace)* had suggested Billy's name for the screen adaptation. This notable novelist of unquestioned talent had deigned to take a meeting with the has-been Billy Byrne-McGuire, probably out of some kind of misplaced obligation to the *Webster's* fan at Warner Brothers, and maybe even a dark curiosity of his own to see what had happened to a writer like Billy who'd gone Missing In Action.

I've heard some profanity in my day. I like to use a fair amount of it myself; it amuses me to do so, but I've never again heard anything like the curses I heard that day after "Mr. Big" left Billy's. Without a doubt, "Mr. Big" had made Billy feel like "mr. small", though I do not know what *exactly* transpired in that brief exchange. I only know that Billy's rage was terrifying. It went on for hours and only got meaner and more frightening when he opened a new half-gallon of Tanqueray. Confused and frightened I watched him rip clenched pages from my book's spine and fling them off the deck. By the time the sun was at the horizon, the whole of *Ivanhoe* had been torn to pieces and scattered to the onshore breezes in a parody of voodoo. Henceforth all novels were to be forever banned under Billy's roof, and it behooved me, "if I knew what was good for me" to agree with him that all novelists were "obsolete, fuckwit, no-talent, pieces of shit". What choice did I have? In uneasy solidarity I agreed with Billy. It killed me to comply (even though I was secretly huffing John Irving, Jean Auel, and Pat Conroy behind his back, down in the Palisades like nobody's business). And, goddamn it, without books, those weekends in Malibu were soooooo long. The only good to come out of the whole affair was that Billy got cable.

Rule #7: The novelist's ambition is not to do something better than his predecessors, but to see what they did not see, say what they did not say.

Funny story: about a hundred years later, just after I signed on at the *Trib*, before my editor decided I could be trusted with features, I was writing book reviews for the Sunday edition – a shabby duty everybody hated and avoided if they could. But when I was low (wo)man on the pole, I had to do it, and by a strange quirk of fate, who should be my very first assignment? You're not dumb. Yeah. Mr. Big. All writers are imperfect and let it be said that while "Biggie" is a fine writer, that last novel of his was just a terrible, pot-boiling dog. But here's the funny part of this story: because I knew that Billy was reading my shit in the *Trib* (the Billy-Roger-Rose-Brenda communication circuit), I wrote that bastard the best review he ever got. *Take that Billy, you obsolete, fuckwit, no talent, piece of shit, mother-fucker.*

Rule #70: Unless you are a Kennedy (or maybe a Kardashian) do not write a version of your family's cruddy history and try to pass it off as fiction. But if you choose to do so in spite of this advice, for God's sake, tell the truth – your truth – whatever you write.

So, the next three years whizzed by. Nah, certainly not. But do you really want to know about my decline into darkness and depression?

Since you asked.

After the Roger debacle, the year just following could righteously be referred to as my Sylvia Plath Period, meaning I was a suicidal poet, but unlike Plath I had neither the means nor, truly, the desire to end my life. (The oven in our campus apartment was electric, and the USC football team was aces just then. So, sue me. I liked college football.) Also, Rose was at Smith and she informed me that if anybody had the right to stick their head in an oven, it wasn't some tailgating moron from fucking USC, it was going to be somebody from Smith for obvious reasons. (I told her to be my guest.)

Next, in my junior year I moved on to my Lesbian Experimental Phase. I went to a lot of k. d. lang concerts, wore Adidas and black tank tops with Meshell Ndegeocello's face silk-screened on them, got a tattoo (think twice, dear reader! And choose VERY carefully. Really!), and I slept with exactly zero women. It wasn't that I wasn't up for it, at least theoretically. And, for sure, I hated men – all men (except for Mike and my brother, Miggs) – so I wasn't doing guys either. It was my first fling with total abstinence. The thing was, I hadn't found sex with Roger all that much fun, and I was pretty sure that intercourse with no dick was going to be even less exciting than doing it with a "pencil dick", so why ever make the effort, can you feel me? Forget eating pussy. Call me a taker but that is a one-way street for me; when it comes to munchin' the rug, in my world, it is better to receive than to give. Just the way it is, but no judgment here for lady lovers. Knock yourselves out.

For me it was an easy slide into Goth from The Butchies. Commence phase three.

Rule #35: Every sentence must pass the v.i.w. test: Did you write something of Value? Is it Interesting? Is it, after all, Worth-

while? Apply this test to all content lest you get to the end of your novel with naught but an accumulation of pages.

Wait, wait just a minute or two. Allow me to give you a little context in terms of family dynamics. A little background that perchance will illuminate my tardy attempts to individuate in such a colorful fashion. If you are very clever you've already deduced that my Joan Jett antics were patently obvious attempts to get some attention. It's fairly classic sibling rivalry bullshit. But, don't you want the details? The background? Of course you do.

I can admit this now: It all *really* started when the little brother made his first appearance onto the world stage. I was six when my sibling ordinal position went from "only" to "oldest of two". When my brother invaded my territory my initial strategy was to be the perfect one. When it was determined that something was not quite right about Miguel Jr., and the whole of the Cervantes family went into crisis mode of unsurpassed proportions, leaving me to feel insignificant and invisible, I was out of my mind with jealousy. But I was Good. When all those test results started coming in...well, everybody, and I mean everybody, thought Miggs was doomed. My job was to provide relief by needing nothing. The illusion of perfection did not come easily to me while the whole world it seemed was riveted on the competition and his developmental issues.

So, The Golden Child. How do I explain what's wrong with my brother? And, I say it that way only because, at first, that was the family's orientation. Everybody thought something was, if not horribly wrong with Miggs, at least he wasn't quite right in the head.

I kind of remember some personal awareness that he was "different" going way back. Definitely by the time he started to talk, but as soon as he had to go to school, that's when I knew that *other people* thought he was different. We *all* knew from birth practically that Miggs had something unusual going on; we just experienced him as "special", but "special" in a good way, not necessarily short bus special.

He had this super quirky way of talking. This in and of itself didn't merit high alert and at first it was kind of cute. Also, lots of little kids have verbal tics, etc. But, as time wore on, Miggs's shit was definitely, shall we say, *unique?* It was almost like he had an idiosyncratic type of communication problem, kind of like a reverse Asperger's syndrome. If you aren't somehow in the know of such things, typically, with Asperger's the afflicted person kind of doesn't "get" routine interpersonal interactions. They can come across as cold and unsympathetic, even robotic. They don't connect. With Miggs it was the exact opposite. You had the feeling when you were talking to my brother that he was hyper-focused on you and what you were saying, and here's the really weird part, you felt like he *knew exactly what you were feeling.* Uber empathic. He stared right into your eyes without blinking and saw through to your soul. It felt as if he was completely dialed in to you neurologically. And, early on, his vocabulary about emotion was odd too, like his neuronal wiring was screwy. His limbic system and his language centers were hotwired or something. Whenever he said anything objective about feelings, it came out funny. It made him sound like Yoda. "Sad, I am, Momma." "Sorry, you are, Tea." "Tired, you are, Papa." And, so on. There's not even scientific or medical nomenclature for that shit. Oh, lots of shrinks (and believe me, there were more than a few) had theories. One called Miggs an "ultra-sensitive". But, that didn't cover his weird speech and other oddities. Like what some referred to as "learning disabilities". He grew out of the weird communication stuff eventually, or maybe he just figured out how to fit in, but school was a misery for him.

He wasn't reading like I was by age three, but, again, nobody got all stressed out about it. Boys read later, right? But, when he couldn't read by seven, the academic Mounties were called in. At first, they were throwing out scary words like "developmentally disabled", and more than once, "childhood schizophrenia", (which Billy called "fucking retarded" and "fucking crazy"). But then, things got kind of sorted out, and eventually it was said to concern more "esoteric intellectual processes". So, even now, Miggs reads *words* only with enormous effort. He can do it, but it's not natural or easy for him. For Miggs, reading English is like you taking your first shot at Vedic Sanskrit every single time you try it. But, Honey, save your sympathy because Miggs has what one specialist called "compensating talents". For everything he found difficult, like reading, he had like super, off the charts abilities in some other area. So, anything to do with numbers? My brother is a human computer. That little fucker will never read this crap I'm writing here, but man, he was doing calculus in the second grade. I don't know about you, but this combo of being able to intuit the electricity of human emotion across the interpersonal divide and also run the fucking numbers like the Rain Man? I would give my metaphorical right one to be able to do that. It makes Miggs uniquely suited for business, so that is why my brother is a goddamn millionaire and he's still in his twenties.

Do you hate him? Shit. You don't hate him enough. There's more. My mom had a clinical supervisor on a rotation she did during her training when Miggs was a baby. She told my mom that Miggs was a "kinesthetic genius", which means that his brain/body connections are wired to function with the utmost efficiency. (Think Michael Jordan and Baryshnikov.) Anything round is his best friend. Balls, wheels, hoops, even yoyos. He could catch a ball when he was nine months old. Truth. (Legal disclaimer: Do NOT attempt this at home with any ordinary mortal child, even your nephew who you think is the next Steve Wozniak.) And, boards. Snowboards, skateboards, diving boards, and more than anything else, surfboards. Give that kid any kind of board and he will show you wizardry. He'll do shit on boards that will make you doubt the existence of gravity. Miguel Cervantes Jr. is one with the sea. By the time he was fifteen he was on the pro circuit. *Sports Illustrated* called him the "Wave Whisperer" in that cover story when he was just thirteen.

And so, after all the early drama about his "development", that is how my little brother ultimately made lemonade out of lemons, and how it has come to pass that he designs and manufactures surf boards for the international surfing elite, and he is opening up his fifth or sixth (I've lost count) surf shop, the next one in Hawaii, and his work day largely consists of taking prototype surfboards out for a spin. Now do you hate him? Wait. I'm not through yet. (Refer to Rule #9.) Miguel Cervantes Jr. looks a hell of a lot like Mr. Brad Pitt, only taller. *Thelma and Louise* Brad Pitt, *Troy* Brad Pitt. Not Brad Pitt in that stupid movie where he reverse ages and spends half the time looking like E.T. (Apologies to Mr. Fitzgerald, but just a stupid premise, and again, sorry about the clunky inter-textuality. What's a girl to do?) Back to my bro and how he looks: both super hot *and* six-foot one barefoot. You can hate him now, or love him as almost everyone does.

Oh, yeah. I'm not done quite yet. Here's the kicker. The proverbial best for last. My brother? My weird, gifted, disabled, quirky, drop-dead gorgeous baby brother is The Nicest Human Being you will ever meet. Abuela said it one time. All the stuff Miggs can *do*. It's *nada*. Miggsy's true gift is who he *is*.

Now. Want to know who his favorite person in the whole wide world is? You can't guess. It's me. Fucked-up me. Go figure. Dude's crazy. Well, you know. I don't mean *crazy*.

Rule #28: The essential cast of your story should be assembled and well known long before the mid-point. Let the reader in on their quirks and their peculiarities. Nothing is more interesting to us than what is flawed about a character. Describe every flaw without mercy in delicious and tantalizing detail.

Here's a little more background for some of the characters who might meet Patty Orloff's criterion for "peripheral" and clearly, make no mistake, I do understand that these are an unnecessary distraction from the thrust of my narrative: Nevertheless I give you, The Fineman Family.

Up the hill at *Chez Fineman*, or what I like to describe as five miles and five million dollars up Sunset Boulevard from the Palisades, the Fineman family lingered on the periphery of our lives like relatives you can't be rid of. Hence, in the most literal sense, they were peripheral. It was sometimes hard to understand what exactly there was between Boo and my mom to keep the friendship going. They seemed so different. Their paths had diverged and then some since that UCLA Extension screenwriting course. And nobody pretended that Mike had anything in common with Eddie Fineman, a competitive and angry man whose wealth and business success did nothing to calm his inadequacy fears and feelings of inferiority. Here's a funny thing. Or, maybe not so funny. While Brenda was always "Aunt Boo" to us (always), her husband never, *never* was "Uncle Eddie". Eddie was always Eddie. Or even Mr. Fineman. I *still* think of Eddie as Mr. Fineman, and truthfully, there's precious little to tell about the guy and what there is to tell is not what you will think of as endearing, I assure you. Eddie Fineman, truth be rendered, is a jerk.

This is all you need to know to form an opinion about Mssr. Fineman.

America's Most Eligible

As a little kid at their house (really a mansion, the kind with a grand staircase and a foyer like the one on *Dallas*), I was crucially aware that Mr. Fineman had a peculiar habit of digging in his nostrils with his thumb. Perhaps in the adult world this was the least of his objectionable traits. To a kid, the nose-picking thing was, no doubt about it, a train-wreck activity. You didn't want to watch it, but you couldn't look away. He performed this simultaneously gross and engrossing function almost constantly regardless of the presence of company. If he got lucky and he scored a big booger he would bring it close to his face for slow and careful inspection before he would then flick the sucker indiscriminately to the floor right where he stood or sat. Not as much of a problem on the ground floor as it was upstairs where the bedrooms were. And this is why: the ground floor was all marble tile and hard woods so you could keep your footwear on your feet. The Finemans' carpeting on the second level cost what Eddie liked to say "five hundie per" (five hundred dollars/yard), and the runner up the staircase had been custom ordered from some Tibetan-virgin-operated loom in the Himalayas or something. So the rule was "shoes off upstairs". (Too bad Mr. Fineman was not so fastidious about boogers on the carpet.) Anyway, nothing, I promise you, no amount of cool Barbie accoutrements in Rosie's bedroom could have enticed me up those stairs in my bare feet or even my socks. Are you kidding me? It was all I could do to keep from puking on the ground floor when Eddie went mining for big chunks of hardened mucous up his nose holes. I sure as hell wasn't going to walk on his boogers barefoot. No sirree. So, I always brought a book over to the Finemans' house so I could entertain myself downstairs by reading, which led Eddie to refer to me as "the brainiac". I don't know how exactly but I understood early that he did this as an attempt to put Miggs down (his reading disorder was well documented), and Miggs's extraordinary abilities in sports drove Eddie bat-shit crazy since he was way over-invested in Josh. (Poor Josh wasn't a complete klutz, but when engaged in athletics, next to Miggs, Michael Phelps looks like a slacker.) It killed Eddie that Miggs was always Joshie's better.

Over time though, I also came to understand that Eddie wasn't just ridiculing Miggs. He was sticking it to Rosie, too. Putting down his own kid whom he thought never quite measured up, and he told her so in so many words in front of people plenty of times. Well, when he wasn't ignoring her. That's what she mostly got. Ignored. It made me feel really bad for her. I felt bad for Boo, too, since Eddie ran a similar number on his wife. He made it a point to call my mom "Doc" or "the Doc", and he made terrible and mean fun of Boo's ambitions to get into casting after she lost her job on the soap for the sin of stilted dialogue. Oddly, or I guess not really when you analyze his behavior, he never, *never*, called Mike "Doc". He always called Mike by his Mexican name, Miguel, because in Eddie Fineman's twisted world, *that* was a put down.

Mr. Fineman was and still is a douche bag. A nose-picking douche bag.

But, let me conclude the college era tales.

Rule #71: Do not unintentionally annoy your reader. For instance, few things annoy me more than the misuse of the word "allude". Do not confuse "allude" with "elude". You allude to a book; you elude a pursuer.

Rose let her "close personal ties" to both Dr. Diana Ward-Cervantes and Dr. Miguel Cervantes be known at Smith early on. (Nobody, I mean *nobody*, can name drop like Rosie.) As my parents both had books throughout our senior year up on the *New York Times* Best Seller List in nonfiction (Mom's newest trilogy holding spots #2, #5 and #6, and Mike's book, *The Shaman's Demons*, at #1 for over a year), the whole academic world was abuzz with their names. It was not surprising when Smith invited my mother to give the commencement address at Rosie's graduation.

Okay, stipulated: I never had any intention to walk at the ceremonies at USC. I did not order the traditional cap and gown. I told my family that I believed that such pomp and circumstance was bullshit. My hair was in a modified Mohawk dyed a color not of the natural world, so a mortarboard was out of the question for me. Still, can you understand my feelings of petty hurt and jealousy that my mother was back east "playing doctor" in her role as Auntie Diana for Rosie in Northampton on the very same day that USC conferred baccalaureate status on me? Just bad timing. I was injured by it.

Rule #72: Re: annoying mistakes: do not use "anticipate" when you mean simple expectation.

Mike was totally cool. He anticipated my disappointment and got last-minute tickets to see Veruca Salt, and like the mensch he is, he went with me and said nothing when I took a couple hits off the blunt somebody passed back to our row. (I will always love Mike for that night. And, it was excellent weed. Not nearly as good as the medical marijuana you can get now, but good enough to dull the pain.)

Rose and my mother flew back to LA from Massachusetts together (upgraded to first class, fuck it all), while after the ceremony the other Finemans went directly on to Florida to visit Eddie's parents in Miami.

I anticipated Rose's expectation that I would be in a snit, so I foiled her by coming on like the very-very-very best friend she sometimes (though this was intermittent depending on her moods) wanted me to be. I mostly ignored my mother, but when I couldn't, I took to calling her "Diana".

Rule #73: You do not need to insert extra articles into sentences where you think they make you seem smarter or grander than you are. For example, don't write "as to whether" where a simple "whether" is sufficient, (unless you are the Queen of England or her upstairs butler).

As to whether or not Rosie's gestures of friendship that summer were genuine, who can say? She went out of her way, I will say, to include me whenever her pals from Smith came to visit. And although, in retrospect, it was not really any great favor to me (considering how things turned out, after all), she *did* introduce me to my next fiancé. Boyfriend *numero* two. I'm pretty sure that Rosie slept with him before passing him along, and then *again*, (for sure-just like old Roger) after we broke up. What can I say? Rose wanted every thing and every one that was rightly mine.

Lover number two. (In correct chronological order.)

Rule #74: "As yet" is likewise a term that conjures images of feeble attempts to seem fancier than one is. Like extra articles in a sentence, "as yet" reveals a pathetic insecurity about one's station in life. If you aren't a member of the royal family, just don't use it.

We went clubbing almost every night that summer. There was a sense that when fall came and when we were both back in school (Rose had been accepted at USC's MFA program and I was headed up to Davis), we were going to have to settle down and get serious about our lives and our careers. Prior to taking on the probity of graduate school (okay, okay, I *know*), we had assumed that all of our youthful, wanton college days of excessive drinking, extreme partying and general misbehavior would be behind us come

August, and so we were whooping it up as if our young lives depended on it. We hadn't *as yet,* seen fit to grow up. We hadn't learned to dump the extra article...*yet.*

Enter Billy the Kid.

My engagement to William (and, really, shouldn't that have been a clue? *Fuck me!*) was my most legitimate engagement in a way since it was the only one that involved the receipt of a precious gem which I wore on my appropriate finger (albeit for less than a week).

Fiancé #2 was William Pryor Winston III, but he called himself Billy the Kid. (You've heard it before: you can't make this shit up.) Billy Winston was better looking than that *Twilight* dude (Boo's casting suggestion), was hugely endowed in the penile department, and flat out sexier than anyone you can name, and I hate to admit it on account of the way it reveals how very shallow I can be, but Billy had not one single other attribute worth mentioning. Truly. The only thing, and I do mean the only thing, that poor boy had going for him was that he looked good and he had a biggie. Okay, he sort of played a passable bass guitar and he was in a band that actually got some local gigs around LA, but, as it turned out, since he had a serious cocaine problem, he was never even close to being solvent. His grandfather was the inventor of the mud flap or something so Billy also had himself a little trust fund, but it wasn't near enough to keep him in guitar picks *and* drugs. I have no idea where the money for my engagement ring came from. After we split up, Billy asked for the ring back and he sold it to cover some of his rehab bills.

Rule #75: It is wholly unnecessary to employ the word "but" after "doubt" and "help". Who speaks like this? I hope you don't. Why would you write this way? I am once again suspicious of insecurities that pile up and force you to insert unnecessary ar-

*ticles of speech into your written text to bolster your self es-
teem. It would be better to seek professional help for this problem as soon as possible.*

Alright, so now you can't help but think, "Athena is not a good person". Get over it. So what? I had myself a little fling with a grunge rocker. So I snorted a little blow up my nose holes. I thought I had my reasons for acting like an idiot, alright? I also needed an overcorrection on the bad sex I'd had with old Roger. (And for that alone I will always be more than a little grateful to Billy The Kid. Size matters. Sorry.)

My mom used to refer to this as my "Yoko Ono period" (though I have warned her that this makes her seem older than she would like). I now can only offer the brevity of the relationship with Billy in my defense, and tell you that I did not know that he was an actual full-scale-Keith-Richards-style drug addict (not a dabbler like the rest of us) until he called me to bust him out of the Betty Ford Clinic.

Miggs had gone off to follow the waves and compete on the World Pro Surfing tour that summer; it was going to be just me and my parents at home, and I guess I was feeling like a colossal loser, so I regressed accordingly and acquired the appropriate consort. I needed a dirty, bad boy; Billy The Kid was perfect for the part. No consultation with Boo was required for that.

Do I even have to tell you how much my parents hated Billy? I hadn't even gotten around to announcing my engagement to the family when Billy and I had a really bad fight. I wasn't keen on the way he wanted to celebrate our betrothal (a boys' weekend in Vegas) and he called me the C-word, told me he had no intention of living the rest of his life with a controlling bitch, demanded my ring back, and went to Vegas without me. In my grief I retired to Boo's in Beverly Hills since Mike was off on some work junket, and my mother was on a retreat in Malibu with thirty-five inner-city high school kids who had lived their whole miserable lives ten miles from the ocean without ever once going to the beach. In anticipation of her empty nest my mom had cultivated a slew of *pro bono* work, mostly with the youthful dregs of Los Angeles society. So, while *Maman* was busy in Malibu trying to rectify social injustice, and Papa was wowing a bunch of his peers at Harvard, and Miggs was nabbing himself a shit ton of money and a four foot trophy, I carted my broken heart off to the solace of Brenda Fineman's lovely home and once again submitted myself to her cure for the broken-hearted. Prescription drugs and Chardonnay chilled to a perfect fifty-two degrees in large quantities is effectively mind numbing, though I imagine it to be a little rough on the liver with oft-repeated treatments. Some of us will only learn the hard way.

Meanwhile, while I was up in Beverly Hills (engaged in legal drug abuse), Billy's frolicking binge in Vegas turned from fun into mayhem and he got himself arrested for running naked down Tropicana Boulevard. Even in Vegas, it turns out, you are under-dressed if you are only wearing a sock, (not on your foot.) Bail was wired from the Winston family trust back east, Billy was released (but ordered to "treatment"), and his father, William Pryor Winston II, flew out to install him at the Betty Ford Clinic in Palm Springs where the dear, well-hung cokehead worked the program hard for about forty-eight hours before he called me from the nearby Denny's. It was sometime before midnight. I foolishly promised to come. My poor mother had only just returned from her retreat that very same evening, weary and spent from four straight days of corralling un-medicated teenagers who all desperately needed Ritalin. To her credit as a mother, she would not let me leave the house alone. I have no doubt but that had she not gone along, I would not now be alive to relate the night's incredible events.

The night's incredible events:

It takes about two and a half hours to drive out to Palm Springs from the Palisades in LA. She drove because I seemed impaired by the activity of melodramatically working my way through a jumbo box of Kleenex.

Get this picture of the two of us: My mother, even exhausted, looks amazing. Boo casts a young Jane Fonda in her fantasy movie version of any Diana Ward-Cervantes biopic. Mind you, in those short, wicked days of my delayed troubled youth I had dyed my one-sided Mohawk jet-black and streaked it with something called "Strawberry Cotton Candy". I wore enough kohl eyeliner and mascara to lubricate a 747. I trust I need not describe my monochromatic wardrobe to you. Suffice to say, I looked, more than anything else, like a deviant member of the extended Adams family. During this lively period of my development, my parents were wisely ignoring my excesses as good parents do since it was, and is, just a phase. (How many forty-year old women do you see wearing ripped up, black fishnets with skunky streaks of magenta in their hair? Well, besides Courtney Love and Madonna? And, now, soon, Lady Gaga?)

We drove all the way through downtown LA listening only to the sound of my piteous weeping until my mother could take it not a minute longer. She glanced over and piped up:

"I know Betty has done some good things, but I will never forgive Gerald Ford." Chalk this up to my mother's attempt to distract me from my misery as we sped down the Santa Monica Freeway toward the desert, because that's what it did. In that moment, I assure you, I wasn't really curious about some old geezer who, I dimly recalled from US History class, used to be the president, but I was grateful not to be alone that night so I tried minimally to hold up my end of the conversation.

"What did Gerald Ford ever do to you, Mom?" She smiled and shook her head and then her mobile phone rang.

"Answer that, please, Honey. It might be Miggs or Dad." I looked at the phone.

"Neither. It's Bobby," I told her.

Rule #76: The word "being" is not appropriate after "regard" as in, "He is regarded as being the best chef in America." Say instead, "He is regarded as the best chef in America."

(Let us now digress momentarily regarding Mom and Boo's internecine relations with the Finemans' household personnel.)

Once upon a time, Bobby Cisneros had been my mother's very first *pro bono* client, going, in a very short time, from cooking meth in a bathtub in East LA to the inevitable stint in a California Youth Authority lock-up, and then to cooking breakfast, lunch and dinner for Brenda's family in Beverly Hills. I believe (though she never copped to it) that my mother paid Bobby's tuition to the Pasadena Culinary Academy. (*Tell me, where would a rehabbed tweaker get that kind of money?*) And I know that when he finished school, Bobby C. apprenticed with my grandmother right there in her kitchen, very much against Mike's wishes, and every second under the watchful eye of my grandfather. (*RIP, Abuela. usted es una Santa!*) The Finemans' other household staff, all but Margarita, the nanny, had been procured in similar ways. The houseboy who commandeered the cleaning staff was Bobby's flamboyant cousin. Practically overnight he had gone from doing tricks on the corner of Hollywood and Santa Monica to the supervision of carefully folded hospital corners with the Finemans' 1200 count Egyptian cotton sheets. The gardener (the Finemans called him the groundskeeper) was Bobby's younger brother, and, well, you can probably guess what kind of horticultural enterprise Tino had been engaged in up there in Humboldt county before Bobby brought him south to trim the hedges for Brenda et al.

"Hi, Bobby, it's Athena...my mom's driving ."

"Oh, hi, Athena, whazzup? Do me one and give the doc a message, yo?"

"Sure, what's the message?" My mother looked at the clock on the dashboard and frowned.

"Tell the doc that Tino got probation. Six months. He tests clean for six, he gets his license back." I relayed the message and my mom smiled. She made a little "okay" with her right hand.

"She says, 'good'."

"Where you guys headed after midnight, yo? It's just you and your mom? Where's the big Doc?"

"It's a long story. And it's just the two of us. The big Doc is in Massachusetts impressing his peers with his genius." Bobby paused while he contemplated Mike's itinerary and assessed our situation.

"I don't like it," he said. "The two of you alone this time of night...you headed home?"

"Eventually. Soon," I said.

"Lock your doors, Athena. Don't let nobody follow you."

"Got it, Bobby. Thanks for calling."

"Not a thing," he said and then again, "Lock your doors. Don't get out of the car for nothin' 'til you get home." Not for the first time I reflected on the undeniably unsafe reality that the people on my mother's *pro bono* caseload lived in every day compared to me.

"Thank you for your concern and advice," I said sincerely. My mother gave me a sidelong glance and a sweet, tired smile.

We rode on in silence until we reached the outskirts of Rancho Mirage. I remember still how fierce my mom looked in the intermittent, sulfurous glow of the town's streetlights. The "Betty" is outside Palm Springs proper. We drove past the clinic's long driveway in search of Denny's and Billy.

Rule #78: Exaggeration is a billion times worse than understatement.

How we almost got carjacked and left for dead (probably raped first) in the California desert:

It wasn't yet three a.m. when we pulled into the Denny's lot. I went inside alone. Although there were a surprising number of diners for the ungodly hour, there was no sign of Billy. A young hostess of the white trash variety approached me immediately.

"Are you Athena?" she asked. I nodded. "Your boyfriend told me to tell you he got a ride."

"A ride?" I repeated. "With who? Whom?"

"He didn't tell me to tell you that, but," the girl looked around nervously and then, leaned close and whispered into my ear. "He left with Fat Sissy." The girl held her arms out to approximate just how fat this Fat Sissy was. Big.

"Is he coming back?" She shook her head and made that face that everywhere means, "*You've been fucked over, Honey.*" I just stood there and blinked back sudden hot tears. Someone was burning French fries in the kitchen.

"Look, if it makes you feel any better, Sissy's brother, Leo, he...well, Leo sort of specializes in the drop-outs from the Center. You know what I mean?" She rested an index finger on one nostril and snorted rancid food scented air into the other in an unmistakable and probably knowledgeable pantomime.

"Leo's a drug dealer?" The waitress made that face again. What could I do?

I cried for the first hour and then my mother decided that we needed to pull off the freeway to find a 7-Eleven to replenish my fluids and get some coffee for her. We got lost almost instantly and pulled up to an isolated, abandoned building on a very remote road in the eastern most part of east LA county. No sooner had she put the car into park and unfolded a street map on top of the dash than an ancient, battered Ford Pinto pulled around the building and blocked our retreat.

"Don't move, Athena," she said pretending to calmly peruse her map. The four gang bangers took their sweet time getting out of their car, and because there was no way we could leave, and also because my mother possessed enough hubris to think that she could actually reason with them, she opened her door and stepped out, her protégé's recently earnest advice completely disregarded.

"Hi," she said sweetly. "I guess you probably can see we're a little lost."

"No shit, lady. I'll bet you're a looooong way from home." The four gangsters – I'm just guessing here – high on crack, laughed like this was the funniest thing they'd ever heard. I jumped out and walked around to stand next to my mother.

"Get back in the car, Athena," she said, but I stood where I was. Meanwhile one of the slouching men reached into our car and took my mom's purse. He dumped the contents on the ground at the feet of the Pinto's driver who immediately stooped down to pick up her wallet. The tallest of the four, a guy with teardrops tattooed on his cheeks, moved forward and reached out to touch my mom's hair. I stepped in and pushed his hand away.

"Don't," I said. He looked at me in a way that communicated quite clearly that people in his world rarely survived if they tried to tell him what to do.

"Hey, *June-yoor*. That bitch got some balls, man." Junior stepped in front of me squarely.

"Naw. She got no balls." He reached a hand for my crotch. "You don't got no balls, do you, Blackie?"

"I wouldn't do that, if I were you, Junior," I said. Junior cracked up like I was doing stand up. I widened my stance and looked him right in his bloodshot eyes. He had that strange combination on his face of amusement and annoyance that in certain contexts looks just like stupidity or confusion, but he slowly withdrew his hand.

"Why not, Blackie? What you gonna do?"

Now, dear reader, I have no doubt that what follows will absolutely strain credulity to the breaking point. In fact I'll bet you're already thinking to yourself, *that shit doesn't really happen, and if it did, nobody would do what Athena is claiming.* But bear in mind that I had already been fucked over by one asshole that night. I wasn't going to let Junior or anybody else do it again without at least some resistance. And, know this: I had spent practically every weekend of my adolescence at Billy Byrne McGuire's house in Malibu watching Bruce Willis movies and the like, committing to memory all of the dialogue from *The Terminator.* (And the sequel.) I had already calculated that my mother and I were pretty likely goners, so I had nothing to lose. I stared Junior right in the eye and bluffed.

"I'm gonna put your mother-fucking, fat, *chollo* ass back in Soledad, asshole." (Obviously channeling *Scarface* there.) Junior cocked his head. I pointed a chipped, black-polished, mean, little finger in his face. "The DEA cops are tracking us. You'd better get back in your gangster-mobile and get out of here pronto." Junior stood there admirably still while he tried really hard to figure if I was blowing smoke up his ass.

"That's bullshit," the fourth guy said, but I could tell that he too had some doubts. I conjured every cinematic bad-guy I had ever seen.

"Go ahead, Junior. Listen to your buddy here. But what he don't know is that I'm undercover for West Valley P.D., asshole. You don't believe me? Good. Just wait. My partner's gonna be here any minute. He's right behind us. We've been setting this white bitch up for months. She's been dealing crystal to her housewife pals in the valley and you wetback mother-fuckers just blew our whole case. My partner is not gonna be happy with you, Junior. I guaran-fucking-tee it." I looked at my Minnie Mouse watch. "You got less than five minutes to get your fat *chollo* selves out of here or my guess is, all four of you will be busted on a parole violation and takin' it up the ass in county before this time tomorrow." My mother had taken a giant step backward, her eyes wide with surprise and what I interpreted was more than just a little awe.

"Hey, Junior, *mira, esse!*" The guy who was rummaging through my mother's wallet pushed it in front of Junior's face.

"So what?" he said.

"Look at this! Look, Homes! It's Bobby. It's Bobby C." Junior grabbed the wallet and scrutinized a snapshot of my mother with her arms around Bobby Cisneros that had been taken the day he graduated from culinary school. Junior looked again at the picture. Then he looked at my mother.

"You know Bobby C?" he asked. "How do you know Bobby C?" One of the other chollos, obviously the smartest of the four, was busy scrolling down my mom's contact list on her cell phone.

I answered for my mother. "I'm trying to help you out here, Junior. I told you. This bitch is Bobby C.'s *connay* in suburbia." Then I got a little crazy. "Are you stupid?"

"She got Bobby's number in her phone, Junior. This bitch ain't lyin'." Clearly a tech whiz, the man checked her recent calls. "Fuck, man, Bobby called this number a couple hours ago!" The smart one held my mother's phone in front of Junior's face and looked up and down the deserted road.

"Call him!" Junior barked. "Get him on the phone!" Wherever Bobby C. was and whatever he had been interrupted from at three o'clock in the morning, he was obviously alert. He must have seen my mom's number pop up. Genius boy fumbled.

"Wait," he said and handed the phone to Junior who got on the phone all BFF.

"Bobby, *hola esse*...it's Junior, your home boy from Eighteenth Street. Hey, man, you know some white bitch...blonde, good lookin'..." Junior looked my mother up and down appreciatively and then at her drivers license. "...Diana Cervantes...What do you know?...The bitch got a Mexican name...You know some white bitch with that name, Homes?" Before he could inhale another single breath, Junior's whole demeanor shifted and he took on the appearance of a middle school student who was getting reamed by the principal for getting caught with pot in his locker. He did everything but stand at attention and salute. His voice was suddenly full of respect.

"Yeah, yeah. Sure thing, Homes. No harm done. I didn't know man. No, she's out of here. Already out of here. No man. I didn't touch her." Junior waved a hand at the other man to give my mom back her wallet. He banged the guy on the head when he started taking the cash. "Okay, peace, brother. Yeah, yeah. No problem, man." Junior closed the phone and looked at me with newfound respect.

"Help her with that shit, man! Put the cash back!" he ordered his underling. Reluctantly the man did as he was told. "You tell Bobby C. we didn't do nothin' to you, right lady?"

Just then a second car – one looking, if possible, even more sinister than the Pinto – cruised by on the highway, slowing but not stopping. All six of us, carjackers and carjackees, stared at the other vehicle until we saw brake lights. When it came to a stop and slowly started backing up, Junior threw my mom's phone on the ground and ran for the Pinto.

"Hit it!" he screamed. "Get the fuck in the car! Get the fuck in! Get in!" Which they all did with ungangsterlike alacrity. My mom and I were still quite frozen so we just watched the Pinto squeal away in the opposite direction as fast as a Pinto with a half a ton of probation inside it can go. The pursuers in the other car, whoever they were, made a quick three-pointer and took off after them. As soon as they passed us by, my mom and I grabbed her phone, and her wallet, and her antique filofax and jumped in our own car and floored it going in the other direction.

Perhaps we were in shock. I don't know, but I can tell you that neither one of us spoke one word for a good fifteen minutes. I felt like my molecules were reassembling or something. I contemplated all the what-ifs. I marveled at my own incredible chutzpah. Apparently my mom was thinking along the same lines since the first thing she said was, "Undercover for West Valley P.D.? You have an amazing imagination, Athena. I can't wait to read your first book." I started to laugh which started her laughing, and I don't know if it was just a reaction to escaping death or what, but that was the best laugh I have ever had. In my whole life.

In retrospect that would have been an ideal time to ask her about *Webster's Peace*. I don't know why I didn't think of it. Perhaps I didn't want to spoil that rare good moment between us. Perhaps I knew or sensed that nothing good would come of the truth. Perhaps, I told myself, I was still just colluding with her to protect Billy and Billy's reputation.

The following morning I scrubbed my face, removed my piercings, and I picked Mike up at the airport in the afternoon. We had a heart-to-heart driving home. I asked him to adopt me legally and he seemed pleased. Neither of us mentioned either of the Billys in that conversation. I had my mom's colorist take my hair back to blonde, got a decent haircut, and when I entered the Davis writing program at summer's end I was a new person: I was Athena Cervantes.

Rule #64: Avoid a succession of loose sentences, especially with the too-frequent use of the word "but".

I wanted Mike to be the one to move me up to Davis but he was in New York that weekend so my mother asked Brenda to go along. It was supposed to be our super fun "girls' road trip", but I was a nervous wreck and my mother was sadly anticipating her somewhat-empty nest. Boo offered to drive; her intention was to give us plenty of opportunity to say good-bye, but all we did with her kindness was antagonize each other. Also, the drive from LA to Davis is about seven hours of scorching mid-state boredom. The Dairy Queen halfway up is the best restaurant on the road. We all got cranky.

I had flown up a few weeks earlier to find a suitable apartment befitting a grad student in the arts, but when my mother saw it her disapproval was obvious.

Boo looked around and made a quick assessment. "Tea, you're going to need a Prozac script if you stay here for two years."

Rule #40: The dismissive "I couldn't care less" is often used with the shortened "not" mistakenly (and mysteriously) omitted: "I could care less." The error destroys the meaning of the sentence and is careless indeed.

It took several hours for my moving helpers to understand that I could care less what their opinions about my new life were going to be. I let them unpack a few boxes, take me out for sushi, and then I sent them to their hotel before they drove me out of my mind. In the morning I was already so homesick I wept, but I had told them to go home, so I had to nut up and find a bar. Which I did.

I had a few days to settle in to the town of Davis and my depressing little apartment before classes got going. I walked around the arboretum. I found a decent pizza place. I hit up the library a couple times and befriended a student worker there who told me about an opening on the *Aggie*, the school paper. He also turned me on to a free lecture series co-sponsored by the school of journalism and the history department.

"The first talk is going to be this dude." The kid handed me a flyer with a grainy picture of an octogenarian in a suit. The man looked vaguely familiar. His name was even more so.

"Jerald Franklin terHorst? Why do I know that name?" I asked my new pal.

"No clue. Guess you'll have to go to his talk to find out." I crammed the flyer into my purse and went to get a smoothie. I didn't give old Jerald another thought.

Rule #62: If you intend to use foreshadowing in your novel, please make it subtle and surprising.

Of all the universities large and small in the good ole' U S of A., is it not a strange and wondrous coincidence that one Jerald Franklin terHorst wound up at U.C. Davis that year? There he was though, in the flesh, giving a talk to the School of Journalism and the History Department on September eighth, the anniversary of U.S. Proclamation 4311. I wasn't yet hooking up with Burke on September eighth and the *Aggie* needed a reporter to cover the event. I volunteered. (Oh, sure, you doubters will poo-poo the possibility, but just suck it and add it to the list of things you'll complain about in your amazon reviews. I speak only the truth here.)

Mr. terHorst was eighty if he was a day, and though not quite frail, he wasn't participating in triathlons either. But mentally the spry old geezer was sharp as a tack. He still had quite a bug up his ass about Gerald Ford, too, and some related ancient history back in the seventies, and that's what he'd come to Davis to talk about. Before he got ten minutes in, I remembered where I'd seen his name and the unbidden memory caused me to sit up suddenly and pay swift attention.

Here's the gist of what that grand old bugger had to say that night. I'm paraphrasing:

For the record: it was October of 1973 when Spiro Agnew's job as the Vice President of the United States of America became Congressman Gerald Ford's job. Spiro Agnew, some will remember, had been forced to resign the vice presidency under enormous pressure because he'd been caught red-handed evading taxes and taking bribes. Agnew was the first, and notably the last, Greek-American to ever hold such a lofty political office in America, and the poor man seemed genuinely perplexed as to why anyone would care that he'd been issuing demands out of the V.P.'s office for kickbacks that he thought he was owed back in his home state of Maryland. Apparently, you could have knocked Spiro over with a feather when he found out that most folks took a dim view. In Greece, payoffs were *why* people sought public office and everybody knew it. (There is a kind of shaky honesty to Greek dishonesty and only now the whole world knows just how true this is. But, let's get back to the story at hand.)

Ford, who was the Republican Party leader in the House at the time, and so next in line to take over for Agnew, seemed to be a pretty decent guy. Even most Democrats liked him. It has been said that he was "eminently likable for a politician". It has, nevertheless, been widely agreed upon that his most notable and possibly only true political accomplishment was that he had a knack for being in the right place at just the right time. The *worst* thing anybody had to say about him up until then was that he seemed to have odd problems with gravity occasionally.

Then Watergate happened, Nixon resigned in ignominy, and Ford became the only man ever to serve America first as her vice president and consecutively as her president without securing one solitary citizen's vote. Thus, whether or not you liked the guy, it was, to most people, more than a bit ironic that the only U.S. president up until then to be a real and true Eagle Boy Scout (Mr. Ford) would come to rule over an epoch in our country's history marred by the worst criminals in the highest offices of the land. (Well, again, up until that point anyway.) Enter the other Jerald, our Mr. terHorst. He was Ford's buddy from Michigan and the Washington correspondent from the *Detroit News*. Ford tapped him to be his press secretary.

This all happened before the Ford family even had sufficient time to move into the Vice President's residence in Washington D.C. And this is precisely the point in relating the story where Mr. terHorst got a little exercised that night in Davis. He claimed that Alexander Haig, Richard Nixon's chief-of-staff and a notorious weasel, paid Gerald Ford a visit and worked out a quid pro quo deal that subsequently pardoned Nixon. I have to be honest. I was asking myself, does it really matter whether Nixon's pardon came because Haig put the screws to Gerald Ford, or that the old crook was pardoned on Ford's own terms? I guess it matters to an Eagle Scout. It mattered to more than a few others too, my mother being only one. (I'll get to that in a bit.) Whatever you believe about that meeting between Haig and Ford, pardon Nixon is what Ford did on September 8th, 1974 in what was called Proclamation 4311.

That single act was undoubtedly what cost Ford the election two years later. On a more personal front, it also immediately cost him the friendship of his close buddy and press secretary. *Voilá!* I give you Mr. Jerald Franklin terHorst who resigned in protest over the whole crummy deal, which as you can imagine, made for some shitty press for the newly-coronated president.

It's interesting, isn't it? Thirty-some years later and this little geezer still had a hard-on for people he said had wrongfully accused him of petty resentment over Gerald Ford's blindsiding him. Jerald Franklin terHorst, with tears in his eyes, told the U.C. Davis J-School students and a few history majors that he was one of the few people in government back in the day who had publicly voiced the opinion that if anyone was going to be pardoned, it should be the thousands of American expats who had left during the Viet Nam war as draft dodgers, and not the scoundrel, Richard Nixon. He blushed, he actually blushed, when the students rose to give him a standing ovation. With a tear in my eye I was among them.

I worked my way through the small crowd around him and made sure my brand new *Aggie* press pass was prominent before I butted in the front of the line.

"Mr. terHorst," I said, "I'm Athena Cervantes from the campus paper. I wonder if I could ask you a few questions for my article about your talk tonight." The old man turned, looked at my press pass for a long moment, and gave me the distinct impression that he was either dubious of the press on the whole, or just disinclined to be interviewed. With sudden unexpected audacity I blurted out why his name seemed so familiar to me.

"I wonder if you might be able to tell me, sir, why my mother keeps a copy of your resignation letter framed over her desk?" The disclosure surprised us equally. Jerald terHorst's rheumy, old, blue eyes widened. His smile turned genuine and about two percent lecherous, or as lecherous as a guy over eighty can get.

"Let's find a bar and get a drink," he said.

Rule # 83: As in rule #73, certain words are redundant and unnecessary. "Case" is one of those words. Why say "It might be the case that mistakes were made" when you can simply say, "Maybe mistakes were made."?

The following day, a little hung over as a result of attempting to keep up with none other than Jerald Franklin terHorst himself, I called home to brag about the honor of doing shots with my mother's hero. Nobody picked up.

The day after that was the day Patty Orloff bade us all to think of ourselves as writers and nothing else and I, henceforth, proceeded to do exactly as she exhorted.

And, so, at last...

Burke. My number three love.

It should be noted, Burke was not without charm. And, as already established, I was not the only one who thought so. He had an appealing mysteriousness about him, and mystery at a certain age virtually means charm, so there you have it. Every female in the program let it be promptly known that he might have his way with them, if he so desired. His looks were imperfect. Irish, not Black Irish like Billy, more like a young Sean Penn maybe, with a similar intensity. He was a little short in the sense-of-humor department. A very serious, no-nonsense fellow. (I guess after the very vapid Billy The Kid, I was ready for some intensity.) He was of average height and he was built like a bantam-weight boxer, all muscle and coiled strength. He rarely smiled, and you would have thought that it cost him dearly to laugh, but when he did, the sun came out. Burke was into austerity in a very big way, hence he used only his surname. *Why use two when only one will do?*

Burke's austerity extended to his writing, and parsimony was his only god. He made Hemingway look like Thomas Pynchon, and nobody in the program knew if he was a bona fide genius or a moron. While the rest of us in Orloff's seminar felt unduly constrained by the five-page max weekly limit, Burke religiously produced a scanty two. Even Professor Orloff (we could tell) did not quite know what to make of his terse prose. It was not unusual for Burke's sentences to be composed of only a single word. When it was his turn to offer feedback to others, his comments were so constipated they often were mere phonemes and vocalizations that sometimes sounded as if a chicken bone had lodged itself in his throat. If another student's work prompted what amounted to genuine animation for Burke, the room would grow pin-drop quiet as everyone turned to watch Orloff watch Burke while she clutched her clipboard to her chest, held her breath and stared at him with a look on her face that said she half expected him to hawk up a loogie on the seminar table. He never quite did that, but, owing to an imperfect dental bite, he was a spitter, so folks generally gave him a little personal space on the rare occasions that he made like he was actually going to speak.

Burke asked me to marry him on our first date. We shared a pizza. We split the bill at Shakey's because Shakey's had a deal and Burke had a coupon. (He deducted the discount from *his* half of the bill.) Too polite to decline his earnest proposal, (it was really more of a declaration that I was the woman he would eventually marry than an actual proposal) I removed an anchovy from my slice and gently donated it to his side. He took that as a "yes". There was, of course, no engagement ring since Burke was devoutly opposed to precious jewelry, particularly the bestowal of it and especially under circumstances whereupon he might be reasonably expected to be the bestow-er. Burke's adherence to austerity as a code to live by meant that he did not believe in giving gifts of any kind. Neither did he ever, once, pick up a check or pay his fair share of any restaurant or bar tab he'd helped to rack up. Instead, he had the uncanny ability to summon generosity in others. Burke was the kind of guy who helped himself to a disproportionate quantity of whatever pitcher of beer or bottle of wine had been floated by anyone else while often times excoriating his benefactor-of-the-moment for what he deemed consumer profligacy. The luminosity afforded by his presence was all Burke ever needed to contribute.

Our engagement lasted throughout grad school. Yes, I did get engaged with alarming and cavalier frequency, but at least with Burke, I now know that I never had any intention to actually get married then. I just liked having somebody want me when it appeared that they had other options available to them.

Burke also, it must be said, was the only one in that seminar who appeared to like my work. At least a little, tiny bit, he said. Well, Patty Orloff did too. But, fat lot of good that did me. If I learned one thing about writing in that class it wasn't how to write. No. What I learned was that it is never a really good thing to be singled out for excellence within any group of writers. That was true in Patty Orloff's class, it was true at the *Aggie*, and it's true now at the *Tribune*. You don't ever want your teacher or your editor to tell you that you're hot shit in front of your colleagues. That is the quickest route to being hated among peers that a writer can take. It can get your tires slashed on a newspaper and I know someone at the *Oakland Trib* that this has happened to. Twice. Both times after he was nominated for a Pulitzer. Such coveted positive attention can also turn your fiancé into a spitting gargoyle and I can attest to this experience personally.

Indeed, it was in Patty Orloff's seminar that I was first introduced to the violence among writers. All these writing courses follow a similar format: Everybody brings their precious pages and takes a turn reading them aloud to the others. Following each piece, the class members are expected to provide "constructive feedback". At least that is the euphemism. In reality, literary criticism in these seminars can range from the politely dismissive to the viciously hostile. So fearful of judgment was I by week two that I wisely aimed for sterling mediocrity in my writing, and in so doing, I avoided the worst of the critical blood sport that my classmates sometimes shared. It is rare in such an environment, as a rule, for a mob to turn downright cruel since everybody fears retaliation, but for my last piece in Orloff's class I decided in a rare burst of creative courage to throw caution to the wind and I wrote a what-the-fuck piece about a little girl trying to survive the mortifying embarrassment of her drunken father's shenanigans on the one and only summer vacation she had shared with him.

Lord, God, I still do not know what nerve I hit, but "uproar" is the only way to describe the ensuing discussion following my five pages of "The Princess of Fire Island". It was all I could do to keep from weeping. And Professor Orloff let them have at me. For way too long, I thought. When the entire bank of possible literary insults had been exhausted, Orloff sat down. A first – since she preferred to pace the room and stare up at the ceiling throughout both the readings and the feedback. She tossed her clipboard onto the table and smiled at me.

"Congratulations, Athena," she said. "You touched a nerve." This was an ambiguous response to say the least, and everybody wanted to clear up the ambiguity right away.

"You *didn't like it*, did you?" It was a virtual chorus of voices.

"No," she shook her head. She waited a beat. She smiled at me. "I adored it." Well, this got a response, though nobody was bold enough to actually call Orloff an idiot.

"Hey, look, you guys, good fiction creates feelings – passion – and makes us feel passionately for the characters. You may hate them, but how did you arrive at such hatred? Somebody convinced you that these characters are real people and they made you care. That's how. That's good writing. That's *great,* good writing." Orloff leaned in and patted the five pages, fanned before me on the table. "Athena, I loved your little girl. And, I hated that father. God, how I hate that father...perhaps he reminds me of someone I know..." She grinned. "This was absolutely your best piece all term. May I keep this copy?" It was the first and only time that Orloff had singled someone out for such high praise and made such a request. I nodded of course and even pushed the five double spaced pages clumsily toward her. She gathered them and smiled benevolently down at them while putting them in order. Then, back to business she went while everybody, especially Burke, glowered at me.

The final meeting of Patty Orloff's fiction seminar was famously held at her house in Marin. It was reputed to be the best unofficial event on the university calendar, and it was when and where she awarded her "Orloff Award" to the best piece of fiction for the term. No one ever missed the party. Every one of my peers would have promised to forfeit sex for a lifetime or turn over a first born child to get the "Orloff Award." I broke up with Burke the day before the party and I don't have a clear memory of how or even why. Sometimes these things happen. But I told him that I would still give him a ride to Marin if he paid for half the gas.

So, jump ahead. Of course my Princess story got the Orloff Award. You'd have to be pretty dumb not to have already figured that one out, but as it turned out, Burke was that dumb. He was so miffed to be snubbed by Patty that he drank too much and demanded an impromptu reading of a poem he'd been working on. It started out true to Burkian form: "She. Broke. My. Heart. An. Animal. She. Is." The last line however represented more words in a single sentence than any of us had heard him utter during the entire two years of the program: "Never, never, never, never, ever fall in love with a woman if her name rhymes with hyena."

So, picture the way the entire room grew as silent as an unvisited crypt. Picture the gaping mouths that gave way to particularly vicious laughter at my expense. I downed my mojito and I told Burke that he was not welcome to ride back to Davis in my car. He would have to bum a ride from someone else, and I was not going to refund his gas money. In short, I grew some balls and sort of just grew up a little bit, or at least in that single, painful moment of humiliation, I outgrew Burke.

A week later I packed up and moved into the basement apartment in Berkeley, again skipping the pomp of a graduation ceremony. I applied to the *Trib* for a day job and, buoyed by the dubious and subjective tide of Orloff's words about my writing, I resolved to finish my good, *great* novel. By sheer chance I found out a few weeks later, from a friend of Rose's, that Burke had slept with Rosie behind my back a couple of times when she had been visiting me in Davis. Truthfully, I felt a little sorry for Burke, and nothing at all, not even anger, toward Rose, but the news deepened my resolve to publish before either of them. Rose made my resolution easier by deciding that she would rather represent writers than be one. Burke made things easy by disappearing.

Rule #85: Kick the wordiness habit. Better to simply and clearly identify "hostile acts" as such, than to refer to negative offenses as "acts of a hostile character".

Corie Skolnick

TWO

"I am a journalist."
   - Howard R. Falkenhorst, Editor, *Oakland Tribune*

Howard R. Falkenhorst is a big, balding, beefy, white guy of indeterminate age, one of those puffy guys who could be any age between thirty-five or fifty-five–you just don't know. If you encountered the very garrulous Howard in a bar one night and, apropos of nothing, he charged you with the task of guessing his profession, "journalist" is one of the last you might reasonably tender, based upon his appearance alone. Never mind his diction or vocabulary, which might instantly provoke images of hard, manual, unskilled labor. He just doesn't seem like the "wordy" type. "Plumber" could be in your top five guesses. At the *Trib* offices Howie wears stained neckties and cheap, buttoned-down, long-sleeved, dingy white, oxford cotton shirts, and slacks that need a cleaning and pressing, so "plumber with a tie" is exactly what he looks like at work. He often seems kind of misplaced there. Like he might have been clearing a clogged drain someplace when he got called hastily to a funeral, and then later he just wandered into the *Tribune* building. He looks like a plumber who keeps a shirt and tie in his truck for impromptu appearances at somber occasions. Whatever. You get the picture. Definitely not *GQ*.

74

In terms of personal philosophy, Howard is, at least to me, something of a twenty-first century enigma as he has been known rather openly (for an educated person, and I must assume that he is) to mourn the day that human civil rights were codified into U.S. law. In fact, on the very center of his trophy wall (every editor has one), Howie has an anachronistic dartboard with LBJ's face painted onto the cork. It was a gift, he proudly tells, from a mentor who went on to work for various Bushes, but who ultimately had to quit them because, like "all those damn Texans", they were "too soft on immigration".

Mostly, though, Howie is pretty much an equal opportunity hater. That is, he has a hard-on for *all* minority peoples, including women and gay people, but, inexplicably, none so much as the "wetbacks" who he says, at least once a week with his bald face hanging out, "should all be sent back over the border to Mexico, *muy pronto*". What the hell? Need I say more about Howie's politics?

I guess nobody in the newsroom challenges his racism or his misogyny lest we be accused of the worst thing a journalist can be guilty of: *having no sense of humor.* Amidst some mystery, it is commonly known that Howie Falkenhorst ascended the paper's ranks through Sports, a true Neanderthal of the Fourth Estate. As far as anyone has been told, he is one of those fifth generation Californians who passionately resents, and resolutely neglects, the reality of California's historical settlement and development by the Spanish, which (note to Howard) predates the Falkenhorst invasion by almost a good four centuries. And, of course, his endurance at the *Tribune* gives those of us who work for him reason to fear his mysterious longevity. One might assume that he either knows somebody or blows somebody, but nobody knows for sure who it is up top that protects him or why.

Corie Skolnick

Nevertheless, as fate would have it, as if part of the greater-great plan of my own little life, at the precise moment when I applied for gainful employment at the *Trib*, just one week out of grad school, Howard R. Falkenhorst was under considerable pressure from the great editorial "above" to diversify his newsroom staff. What got ultimately related to me regarding my hire was the story that Howard's boss made it crystal clear on the very same day: *Get some skirt and some color on the team.* I believe, left entirely to his own devices, Howard's people would forever resemble—to a man —the demographics of the *Wehrmacht Newsletter* staff, i.e. universally male and pale. So, even though Howard R. Falkenhorst told everyone who gave him the opportunity to do so that he would have sooner had two root canals that hot June day than hire a "*beaner chick*", he jumped at the chance to acquire one who looked more Jenny McCarthy than J.Lo – one whose veins contained not a drop of Latin blood but who had merely borrowed her Spanish-sounding surname. At any rate, that is how I became a professional journalist. I was hired on by Howie as a token, fraudulent Latina with sketchy writing skills, no legitimate work experience really, and zero journalistic credentials if you didn't count my stint on the *Aggie*. "Athena Cervantes", however, looked good on the masthead and hiring me put both "skirt" and "color" on Howard's newsroom team.

Oh, and there was that personal letter of recommendation from one Jerald Franklin terHorst written on my behalf to an old mentee of his working up at the tippy top of the *Trib's* news syndicate. That probably didn't hurt my chances. (I'm just keeping it real.)

Rule #52: Transporting a reader across time in a narrative or story that spans years, decades, even lifetimes is tricky, tricky business. Especially if you are telling a tale that requires some

back and forth on the timeline. This movement requires more skill than any other story telling feature. Beware the lazy segue. Terms like "Meanwhile", "So, anyway", "Over time", etc. are worse than cliché. Steer clear.

Moving right along... too many years of my young life evaporated rather unproductively at the *Trib*. Against all odds, Howie and I attained a workable détente. Without conscious intent to do so, he conferred upon me a certain dubious status as the resident "minority" columnist by giving me every assignment that featured somebody with a "funny" sounding name - "funny" being his operative word for "foreign". In that way, the human interest stories became, in time, my special province. I made a little name for myself locally and established a minor following among Bay Area readers. I got some fan mail and some death threats, the surest sign of success as a journalist. I never got a by-line or even a promotion until the Fremont Rodeo Queen story put my name on the national radar, but over the years, Howard did hire a number of other women, calculating that he could get away with paying them less (which he could and did), and so things were not absolutely bleak while he had more "skirt" to bother than just little ole' me.

My long, lonely nights during those years were spent expanding (with a depressing dedication to futility) the manuscript I had begun in grad school. I took up running to offset the Malomar/chardonnay diet I was on, and I dated sporadically and casually. Nothing that got remotely serious. Three strikes and I was out as far as men were concerned. As a writer I was, at best, treading water.

On the home front, down in southern California, Little Brother had moved into his own house in Santa Monica and he was rapidly becoming a surf shop mogul. My mother was feathering her empty nest with more and more pro-bono work in the LA ghettos, and Mike's research had put him on the short list to head up the National Institute of Mental Health ethics committee. Both Mike and my mom continued to put best-selling books on the *New York Times'* nonfiction list. My mother effortlessly published a whole new series having something to do with the endurance of menopause, and Mike's latest book of essays got so white hot it was out on audiobook. So, while I labored without much progress on America's next greatest novel up in the Bay Area, it was just over-achieving business as usual down in the Palisades for *mi familia.*

Regarding Rose and her family, I'll admit this much: it was meanly gratifying that neither she nor Brenda nor the other Finemans had major status changes to the better. Eddie continued to make oodles of mysterious money; Brenda was still struggling to keep her casting agency above water; Joshie worked part-time in Miggs's Hermosa Beach shop while taking film classes at Santa Monica Community College at night (and defending various narcotics possession charges by day); and Rosie was at her fourth New York literary agency since grad school, having given up writing altogether and going over to the dark side – publishing. She convinced herself that mobility was a good thing and that her success as an agent was only that one best-selling author client beyond her grasp. We kept in touch via infrequent emails, but she never asked about my book and she certainly never offered to represent me when it was finished. I never suggested as much either. I never mentioned my book at all to Rose.

I did get a sad, needy email from Billy once, but otherwise we were completely incommunicado except for a few nuggets of gossip that made it through the extended Fineman Family pipeline.

Rule #17: Do not inject opinion. Your opinions are no doubt important to you. Your readers, however, may not share your enthusiasm about them.

Of course the nation went to war again, but you would hardly notice that. Except for a certain stale bitterness about the inevitable war profiteering by Halliburton and the rest of the defense industry, even my mother seemed quietly resigned to the domination of the United States by the military industrial complex war machine. I guess you could call it a lucky stroke of fate for Billy though that when war was declared against Iraq, *Webster's Peace* got dragged out of mothballs and re-shown at art houses all over the country. Even I ordered it on Netflix twice, but I found both times that I just couldn't watch *Webster's Peace* all the way through.

You'll think it strange that I never confronted my mother about covering for Billy throughout my childhood, nor did I ever ask her outright why she'd allowed him to steal her script. That's how those terrible secrets go I've learned. There's an awful kind of collusion involved and I did not want to be the one to upset their stupid apple cart of secrets and lies. I happened to be down in LA when Billy got interviewed in the *LA Times Calendar* about "his" inspiration for his one and only screenplay. I pointed to the full-color photo of an aging Billy on the *Calendar's* front page after Sunday brunch but Mother's only significant comment was, "Just like in Viet Nam, the burden of war will be carried by the silent underclass and the young". That sounded just like something Jerald ter-Horst had said to me, but I wound up never saying anything to her about my night with him either. I knew how to keep secrets too.

Rule #95: It is my most earnestly held opinion that to embark on the composition of a major work of fiction is a matter of pri-

vacy. Tell no one that you are writing a novel or what it is about lest you spend inordinate amounts of time fending off questions related to your progress. "How's the book going?" is a writer's most dreaded inquiry. Number two is, "What's your book about?"

As time dragged on I started a list* of famous authors who had labored for many years before publishing their first novels, which I consulted almost daily. It was ammo for the inevitable inquiry, "How's the book going?" The funny thing was that as time marched on with no published book to my credit, people stopped asking. Spending so much time on a book that never materialized wasn't unlike having an unmentionable disease, awkward silences and everything.

*Just fyi:
- Salinger, 9 years for *Catcher In The Rye*
- Mitchell, 9 years for *Gone With The Wind*.
  Then there are the whiz kids:
- Stephen King, only 2 years for *Carrie*.
- Harper Lee took 2 years to write *To Kill A Mockingbird*.
  But, thank God for Kafka.
- Kafka would still be working on *The Trial*; he never did stop working on it.
  My absolute favorite:
- Nabokov spent 16 years from starting *Lolita* to getting it published in France (by a publisher that mostly put out pornography) first, and then 3 years later in the U.S., so in total, 19 years to publication...so the manuscript was 7 years older than Lolita herself was by the time the book saw print.

Anyway, *the list** was ever ongoing, and in my darkest hours, some-how reading it over and over heartened me to think I was in good writerly company.

And so I labored on, convincing myself daily that my slavish devotion in obscurity to the manuscript of *Wooden Nickels* seemed a small price to pay to produce a readable novel. It was a kind of literary treadmill.

Until one fine summer Saturday morning when I opened my trusty, old laptop again for the gazillionth time. Just like always, I loaded the *Wooden Nickels* file for another session, and stared at the ancient cursor blinking slowly and greenly on the screen for five unproductive minutes before touching the keyboard again. At the first keystroke, the entire machine, now ridiculously obsolete, impossibly slow, and virtually useless for any task other than pure word processing – forget accessing the internet with it – simply gave up the ghost and died. The screen went utterly black. I'd heard of computer crashes, but I'd never actually witnessed one. Until my own ancient Dell laptop crashed before my very eyes. In that horrible single moment I had regret. *SO MUCH REGRET!* I was forced to entertain the possibility that all was lost. But, what was lost was surprising. I simultaneously felt an odd sense of libera-tion. And a question arose. Unbidden and definitely unwanted, yet undeniably there. Had I squandered my best years to date on noth-ing more than a mewling, uninteresting and now inaccessible dia-tribe against one Billy Byrne McGuire? When *Wooden Nickels* evap-orated into thin virtual air, I finally saw it for what it really was. And with not a whit of doubt, I knew that at its heart it was noth-ing more than a lengthy indictment of Billy for his crime of plagia-rism, and the lesser offenses of marital infidelity and parental ne-glect, and I also knew in that single second it would never be any-thing else no matter how hard I worked at it. But, I still couldn't let it go. I wanted it back. Like a crummy relationship that comes to an end only after you've spent too much time in, I desperately wanted my manuscript back.

I sat staring at the empty screen stunned into immobility. Every word I had written had instantly vanished. Where do all those words *go?* I turned the computer off, waited a full minute, then turned it on again. I let my trembling fingers hover over the impotent keyboard. Like an addict, my whole body craved the re-writing process. Fact: you cannot rewrite what you cannot access. I simply closed the Dell, put on my running shoes and went out to log 10k and contemplate the wisdom (or lack thereof) of backing up your files.

Rule #49: Place yourself in the background. Write in a way that draws the reader's attention to the sense and substance of the writing, rather than to the mood and temper of the author.

I am not able to relate to you with any clarity at all what happened to the rest of that weekend. I suspect that it involved co-pious amounts of cheap white wine the quality of which probably declined right along with my mood. I demolished the remaining stash of Malomars, probably three or four packages. I confided the loss to no one. I may have taken to my bed.

The following Monday morning, sheets of unseasonable freezing rain flooded the freeways, sent most reasonable Bay Area commuters to the BART, and kept almost the entire *Trib* writing staff at home. I myself put on a bright yellow slicker, my fat jeans, a worn-out UC Davis hoody and old rubber waders only so I could relinquish my laptop to Ronald from Security who was rumored to possess mad computer salvation skills. Like a grieving, un-recon-ciled lover, I dared to hope that such rumors were true.

"I'm only interested in recovering one file, Ronald," I told him. "If you can copy the *Wooden Nickels* file I will give you anything you want."

"Anything?" Ronald's glasses fogged a little bit when he stroked my ancient computer. "This baby's a dinosaur," he sneered, but his appreciation for its vintage was obvious. "If I can get your file off of here can I keep the hardware?"

"Hell, yes!" I yelled too loudly. I almost hugged him.

Ronald smiled slyly and slunk off to some secret interstitial space in the *Trib* building to industriously shirk his building security duties and to try instead to recover my manuscript.

Around four-ish with the rain still sheeting on the windows, Howard dropped by my desk with a last minute assignment. He pulled a late-lunch toothpick out of his mouth and stabbed the notes he held in his grubby other hand.

"Dimitriou...? What is that? Is that Mexican?" When Howard asked me such a question it was tempting to try to think he was only issuing a friendly insult. I hated to have him reveal his spectacular ignorance while simultaneously asserting his authority. It made me feel a little sick that I worked under such a moron.

"It's Greek," I said. "You know...like *Alexis Dimitriou*? The Greek Minister of Finance? That guy?" (For a veteran newspaperman and an editor on a major city daily, Howard R. Falkenhorst remained scandalously ignorant of foreign affairs.)

"Yeah, whatever." He threw the summary across my desk. Before he replaced his toothpick he belched. "It's all yours. Right up your alley, *Cervantes*." He made my last name sound like a filthy epithet.

I glanced at the deadline.

"Howie, wait a sec. This is due Wednesday for the supp. I can't do this. I've got four features stacked up like jets. You've got to give this to somebody else." I gestured to the mess on my desktop. Howard swiveled his fat head and squeezed his man boobs theatrically.

"Oh, hey, do you *see* any other writers here, Cervantes?" The only other reporter to have braved the storm that day had already left with a photographer to cover the flooding in Alameda. "It's yours, *Chee Ka*. And, get on it. Someone upstairs is very interested in this guy Dimitriou." Howard swirled his pointed finger aloft to indicate his boss's boss. "Oh, and F.Y.I....*El Heff Ay*," he said over his shoulder as he minced away, "said he wants YOU, specifically, to do this one."

I didn't know that our editor-in-chief knew even of my existence but I didn't have time to wonder about it with a deadline of Wednesday. I scanned the newsroom clerk's scanty assignment notes. As per usual, Lupe had included a thumbnail photo of the subject of the piece, Dr. Nikko Dimitriou, up at the top of the page in shadowy photocopy quality. It showed him to be a man who bore a striking resemblance to Albert Einstein.

I fired up the search engine and typed "Nikko Dimitriou". A picture, not remotely resembling Albert E., flashed at the top of the search. I clicked on it.

Holy dear mother of god! I clicked again. The screen photo enlarged. Now, do this for me. Sit back and take a deep breath and close your eyes and try to remember the first time you saw the likeness of the person who could very well be the love of your life. Remember that fluttery little response deep in your chest? A feeling that any cardiologist can tell you is your heart literally skipping a beat. The photo on my seventeen-inch desktop monitor was from a two-month-old cover of *Wired* magazine; the article was titled, "*AMERICA'S MOST ELIGIBLE GEEK*". Nikko Dimitriou's picture was the kind of photograph that could make a person buy expensive hair products and dental hygiene paraphernalia in quantities they can't possibly use up in one little lifetime. His smile was equal parts young John-John Kennedy, James Dean, Paul Newman, and Johnny Depp. With a big, healthy dose of Ryan Gosling. Powerful. Sexy. But somehow friendly, too. Iconic. I read the *Wired* article. Then I read the *Times* article and pulled up a few more with even more pictures from the internet. One from the *Chronicle* showed Nikko Dimitriou in between Warren Buffet and Bill Gates at some fundraiser from the previous year. Another one had him on a stage behind microphones, Bono's arm reaching up to embrace his shoulders.

"Who the hell *is* this guy?" I asked myself in a breathy whisper. Within an hour of diligent study I knew what apparently every other sentient being in the free world (at least the females) already knew about Dr. Nikko Dimitriou.

Rule #81: The subject of a sentence and the principal verb should not, as a rule, be separated by a phrase or clause that can be transferred to the beginning.

At the bottom of the clerk's notes no fewer than six contact numbers were listed for the good, young doctor. Stanford University's Department of Medicine was listed and a second Stanford number under something called Stanford University's School of Integrative Studies in Cancer Detection and Technology. Two for Naxxos International, one in Toronto, Canada and one in San Francisco. Another two simply listed "Dr. Nikko Dimitriou, mobile" and "Dr. Nikko Dimitriou, home". I did the eenie-meenie and landed on "home" so that's the first one I dialed. It rang six times and then a voice mail message instructed me to leave a message. The voice was female and sounded young and sexy. I told myself that she was not a significant other since nowhere in my research did I find any mention of a wife or even a long term girlfriend. Probably his assistant, I found myself hoping. The *Wired* article seemed to make a point of Nikko Dimitiou's single relationship status, noting a long list of adoring female "associates" who had been interviewed for the piece. It was clear from their quotes that they were all smitten with Nikko Dimitriou. I didn't leave a message on his home number voice mailbox. The clock said it was after six so I didn't try the work numbers. I dialed his cell.

"Nikko here." He picked up on the second ring and he sounded nice. Well, I imagined he did.

"Dr. Dimitriou, this is Athena Cervantes from the *Oakland Tribune*." Dr. Nikko Dimitriou didn't skip a beat.

"Athena," he said, "I'm a huge fan!" *Whaaaat?????* "The Rodeo Queen story last month was your best! Is it okay if I call you Athena? And, please, you should call me Nikko." I scanned the screen on my desktop with his celebrity pals all over it. *First names? Really?* I tried to bring my voice into a reasonable register but I think I sounded a lot like Minnie Mouse.

"I'm actually calling to get some quotes for the supplement piece we'll be running on Sunday about you. Did the clerk tell you that I'd be calling?" I could feel sweat trickle down my back.

"Yes, Lupe, wasn't it? Did she tell you how honored I am that you're going to do the article?"

"Well, Dr. Dim...Nikko, the National Science Award is a pretty big deal. I'm actually the lucky one. Usually these kinds of profiles go to a much more senior staffer."

"Well, when can we meet?"

"Oh, no, sir, I can just get some quotes right now on the phone if you have the time." *Sheeesh, what a totally nice guy*, I was thinking.

"You know, I'm not really a phone guy. But, I *am* really close to your office right now. I'll swing over." He hung up before I could even make up a good lie.

Rule #4: Concentrate your narrative energy on the point of change. When your character is new to a place that's the point to step back and fill in the details of their world. People don't notice their daily routine, so when writers describe them it can sound as if they're trying too hard to instruct the reader.

Let me be completely honest about this one thing: My cubicle is not what you would call "tidy". And, unlike my colleagues, I don't hang pictures of myself with every celebrity (like the rodeo queen) I've ever interviewed. No ferns or struggling dieffenbachia, and my cube walls are bare. I looked around as I imagined Nikko Dimitriou might and my workspace looked not so much neglected as much as it seemed that on any day I was expecting to get the boot. It certainly did not look impressive by any stretch. So, faced with the imminent arrival of an actual and real "Greek God" I had to choose between a quick housekeeping flurry or a mad dash to the ladies' room to try to improve my personal appearance. I calculated that at the very least I had to clear a space for Nikko Dimitriou to sit down for my interview before I could consider running a comb through my hair or even checking my teeth for stray bits of the tabouli salad that had been lunch. Three sticks of hastily ingested and diligently chewed Double Bubble provided a modicum of dental hygiene while I tried to locate the guest chair that no "guest" had ever previously occupied. There wasn't a thing I could do about the day's wardrobe choice. Never what you would call a fashionista, I had a sudden sinking realization that my once bohemian "style" had devolved into something that could accurately be described as "bag-lady un-chic". Magically, a long-forgotten, spare pair of running shoes materialized from under a stack of old copy so at least I'd have shoes on my feet and not storm boots.

I heard the doors whoosh open and immediately Security Ronald materialized inside the newsroom with Nikko Dimitriou in tow. Wow! He *was* close by! And, double wow! Living and breathing, the good doctor was even more gorgeous than his two-dimensional self. I crouched down to switch footwear and cursed. The gigantic wad of pink gum flew out of my mouth and like magic it disappeared somehow between my legs. I spent all of ten seconds trying to locate it before I sank down to the floor and quickly made the switch from rubber waders to athletic shoes. Then I jumped up and peered over the cube's wall. Ronald had engaged Dr. Dimitriou in what seemed an intense conversation as he escorted him slowly over to my workspace. A dedicated nerd like our Ronald had no doubt recognized the young tech wizard on sight and found it necessary to explain to him why it was that he himself was working a security job for the *Tribune* instead of writing code for one of Silicon Valley's finest firms. They approached the opening of my cube while I presented my backside. Bending over a tall stack of empty file folders I tried to feign something between industry and importance.

"Cervantes..." Ronald rapped on the glass wall. "You got somebody." I straightened up, turned and brushed the falling hair out of my eyes.

"Oh," I smiled and extended a hand. "Dr. Di - "

"Nikko," he cut me off with a dazzling smile. "Thank you, Ronald," Nikko dismissed him, lowering the wattage a bit and Ronald saluted before ambling off. When Nikko Dimitriou turned his attention back to me and touched my hand, a sensation unlike anything I'd ever felt coursed through my whole body. I thought my knees were actually going to buckle like a heroine in a cheesy chick lit novel. I just stood there stupidly shaking his hand and staring into his gorgeous face for an impossibly long moment before he put his other hand around mine and gently squeezed. It was the most incredible sensation of déjà vu I'd ever had.

As if he were echoing my very thoughts he whispered, "You are absolutely gorgeous, Athena." He studied my face and continued to hold my hand in both of his. "But..." Before I could resist, Nikko twirled me 180 degrees and reached forward to peel the wad of pink gum from my left butt cheek. Then he spun me back around and deposited the offending item into my palm. He pointed to my waders on the floor. "It's really coming down out there. Why don't you put your Wellies back on and we'll go someplace we can talk, eh?"

Rule #19: Do not use dialect unless you have a talented ear for it.

"Someplace" was Yoshi's over near Jack London Square. The place was almost empty because of the weather. The jazz "combo" had been diminished by the storm to just one lone guitar player. We ate sushi and drank *sake* and talked until I checked my watch. It was almost two a.m. We'd been there nearly six hours and I had not asked a single question that I could put into a Sunday profile about the youngest recipient of the National Science Award for computerized cancer detection innovation. Most of the conversation had in fact been in the other direction, as if Nikko Dimitriou had been interviewing me.

"Athena, these guys want to close but I just don't want the night to end," Nikko said. "I know a little Russian place...stays open all night sometimes...we can go get some coffee...?"

"Actually, I still *do* need to get some usable quotes. Where's the place?"

We drove in Nikko's Prius about a mile or two to his little "Russian place". The joint was packed. But oddly quiet. Each tiny, candle-lit table seated only two. The place reeked of romance. The owner, a young guy around our age, clearly knew Nikko well and I felt an instant twinge of jealousy for every other woman he'd ever brought to this super sexy after-hours spot. The owner locked the door behind us. After they exchanged fond, familiar embraces Nikko put his arm around me.

"Alexi, *this* is Athena Cervantes." I expected Alexi to nod politely and pretend that he recognized my name, but instead he fawned all over us with a heavy Russian accent.

"Theees? Theees is Athena? My gawd! She is so bee-you-ti-full! You don tell me dat she looks like da moveee star!" Nikko beamed. "I breeng da best vodka to sell-ee-brate!"

"Really, Alexi? It's long after two." Nikko looked around at the other table tops. It seemed that only coffee and tea were being consumed in ceramic mugs and delicate china.

"Yah! Teck-nik-lee vee are closed! Only da fambly ees heeer at deees hour." Alexi winked. "And I don need no dam leeker li-seens for da fambly!" Tiny icy jelly jars materialized and Alexi filled them to the top with strong Russian vodka. He took the bottle on a circuit around the room and then he sat down and joined us for a toast.

"To fambly!" he said, raising his own cup and swiveling around to include everyone in the toast. The patrons at the other tables raised cups and glasses. As my eyes adjusted in the dim light I could see that half the people were clearly not Russians. No two people at any one table were of the same race. So, Alexi had either a multi-ethnic family like no other or he used the term "family" in an extremely inclusive way. "To *family*," I echoed. I immediately wanted more than anything to be an insider. To be included in this cozy "fambly" tableau.

Alexi downed his own sparkling jar in two quick gulps and then he leaned toward me. His voice was conspiratorial. He smelled like anise and he spoke as if he was picking up the thread of a perpetual conversation.

"So, Athena, dees girrrl, da ro-day-oh queen? She has no mudder?"

"Her mom died when she was born." I told him what he already knew from the *Trib* feature. He clucked his tongue and shook his head.

"And da papa, he verk in da feeelds still, yah?"

"Yah, yeah, yes," I told him. Alexi looked up at Nikko and gestured with extravagant hand motions.

"Nikko, vee must help dis girrrl, no? How dis papa pay for her to go to da colidge?" Alexi's consonants rumbled across the table. Nikko reached out and squeezed the Russian's shoulder.

"Done," he said simply and smiled.

"Yah?" Alexi grinned back. "Dees is dun? Dees already hoppin?" He leaned back beaming. "Ahhh, dees eees vye you bring Athena to Alexi's! Vee are sell-ee-brate-ing for da leetle queen!" Alexi jumped up, leaned over and kissed my cheek with wet lips. "Hay!" he shouted. "Ev-ry-bud-dee! Deees is my friends, Nikko and Athena! Vee sell-ee brate-ing da queen of da ro-day-oh!" Another frozen bottle came out of the kitchen and was passed around.

What happened next was utterly amazing. As if on cue, seemingly from thin air, musical instruments appeared at every table. A banjo, a violin, an accordion, guitars and a mandolin. Even some bongos and a tambourine popped up as if by magical decree, and suddenly the dim, romantic restaurant transformed into a lively party. In short order, everyone who wasn't playing or singing was out on the floor dancing wildly. I'd never seen anything like it. I felt as if I'd been cast by Boo as an extra in a movie about beautiful gypsies. I kicked off my Wellies and danced like I'd never danced in my entire life.

Just before dawn people started pooping out and Alexi finally unlocked the front door to let them head home to bed, or off to work, depending on their luck. I went to find Nikko and when I did he was having an exchange in a dark corner with the pretty, young violinist. I watched him extract a handful of currency from his jeans. *Oh Lord!* I thought. I don't exactly know why, maybe it was something about the unusual setting coupled with Russian vodka and distant memories from my history with Billy The Kid, but something provoked a sudden weird suspicion. *Drugs!* my intoxicated mind screamed silently. My heart sank. I watched them a minute longer as Nikko patted the girl's head affectionately and whispered in her ear. I slunk back to our table and downed the dregs of my vodka glass. When Nikko found me a few minutes later he had my discarded waders dangling from his hands.

"I have to be in Palo Alto at eleven so I'm going to send you home in a cab and then you can have the driver wait if you want him to take you to the office. Does that sound okay?"

"Fine," I said stiffly. I pulled my boots on. "Well, thank you for a really interesting evening. I'll call you later or tomorrow to get those quotes. If you don't mind." I made my voice sound hard and chilly. Nikko looked puzzled for a second but he shrugged and nodded okay.

"Good," he said. He leaned forward and kissed both cheeks. Then he left me to wait for my cab. I used the ladies' room before I went to say my goodbyes to Alexi whom I found in the same corner arguing with the violinist. He hugged her hard and I could see that she was crying. I couldn't help but hear.

"I vill pay for my own needles, Alexi," she choked. "I do NOT use dirty needles!" *Oh, my god,* I thought. *It's heroin!* I cleared my throat and Alexi released the girl. I could see then how very young she was. And so pale and so thin. Terrible things went through my head. Things I did not want to imagine about Alexi, never mind Nikko Dimitriou. Alexi looked up. He saw me and held up one finger and then gave the girl a quick kiss on the cheek. He said something in Russian and she laughed and wiped her cheek.

"Let me vok Athena out," he told the girl. He fell in step beside me. Out on the sidewalk I remained silent. The sun was just starting to rise. I could smell the bay. I was exhausted and sick and sad. Alexi reached into his pocket and withdrew a pack of cigarettes but he just fondled them without lighting one. He looked at them ruefully for a bit and then grinned.

"I qweet da bastards, but I carreee dem. Just in case I change my mind." I just nodded. I was overwhelmed suddenly with a fatigue that is beyond physical. *God*, I thought. *What a strange complicated world this is.* Alexi read my mind.

"So, you catch us, huh?" His smile was anything but that of a sinister, drug-dealing pimp of young prostitutes. He sighed. "Nadi has pride. Too much of eeet." Alexi looked down the street and then down at the puddle beyond the curb. He shook his head. "Nikko, he find out dat sometimes, Nadia, she ree-hewsing her needles. He get very upset about it."

"How kind," I said. The sarcasm floated right over Alexi's head. He nodded.

"So, sometimes now vee do a leetle treeek on her, me and Nikko. But, sometimes eeet don't verk on her so good." I looked at him, incredulous that he could discuss the exploitation of a drug-addicted, teen aged prostitute with me and be so cavalier about it too. He misunderstood the look of horror on my face and chuckled. "Nikko tell her tonight dat I vill not let heem pay for da vodka. He say dat she must give me da munee and make a story up that she make beeeg tips dis veek." He leaned against the front window and inhaled as if he was taking a drag off one of those unlit ciggies. "I tell her I cannot take dis money. It is bad luck for a Russian to take money for vodka. She must keep it and never tell Nikko. But Nadi is from the Ukraine and she knows dees is big Russian boool sheet." Alexi laughed outright. "My job? My job is to make her take da muneee." He shrugged. "She need it for da drugs, you know? And

93

da needles." We stood side by side, me seething in anger, Alexi oblivious. "Poor keeed," he said. "She was eleven when she find out she got da bad blood disease." I almost could not believe my ears.

"What?!" I yelled. "What?! That kid has HIV?" At that instant my cab rolled up to the curb and splashed our feet. At least I had on rain boots. Alexi cursed his drenched pant legs and ruined loafers in Russian. I thought I was going to vomit but I managed to open the cab door. Alexi looked up, suddenly truly alarmed.

"Don't tell her I tell you, Athena. Nadi is very ashamed of dees!"

"*She's* ashamed? *She's* ashamed?" I slammed the door hard. "Berkeley, fast," I ordered the driver. I saw a light bulb go off for my new not-ever-now Russian friend standing in a puddle. He pounded on the window as we pulled away.

"No! No! No!" he shouted frantically. "Not dee haytch eye bee!" he yelled. "Nadi is ..." I turned around and lost the final word but I had suddenly no interest in slime like Alexi, or Nikko Dimitriou. I let the driver get on the Berkeley freeway before I could stop crying enough to give him my cross streets. When I arrived on my corner and tried to pay the fare, the driver refused to take the money.

"Nope," he said, "the doc's got an account. We settle up later."

"I don't want his filthy money," I spit the words out and threw two twenties over the seat.

"Hey, I can't take this, lady," he tried to hand my money back to me. "I told you. The doc takes good care of me."

"Keep it!" I screamed. "Think of it as a tip." I managed to open the door and jump out, falling to my knees instantly on the sidewalk. The driver got out and ran around the car. He tried to help me to my feet, still pushing the bills at me.

"Stop it!" I yelled. "Keep his filthy money!" The young man stepped back gesturing as if he thought I might do him bodily harm.

"You got a problem, lady, you know that?" He looked at me and wiped his brow sticking the money into his pocket. "I'm gonna take this, but I'm not gonna keep it. You tell the doc I took this money and I gave it to the little fiddle player for her insulin!" His tires screeched down the street.

Rule #25: Place the emphatic words of a sentence at the end.

I did not put two and two together until hours later when the vodka wore off.

Once I figured out exactly who Nikko Dimitriou really was, i.e. NOT an exploiter of teenaged, drug-addicted, terminally ill girls, but instead an anonymous and kind benefactor to anyone in need, I didn't really require any quotes to write the puff piece I'd been assigned. I filed his profile with the header: DOES NIKKO DIMITRIOU WALK ON WATER? And Mr. Big (Howie's boss's boss) loved it. I got a raise and Ronald was told to hang a fern in my cube.

Rule #30: Do not attempt to emphasize simple statements by using a mark of exclamation. The exclamation mark is to be reserved for use after true exclamations.

Two weeks to the day after my night out with Nikko Dimitriou an anonymous benefactor sent a brand new MacBook Air to the *Trib* with a terse message: *Ms. Cervantes – your stories bring us all in the Bay Area a little bit closer. Keep them coming.* And it was signed simply, "a fan of the Fremont Rodeo". I wanted to – come on! of course I wanted to – imagine that my "fan" was Nikko Dimitriou.

I even called the Apple store and begged them to reveal the identity of the sender, but no dice. Those guys at Apple have better espionage skills than the CIA.

Then, miracle of miracles, Ronald came through that same day with a recovered file of *Wooden Nickels* and he even helped me with the re-formatting from the obsolete PC program that had harbored six years of my sweat, tears and labor. (I guess he was feeling generous because I gifted him the old Dell.) At first, I was ambivalent about his technological success, almost resigned to the loss of my novel. Then I saw it uploaded to my brand new laptop and I resolved to finish the sucker after all. Don't ask me why. I set to work that very night re-writing, which really meant un-writing, the *Wooden Nickels* manuscript.

I was a writer on fire.

Rule #38: Regarding the use of a colloquialism, I advise that you simply use it. Do not draw attention to it by encasing it in quotation marks. When you do so it just looks like insecurity. Are you worried people won't think you "know better"?

Nikko's profile came and went in the Sunday Supplement without a word from him. I was disappointed (crushed). But I kept myself busy with a dedicated schedule to rewrite *Wooden Nickels*. After such a close call nearly losing years of work, I promised myself, that for the good or the terrible, I was going to finish it and get it out there. I was even toying with the probably-stupid idea of letting Rose Fineman read it. The following week I brought Security Ronald a fancy pastry from Nabalom's bakery every morning. I backed up all my files. I wrote a lengthy piece for the mid-week feature section about Nadia. The day after her super-sad life story ran, I got a phone call.

"Is this Athena Cervantes?" The voice had "busy" and "important" all over it.

"Yep, I am she. I am her. This is Athena."

"I would like to contact Nadia Pusenkoff, from your article yesterday. I assume that you can help me with that." All business, that one.

"Assumptions aside, who might you be, and why do you want to talk to Nadia?"

"My name is Rachel Wertz. I am Michael Tilson Thomas' assistant." *Who?* Clearly she thought I would recognize the name, but people often over-estimate how knowledgeable journalists are. Or sometimes they are over-estimating their own importance and fame. The effect is exactly the same.

"Of course, excuse me, will you hold just one moment?" I hit mute and Googled the name. *Holy shit!* This all took less than twenty seconds, tops. "I am so sorry, Miss Wertz--"

"Mizzz," she corrected. Annoyed. People did not often put Michael Tilson Thomas's assistant on hold. So it seemed.

"I'll be in touch with Nadia today. I'll ask her permission to supply you with her contact information. Would that suffice?" Suffice it to say, I never use the word suffice unless I'm speaking to the assistant to the director of the San Francisco Symphony Orchestra or the Queen of England.

"Tell her I look forward to speaking with her immediately." Rachel Wertz did not say goodbye.

Before I could call Nadia a text popped up on my iPhone. The number was strange. It had too many digits.

"I owe you an apology."

I texted back.

"WHO owes me an apology?"

"N.D."

No way!

"And for what exactly are you apologizing?" *Heart thumping wildly.*

"Not being in touch. Have a great excuse. Had to leave the country after our night. Still in Greece." *That is a great excuse and it explains the weird number.* Before I could come up with a response, he texted again.

"Had a family emergency. Will be back on Friday. Dinner?"

"Ok."

And that was it. I was so excited that I almost forgot to call Nadia. When I remembered to do it, *she* knew who Michael Tilson Thomas is. I gave her Rachel Wertz's number, cutting out the middle man.

"Nadia, call her today. It sounds urgent."

"I do eeet now," she promised and then hung up immediately to keep said promise.

I sat at my desk for a long time reviewing my text history with Nikko Dimitriou. "Our night" sounded distinctly romantic to me. *Doesn't it?* I read it a dozen times. Was I too terse? Did I sound like a bitch? I fretted all week. I didn't hear from him again until Friday morning. Lupe interrupted the staff meeting. Interruptions were big Howie no-nos. He made everybody submit their cell phones to Lupe while the meetings went on.

"Athena, *your source* is on the phone," Lupe said significantly.

"Cervantes, you know the rules," Howard snapped his fingers. "Lupe, tell her source she'll call him back."

"He says it's now or never, Howard. It sounds like the guy from the mayor's office, Athena. You *know...*"

"Oh, that guy!" I jumped up and ran out before Howard could stop me.

As soon as Lupe and I were out of earshot we snickered.

"Fuck that fat, racist bastard," Lupe said laughing. "Your cell has been ringing off the hook. I guess he gave up and finally called the land line...he's on line four."

It didn't start out good.

"Athena, I'm really sorry about this," My heart sank. "I've been on boats and planes for two days now and I'm beat. I wonder if you'd mind coming over to the city and having dinner at my place." I'm telling you, that short little conversation was a roller coaster!

"Mind? No. That sounds great. I love the city." *Too* enthusiastic? *Too* eager? "I mean, that's not a problem. I'll need your address though."

"I'll send a car at seven," he said and hung up. Right. He's not a phone guy. At exactly seven p.m. the same cab driver who had dropped me off the morning after "our night" pulled up in front of my house. I got in sheepishly.

"Hi," I said. He didn't say anything. "Look, the other day..." He held up a hand.

"No worries," he said. "I'm what you would call 'discreet.'" We rode along in silence for a while.

"Thank you," I told him. He made a little gesture with his hand that told me all was forgiven if not forgotten. The traffic into San Francisco was awful. Typical for a Friday night. I had no idea where Nikko Dimitriou lived so I just sat back and enjoyed the ride. Nikko's building was in the financial district on the waterfront.

"It's the penthouse," my cabbie told me, stopping in front of the Gateway building.

"Of course it is," I said. "Will you be driving me back to Berkeley?"

"That's up to you and the boss," he smiled.

"Right."

Materializing out of nowhere, a handsome, young man wearing culinary whites hopped on the elevator with me at the very last possible second. He was balancing a large wicker basket. "Can I press your floor?" I asked. He looked at the penthouse light on the panel.

"We're good," he told me. Fellow travelers to the penthouse, we smiled at each other.

"Mind if I ask what's in the basket?" I ventured. The young man grinned.

"No, I don't mind. I have in this basket the means to change your life and rock your world."

"Mine specifically?" I asked.

"If you're going to the penthouse, yeah." His smile was as blinding white as his jacket.

"Just what I need," I said. The doors to the penthouse suite were open when we reached the top, and the chef took his delivery immediately into the kitchen without hesitating so I followed him inside. I could hear Nikko's voice, muted and speaking in a foreign language rapidly. I rounded the corner and found him out on the balcony overlooking the Golden Gate Bridge and the Bay beneath. Everything, including Nikko Dimitriou, was breathtaking through floor to ceiling glass. His hair was wet, he was shirtless, and he had a towel draped around his neck. His face lit up when he saw me and he nodded and waved me in. He pointed to the phone and made the universal sign for "blah, blah, blah", then "one sec". He mouthed the words "make yourself at home" and then he pointed to an open bottle of Proseco in an ice bucket on the bar. I made my-self at home with the bubbly and took a seat facing the bridge.

"Ohhhh, sorry, sorry, sorry!" Nikko pulled the towel from his neck and dropped the phone on the eggshell-white suede couch. He bent to kiss my cheek like an old friend. "Wow, what a week!" he said.

"Yeah, you said you had a family emergency? In Greece? I hope everything is okay." I tried not to stare at his naked torso. Nikko plopped down on the couch next to a waiting t-shirt. He slipped it over his head and toweled off his hair. I felt a tiny bit of disappointment that he didn't seem to notice how gussied up I was. (Compared to gumboots and fat jeans anyway.)

"Yep, it is...it's okay now. How's the Proseco? Is it cold enough?" Before I could give him the temperature report of the wine, the young chef appeared from the kitchen with a small tray.

"Tapas?" He leaned over, handed me a small plate and napkin, and extended little morsels of wonderfulness in my direction.

"Pablo, this is Athena. Athena, Pablo."

"We met in the elevator, Doc." Pablo smiled his swell smile again. I complimented the tiny pie.

"What *is* this?" I crooned.

"I would tell you but then I'd have to kill you. Old family secret." He smiled at me and then turned to Nikko and shrugged. "We all have a few of those, eh, Doc?" Nikko jumped up and grabbed the Proseco bottle to fill my glass.

"Indeed. What's on the menu, Pablo?" I felt a tiny current of information ripple through the room but I could not decipher the message.

"Right," Pablo nodded knowingly and then proceeded to describe the dinner he'd delivered from his family's stall in the Ferry Building Farmer's Market just across the street. "And, dessert is a surprise, but I'll give you a hint: chocolate. Do you like chocolate, Athena?"

My mouth was full of something delicious so I just pointed and nodded. The men laughed and Nikko offered a glass to Pablo.

"Not on duty!" he demurred. "I can stay and serve if you like, but otherwise I'll head back to work and close up shop." Nikko gave Pablo his leave. Nothing was said about a check for the delivery and I reasoned that this must mean that Nikko Dimitriou kept a running tab with Pablo. I didn't like the instantaneous jealousy I felt, one more time imagining a steady stream of chocolate-loving beauties in the elevator heading up to the penthouse. By the time Pablo had departed and we filled trays with various delicious-looking items and more wine, the sun was setting and Nikko led me outside.

"Wow!" I breathed involuntarily. "I don't get this view in my Berkeley basement."

"It is special," Nikko said. He looked at the bridge for a few seconds and sighed. Then he raised his glass. "To Athena, my new best friend." I shivered before our glasses touched. Nikko downed his drink in one long pull. "I wish I could show you the sunset from Mytilini in Greece. It is also spectacular." He smiled and touched my hand. "Maybe someday...soon." What can I tell you? Every nerve ending, especially those in certain unmentionable zones, was on fire. *Was this man EVER going to kiss me?*

Right away Nikko engineered the conversation over to me again.

"Tell me a little bit about your brother," he began. By midnight we'd consumed everything in Pablo's basket and we were back inside the condo on the white couches sipping something Nikko called "*skorpinos*". I had kicked off my shoes and bared my soul. I filled Nikko in on my entire family and somehow doing so felt completely natural. But, again, I hadn't asked him a single personal question.

"You'd make a great reporter," I told him, "if you ever decide to give up being the number one dude in the whole world in computerized cancer detection." Nikko sat back.

"Have I asked too many questions? I'm sorry." He put his glass on the coffee table, rubbed his forearms and looked across at me with what I hoped was desire. Instead he yawned. "It's just that...I'm really interested in everything about you." I'll admit that under the influence of sparkling wine and whatever goes into a *skorpino*, not to mention the extremely romantic view from Nikko's living room, I could have done something uninhibited just then that I would have regretted almost immediately, and maybe for the rest of my life, but, partially due to the paralyzing effects of the alcohol, not to mention the atrophy of my boy-girl skills, I just sat on the couch and blushed. Nikko looked at his watch for the first time. "Oh, hey," he said yawning again, "we've got to get you home. I'm sorry I can't take you myself tonight. I'm a little jet-lagged still and I have an early meeting tomorrow. I've got to get some sleep."

So that was it. He was, to my dismay that evening, a complete gentleman. He walked me downstairs where a cab was waiting. I stood very still for a full minute before getting into it giving Nikko one final opportunity to give me a proper kiss good-night, but he kissed only the top of my head and helped me get inside.

"I forgot to tell you. Nadia has an audition with the San Francisco Symphony next week. Thanks to you. Thanks to your story." I wanted to say something humble but before I could summon words he produced a small gift box from his back pocket. He tucked it into my hand.

"I will call you soon," he said.

"What's this?" I shook the box.

"Just a token of my appreciation...for your work." I gave him a puzzled look. "I'm your number one fan, Athena. I hope you will let me add to this. Good night." He walked away before I could say thanks. I held tight to the unopened box all the way to Berkeley and only opened it once I was tucked into bed. A delicate, silver charm bracelet held two exquisite charms. One was a tiny Arabian horse and the other was a finely detailed violin.

Rule #16: Be clear. Clarity, clarity, clarity! When you become hopelessly mired in a sentence, it is best to start fresh; do not try to fight your way through against the terrible odds of syntax. Try breaking the sentence down into two or three really clear shorter sentences.

I spent the entirety of Saturday morning analyzing the meaning of every single thing Nikko Dimitriou had said to me. Mostly he had asked a lot of probing questions. But when he said "soon" as in, "I'll call you *soon*" – exactly what did he mean? By Sunday night I knew he hadn't meant "I'll call you this weekend". I wore the silver charm bracelet constantly. I analyzed the gift, too. Surely jewelry designated some kind of significant intentions. Didn't it? But what to make of his remarkable decorum? Was he simply being a gentleman? It was painfully unthinkable to believe that he was not attracted to me, but he hadn't so much as kissed me or even held my hand for more than a minute. I concluded that his propriety was a good thing in light of my own rusted romantic apparatus. But, oh, how I did fantasize about him. It's downright embarrassing how much.

Saturday afternoon I decided that I should call my parents. Did not my family need to know that I was in love? At long last I had a status update worthy of a phone call! I had news to share! Good news.

I got my mom's voicemail and hung up. Same thing on the house line. Mike didn't answer his cell phone either, so I tried my brother. No dice. I called his Hermosa Beach shop and got Josh who said that Miggs had been in earlier to make a bank deposit, but I'd missed him by a few hours. Josh sounded stoned so I didn't bother leaving a message with him.

Superb. As soon as I had something swell to call home about, there was nobody at home to get the call. I kept trying throughout the day but my anxiety just ratcheted up with every subsequent unanswered round of calls to them.

By late Sunday night, with untold attempts to find someone, anyone, in my family I finally capitulated and called Boo in spite of the indecent hour, because she almost always knew of my family's whereabouts.

"Your mom's here, Honey," she said. "Everybody's okay. Nothing to worry about." *Uh oh.* I braced for the worst. *"Nothing?" Like last year when Eddie collapsed in a gutter in the middle of LA's jewelry district?* (He wound up having an emergency triple bypass the next day, which Boo described as "nothing - just you know, a little heart thing.")

"How come nobody's answering their phones?" I demanded. I should have been apologizing for the late hour, but, I could tell right away there was something going on down there. Something Boo wasn't talking about. "Can you put my mom on?"

"Uh...I think she might be sleeping...or..."

"Boo, can I just talk to her, please?"

"Well..."

Fact: you cannot have a coherent conversation with a woman who has knocked back twenty milligrams of Valium with any amount of alcoholic libation. A woman under the influence of the Brenda Fineman Cure makes no sense. Boo reclaimed the phone and hinted broadly at some kind of marital strife between my parents arising, she alleged, from possible – *no! not Mike!* - indiscretions perpetrated by my stepfather. Boo was deliberately stingy with any specifics. I hung up feeling heartsick and then I took a few minutes to get pissed that my good news had been eclipsed by my mother's bad news. I sent Howard an email telling him I was called to LA on a family emergency and then I went on line to make a reservation for the earliest Southwest flight down to LAX the next day. I called Miggs to bring him into the loop and to ask him to pick me up from the airport.

He answered on the first ring.

"I think Dad's fucking somebody," I told him without preliminary niceties. Miguel's silence made me instantly uncomfortable. I suddenly experienced a distinctly alienated feeling, one I used to get when we were kids, an ancient feeling, but nevertheless all too familiar and very, very painful. It tripped Rosie's voice on an old tape in my head. *You're not REALLY a Cervantes, Athena. Your REAL father is Bil-ly. Mike is Miggs's father, not yours.*

"Uh...Dad's fucking somebody? Uh...who?" Miggs sounded stoned. Or, evasive. I couldn't tell which.

"*Uh*...Miggs, does that really matter? Mom's been at the Fineman's all day and she's totally zonked on Boo's tranqs. I got less than half of a half of the story out of Boo and Dad's not answering his phone."

"Uh..."

I could sense the guilt via satellite.

"Why do I get the feeling, Little Brother, that I'm not telling you anything you didn't already know?"

"Uh...I dunno."

"Miggs? Where's Dad?"

"Uh...He's sleeping on my couch." I was struck dumb. Miggs drew in a long breath. "Sissy, I'm not taking sides...but..."

"Miguel Valles Capuano Domingo Cervantes, Jr." I told him. "Southwest 669 at eight thirty tomorrow morning. LAX not Burbank. Do not be late."

I spent the night clutching my iPhone, hoping that my parents' situation would turn out to be a funny misunderstanding – *please, God!* – and fruitlessly checking for any kind of electronic message from Nikko. By dawn, fifty-four hours and then some had gone by without any kind of communication from him. I had begun to indulge in my truest talent: the construction of inglorious rejection fantasies.

The one-hour flight from Oakland International to LAX felt like ten. With my iPhone on airplane mode I spent the time examining my new, silver bracelet and charms for some meaning beyond the obvious. Sleep deprivation made me feel unduly fragile. As soon as the jet's wheels touched the tarmac I pulled out my iPhone and checked again. The gathering tears succumbed to gravity and splashed on the screen apps. Nothing.

The passenger in the aisle seat next to mine waved a white tissue toward me and cleared her throat. I received her offering mutely and took in her stern look and expensive suit. She peered at me over the slender lenses of her reading glasses. Though I had been oblivious to her during the flight I understood right away that this was not a woman you should ignore under any circumstances, stranger or not.

"I was admiring your bracelet," she told me and handed over another tissue.

"Thanks," I sniffed, "It was a gift." She nodded for a full moment.

"From the person who has made you cry?" I swear she was smirking. Really, I have no idea why I let her interrogate me. I nodded and wiped my eyes with her second tissue. A whimper escaped without warning and I clutched my iPhone to my chest. She snorted.

"Cute?"

"Unbelievable," I croaked.

"Charming?" Her voice oozed sarcasm.

"Ditto."

"Seemingly kind. Considerate. And generous?" I could smell her disdain. I sobbed. The woman folded up her glasses and put them in her slim, Italian leather shoulder bag, jerking one final tissue out and handing it to me. "Let me guess," she said, her voice the growl of a pissed off pit bull. "Until very recently, you've had a rather long dry spell following a succession of real losers." I nodded miserably and blew my nose into her tissue. She flicked a manicured finger at my iPhone. "Then this one comes along all gifts and heartache." *How did SHE know?* "They're all bastards," she whispered with real cruelty. "Especially the ones who bear gifts." She stared forward and shook her head, her orange painted lips curling meanly.

"You don't know the half of it," I told her, sadly thinking suddenly of my parents and how the real tragedy *du jour* was theirs, but then she gave me a look that said, "Oh, yes I do, Dearie," and bam! She was unbuckled and up and running for the door, her very expensive laptop bouncing at her hip, and the passengers in rows one through six glaring at her as she jostled past them. She paused and turned at the plane's doorway. Our eyes met again and she shook her head as if, though we were complete strangers, she was sorely disappointed in me.

"Get a grip," she sneered. Then she was gone.

LAX on Monday mornings is a nightmare. I stood at the curb outside of baggage claim and scanned the traffic for Miguel's vintage, black 4Runner, easy to spot encumbered under a roof rack loaded with up to a half-dozen surfboards. I was beyond annoyed that my brother's SUV was not among the four lanes of cars, taxis and limos all weaving in and out, intent on picking up some anxious commuter like me. I violated my oath to Oprah to treat my car and the cars of others as a "NO PHONE ZONE" and I texted him.

"where r u?"

His response arrived precisely as a sleek, silver Maserati Quattroporte pulled up in front of me.

"boo's on the way"

The Maserati's horn bleated. It was a baleful sound impossible to ignore.

"Jesus!" I jumped back and bent over to come face-to-face with my own reflection in the Maserati's tinted window as it purred slowly open. Brenda Fineman leaned across the console.

"Sorry, I'm late, Sweetheart!" She unlocked the door and I got in, conscious of my fellow air travelers futilely looking to see who was behind the wheel of the beautiful sedan. For a woman her age, my Aunt Boo looks damn good. Great, even. Plus she always wears those big Prada sunglasses that can make anybody look rich and famous even when they aren't behind the wheel of a hundred-thousand-dollar-and-change vehicle. I ran my hand over the soft leather seat.

"New wheels?" Boo leaned over and air-kissed me on both cheeks.

"Oh, this is Eddie's newest toy. He's out of town. Don't tell him I used it. I'm not allowed to drive his new cars until he gets his first scratch." Boo had no worries about me ratting her out. I had hardly exchanged a civil word with Eddie since the night of the Fineman's twenty-fifth wedding anniversary party when the scumbag had (unbeknownst to his wife, of course) tried to put a serious move on me.

"He won't check the mileage?"

"Pfffffft!" Boo swatted the air in salute to what she believed was Eddie's incipient Alzheimer's.

"So. Where's my mom?"

"Let's get out of the airport first, okay?" Brenda executed a few maneuvers that would have made Eddie Fineman's head swivel Exorcist-style. When we were finally on Century Boulevard I asked again.

"Mom?"

"I just dropped her off at your brother's house."

"But *Dad's* staying at Miggs's house."

"I know. They're *talking.*"

"Okay," I said. "Talking about *what,* Boo?"

"You FUCKING COCK SUCKER!...oh, not you, Honey...*that* asshole!" Brenda waggled a French-tipped index finger impatiently at the van in front of us and I exhaled. "This city is FULL of assholes that can't drive worth SHIT. Do you have any idea what Eddie would do to me if I got the first scratch on this car?"

"Boo," I said trying to get her back on track. "Mom and Dad?"

"Oh, yeah, well, I think I'd better let your mom tell you about all that."

"About all *what?*" I knew that my voice was edging into the hysterical zone and I was *trying* to sound chill. "I just want to know what I'm walking into."

"Well, you cannot tell your mother that I told you anything." Boo turned the Prada shades in my direction. "I mean it, Tea. You have to promise that you'll pretend you know nothing." I zipped my lips closed tightly and threw an imaginary key into the back seat of Eddie Fineman's new car.

"Diana caught Mike *in flagrante* with a younger woman."

"*In flagrante?*"

"You know..." Boo pulled her shades down and rolled her eyes.

"In bed?" She shook her head.

"No, no, no!"

"Naked?"

"Oh, god no!"

"Well, what then? *In flagrante,* how?" Brenda's short stint on that soap opera left its mark on her day-to-day speech. She laces her language with terms better suited to nineteenth century romance novels, a quirk I mostly found amusing, but, not just then as she was applying it to events that might be leading to the destruction of my mother's second marriage. It made me queasy to hear such a phrase applied to my stepfather whom I loved and trusted beyond all reason.

"Mike wouldn't cheat on my mom," I said stubbornly. "I don't think that could happen."

"I'm going to let your mother give you the details," Boo said. She turned the car north onto Sepulveda Boulevard and we rode a few blocks in silence. I was remembering my strange conversation with the strange woman on the plane. I don't know what Boo was thinking. We were almost to Venice when my iPhone rang. It was Nikko's U.S. number. Which meant, if you are paying attention, that he was in the country and had no good reason not to call me all weekend. Monday morning. He was calling ....? I didn't have a theory at the ready but neither could I jump off the rejection train quite that quickly. Why was he calling?

"Aren't you going to get that?" Brenda again flexed her manicured index finger like a weapon and flicked my iPhone. I thought about choosing to ignore the call, but I have never been one who can postpone the inevitable – neither good nor bad. My hand was shaking when I drew a slow, doomed finger across the bottom of my screen.

"Hello?" My voice sounded strained and hollow and, I'll admit it, slightly pissed off.

"Athena? Are you alright? You sound ...strange."

"Oh, hi, Nikko," I winced at the strain in my voice and Brenda's un-signaled lane change caused the driver behind us to lay on his horn.

"Fuck YOU, cocksucker!" she yelled. "Oooops! Sorry, Honey." She patted my knee and then zipped her lips and threw her own imaginary key into the back seat.

"Athena?!" Nikko sounded alarmed. "Where *are* you?"

"I'm in LA. There's been…I've had…"

"Is that your *mother*?"

"Oh, *god no!*" I gave Boo a guilty, sidelong glance and I knew she was squinting at me behind her Pradas.

"Are you okay, Honey?" The rushing sense of relief I felt at the obvious affectionate inquiry and concern in Nikko's voice cannot be overstated. I was silent just a beat too long, trying not to break down and cry.

"Athena, what's wrong? Is there something I can do? Listen, I'm at the airport in Toronto right now. I'm supposed to leave in an hour for Athens. That's why I haven't called. Something came up and I've been in meetings every day into the wee hours." He paused and I stifled a sob that was more relief than anything else. "Athena, please, tell me what's wrong! Do you need help?"

"No, no, no, Nikko! That's crazy. I don't need you. I mean, I need you, I *do* need you, but, not about this. I'm fine. Really. This is just a little family drama. No big deal. I'll probably be back in Oakland tomorrow night. But, why do you have to go back to Athens so soon?"

"Oh, Jesus. It's a long story. Family drama would be a great description here, too. Believe me I wish I didn't have to go. But, I'll be back on Friday. Early on Friday." He paused for a second.

"Hey, can I ask you a really personal question? I know you aren't alone, but…"

I looked uneasily at Boo who was resorting to single-finger sign language to communicate with her fellow freeway travelers.

"How personal?" I reached out and kicked the controls on the Maserati's AC up another notch.

"Very," Nikko said.

"Very? How very?"

He hesitated. I could hear a boarding announcement on his end for a flight to Montreal.

"What size are your feet?"

"Huh?"

"What size shoe do you wear?"

"Six. And a half. Why?"

"No, I'm just kidding. That wasn't the personal question."

"Oh," I said more than a little disappointed but kind of relieved too. Nikko was quiet for a moment before he took in a big noisy breath.

"The really personal question I have for you is…oh, damn, they called my row. I've gotta run. I'll call you Friday."

I held my breath and listened to another announcement for a canceled flight to Copenhagen.

"Absolutely." I was no longer crying.

I stared at Nikko's number on my iPhone's screen before finally hitting END CALL.

"Okay," Boo said. "Tell."

"Tell what?"

"For starters… who's the boy?"

"Listen, Boo. My love life is not on the agenda for today. Can we just deal with the local crisis at hand?"

"Okay," she said. "Fair enough. But, later, you'll fill me in, yes?"

"Sure," I promised, knowing that if Brenda had anything to say about it, I would definitely have to do it before I went back to Oakland the following day. Brenda lived for tragic events.

My brother's 4-Runner was parked lower than usual in his driveway. Three days of throwaway circulars were accumulating on the porch, his gate was ajar, and all the shutters in the front were closed in an erratic pattern that gave his house an air of definite chaos. Adding to the "state of emergency" look, my stepdad's old Beamer was parked crookedly across the street as if he'd been chased into the house.

"You're not coming in?" I asked Boo. She shook her head. I looked again at the crooked shutters. "Okay, well, thanks for the ride," I told her. I was moving at glacial speed. She held up her hand in the "call me" sign and I nodded that I would. My limbs felt too heavy to attempt a wave as she pulled out.

I knocked tentatively on the uniquely-carved wooden door of my brother's Santa Monica bungalow, but no one answered. I turned the handle, pushed gently and the door creaked open. A rumpled blanket and a ratty pillow from the seen-better-days category were still on the couch. In the kitchen I poured myself a mug of coffee from a full pot before I peered out the window into the little garden. My parents were squared off in Adirondack chairs and surrounded by ostentatiously blooming rose bushes. If I didn't know the circumstances, it would have been picturesque, almost romantic. Both my mom and my stepfather were utterly still and looking down at the ground between them. I saw my mom swipe at her cheek and my stepfather reached up and squeezed her shoulder gently. She turned her head and sighed before her lips brushed his knuckles. She gave him a weak, teary smile. I couldn't have felt more embarrassment if I had walked in on them doing it doggie style. My mom looked up to catch me staring.

"Hi, Honey," she yelled. "Give us a minute, okay?" I backed away from the kitchen and went to search for Miggs. In his bedroom the closed shutters blocked out the bright daylight and a fifty-inch flat-screen on the wall featured Tiger Woods playing a TiVo-ed tournament from god knows when. My brother had iPod ear buds in his ears and another set of expensive Dolbies around his neck. He made space for me next to him on his big bed and held his arms out. I put my coffee cup on his nightstand.

"This sucks," I said nestling in under his arm. Miggs removed one of the little white buds from his ear.

"What?"

"This sucks!" He blinked and nodded once, biting his lips in a gesture I knew to mean that I should not pursue conversation. Instead I lay silently next to him and studied the walls of my brother's bedroom feeling a little like a voyeur. A recent girlfriend, one who was already a footnote in my brother's very crowded romantic history, had convinced him that the many posters of his favorite rock bands and the others of his most revered surf legends were indications of his resistance to maturity. The poor girl was shocked when he agreed with her and then even more shocked when Miggs had the best of these posters expensively framed to be re-hung by a professional curator. No doubt that was the beginning of the end of their relationship.

Tiger sank a bogey, Miggs raised the remote wearily and tapped the pause button. I was unprepared for the direction his thoughts had gone.

"Man, I'm glad Papi and Abuela are dead."

"Miggs!"

"What?" He shrugged. "Abuela would fuckin' kill him. You know it."

"Miggs!" I said even louder, but it was the truth and we both did know it. It had taken my stepfather's parents more than a year to accept my mother as his choice – a woman divorced with a child – but once they had, we had both been as cherished as if they had arranged the marriage themselves. I suppose this episode planted the seeds of my rejection sensitivity and compounded the insecurities I inherited as a child of divorce, but both of them had tried to rectify what they called *a mistake*. In their own ways each of them had taken me aside to let me know: I was just like blood to them. My mother was their daughter.

Abuela's heart had blown out in a split second when I was in high school with no warning and no illness prior of any kind. Papi died slowly of another kind of broken heart, and it *was* a good thing that they weren't around to see this shit between our parents. It would have broken their hearts and killed them all over again.

Miggs and I lay silently next to each other in the center of his king-sized bed looking around the room at his posters and the dozen or more surfboards that were too good for the garage. The bedroom door squeaked open and our parents filed in, one behind the other, Mike looking sheepish and guilty, my mother looking just tired. Mike glanced up at the big flat-screen where Tiger's face stretched across it in a big smile from better days.

"Whooo boy," Mike said. "Whooo boy!"

Nobody else said a word when Mike and my mother climbed up onto Miggs's big bed, my mom on Miggs's side and Mike next to me. We curled toward each other and I felt Mike's arm wrap around me and reach across Miggs until he could put his hand on my mom's shoulder. She did the same and I felt her hand push my hair back and stroke my cheek. I started to cry and then Miggs did too.

"Are you guys getting a divorce?" My brother sounded so young and so scared I squeezed him tighter. My family had not been together, the four of us, in a king-sized bed like this, in probably twenty years, not even when the *abuelos* died, which had killed all of us in different ways. Once upon a time though, when my brother and I were little kids, sandwiched in between the two of them on our parents' bed was how we had begun practically every day. A Miggs and Tea sandwich, they called it.

The sensation of true pain coursing through my brother's body in my arms, my baby brother, a man now, six-feet tall, a competitive professional surfer and a businessman with his next surf shop scheduled to open on Maui any day, his pain just felt so wrong and so terrifying I thought I would lose my mind.

"You're gonna be okay." It was my voice but I heard it from some other place far away, and I felt strangely removed like my consciousness was hovering high over the big, crowded bed looking down at the four of us, where I could see myself. I was up on Miggs's ceiling where big, white, fluffy clouds and gray seagulls were painted into the sunny background blue. I felt as if I was floating or flying up there looking down at the four of us and I felt that if I wanted to I could just fly away, right out the window with those gulls. But, then I had the simple thought that those closed shutters would present a problem and WHAM! I was back on the bed and my mom was standing up at the doorway while my brother and father and I still lay sniffling in a big, tangled mess.

"Come on now, kids," she said. "You guys have to get out of the middle of this. This is private between me and Dad and we have some work to do, but we're going to do it and everybody is going to survive."

"You fucker, Dad!" Miggs wailed, "You fucked up!" I elbowed my agreement into Mike's ribcage.

"Oww," he said. "You're right. I fucked up. I fucked up big time." Mike had shed a few manly tears when Papi died, maybe a bit more than that for Abuela, but nothing like this. It scared me.

"Come *ON*, you guys," Mom said again. "This is not going to help anybody."

I glared at her and it occurred to me, not truly for the first time in my life, that my mother was a colossal martyr. *Are you crazy, Mom?*

"Are you crazy?" I screamed. "He fucked up SO FUCKING BAD!" My voice was so shrill and my hysteria so over the top that everybody froze. In a second my brother was laughing and then the rest of us started to laugh too. Not my mother, but Mike and

Miggs and I were laughing *and* crying, and then, just as suddenly, it was completely quiet again. Just the birds chirping outside in Miggs's backyard.

"Come on, you guys," Mom said softly. "Come on. You guys have got to get out of the middle." Then she left the room and Mike whispered into my hair, "She's right. She's right." He got up and patted my head and then he followed her out and Miggs hugged me hard and said, "Man, Sissy, they are *fucked* up."

"Yeah," I said holding on to him as hard as I could. Another minute went by until I finally released him. "You gonna get out of the middle?"

"Yeah. I have to. I got a shop to open in Maui. I'm leaving tonight."

"Oh, Dude!" I said while he gave me one final squeeze before he too left the room, and I was all alone again, and they were all somewhere else, but together. I laid in my brother's bed for a long time alone feeling sorry mostly for myself because this was the second time my family had come apart at the seams. I got mad that my brother was going to get on a plane and get out of the middle just like my mother said he should. And then I had this terrible thought: *Now YOU are going to know what it's like,* is what I thought. And in that one horrible, shameful moment, I was not altogether unhappy about the fact that finally, he was.

Brenda called my mother's house in the early afternoon. We'd been back for several hours, both of us trying to nap.

"You promised to call me," she whined.

"Oh, sorry, Boo. I was just going to do that, I just got back to the house this minute." My scrupulous mother frowned.

"Why don't you and your mom come over here for dinner? I'll have Roberto make us some tapas."

"Who's Roberto? What happened to Bobby C?"

"Oh, Bobby wants us to call him Roberto now. I think he's embracing his Latin heritage or something. Whatever. But his tapas are to die for."

"Tapas? Okay, maybe," I said. "Let me check with Mom. She's lying down."

"She hardly slept a wink last night," Boo reported.

"I'm sure. I'll call you back when she wakes up."

"Do it," Boo said and hung up.

"Liar, liar," my mother shook her head. "You know what happens to little girls who lie?"

"Yeah, they get out of unpleasant circumstances, like dinner with the Finemans."

"Remember, Eddie's not home," Mom reminded me.

"What about Joshie?" At twenty-four the immensely unlikable Joshua Fineman was in his sixth year of junior college, at Santa Monica Community College. Since Eddie traveled so much for work, and Boo and Margarita both doted on the boy excessively, it was beginning to look as if Joshie would never leave home and he seemed destined to make it into the Guinness world records as the oldest living person to still have a nanny. His part-time gig in Miggs's Hermosa Beach shop, was a concession to our mothers' friendship, but Joshie was allowed nowhere near the register because he'd been caught stealing – pilfering – at least twice. I never liked him. Miggs feels sorry for him. Eddie Fineman will not let his son work in the family enterprise unless he has at least an undergraduate college education. Eddie's own father was an uneducated, immigrant diamond cutter in New York and Eddie's success has been a product of timing, guts and luck instead of a formal education. He never went beyond eleventh grade, so he has some compensating to do, and Joshie, goddamn it, is going to do it for him. Rosie Fineman's MFA degree from USC isn't worth the paper it's written on as far as her father is concerned. ("What the fuck are you going to do with that worthless degree, Rose?")

"I'm positive Joshie has class on Monday nights," Mom said. "I'm sure he won't be home."

"Well, do *you* want to go over to Boo's for tapas?" I asked.

"Do you want to suggest an alternative?"

"We could stay here, order in, and you could tell me exactly what the fuck happened between you and Dad."

"Tapas sound good," she said. Then the house phone rang again and she took it into her bedroom.

For a woman whose second marriage had been threatened to its core within the previous twenty-four hours, my mother seemed pretty perky as she drove me up Sunset Boulevard toward the Fineman's. The sun was setting in the Pacific behind us, she had the top down on her Mini Cooper, and I had yet to hear a single significant detail of what had happened to precipitate the crisis at hand which had seemed critical enough to me to hop a plane home.

"You look good, Mom," I told her.

"Thanks, Honey," she said. She peeked at her reflection in the rear view mirror as if to check the reality of my assessment and then she gave me what I tried to interpret as a stoic smile.

"No, I mean, you don't look stressed out." She laughed a quick little laugh that sounded like the bark of a Pekinese.

"I didn't mean it that way. You *do* look good..." And she does. She looks incredible for her age. She still runs five miles every day and she still weighs what she weighed in high school. But, I wasn't talking about her condition or how pretty she still is. "I'm just wondering how you've made this amazing recovery. You know? In such a short time. I mean, you were *humming* a minute ago. You did *laundry* today. Just last night you were sequestered at the Fineman's and Boo was feeding you tranquilizers. You had me so worried I hopped the first flight down. Am I missing something here?" She glanced in the mirror to check the traffic, then signaled and pulled the car over to the curb. She killed the engine and turned to face me.

"Tea, I really meant what I said today about you and Miggs staying out of this." She softened when she saw tears well up. She sighed and put her palms together in front of her chest like a Catholic girl at mass. "You know, Honey, things change between partners. Even when people love each other."

"So, you *are* getting a divorce?" She reached out and took my chin in her soft hand.

"Oh, Sweetie, I don't know." I pulled away and failed to stop two fat tears from rolling down my cheeks.

"Well, what *do* you know?" I squeaked. She pulled a creased Starbuck's napkin from inside her console box and touched it to my cheek.

"Honey, you've been gone from home a long time, now. Dad and I have been...well, we've been drifting a little bit. He's been very busy with all that ethics committee work..." *GOD, MOTHER! I WISH that you would take some responsibility. Just a little!* "...I've been super busy too. We've both just been caught up in things. You know, we've both been putting everything into our careers and our work since you kids left home. There's not a lot of overlap there." *Well, sure, no understatement there, eh?*

Let it be known here that my stepfather, Miguel – Mike to his compañeros – Cervantes has been short listed twice for the most prestigious scientific acknowledgments in his field. He was in high demand on the speaker's circuit all over the country and even internationally more recently. The university put a ton of pressure on him to do these high profile speaking gigs because it bought them a hell of a lot of prestige. I knew that and also that my mother's clinical work, especially the *pro bono* work she did in east LA with "high risk youth" had precluded any possibility that she would be a good, little faculty wifey and go along on every one of his trips. She had a teaching schedule of her own besides and all the clinical work she could take on. This had been a real bone of contention between them going way back to my high school days. I had just assumed they had worked this out. Apparently not. *But why is it a crisis only now?*

"But, you know, Sweetie, sometimes these things can be a good thing for a relationship." I looked at her with naked doubt. *Please, do not tell me that every crisis is an opportunity.*

"And every crisis is an opportunity," she said.

"Fuck," I said.

"Tea, c'mon, Honey. I realized this morning and I think that Dad realized it too, that he and I haven't really talked to each other in years. Years! We hardly know each other anymore."

"What are you talking about? You talk to each other every day."

"That's just bullshit about the house and who's going where when and who needs a ride to the airport and nonsense. Just utter nonsense. Dad told me this morning in Miggsy's backyard that *he's lonely.* Do you have any idea how I felt when my husband of twenty five years told me that he's been *lonely* for the last ten?" Now it was her turn to cry big, fat tears and I wished I could take back my other wish about her taking responsibility. I handed her the Starbucks napkin even though it was a damp, useless wad. And suddenly, watching her wiping her face so pathetically, instead of feeling sympathy for her, I felt the same surge of familiar rage that I had felt toward her that morning for being such a victim. *Mom! You are such the martyr!*

"Can we just go, now?" I asked her. The sun had set and I was shivering.

"Sure," she said. "And you're going to stay out of the middle?"

"Sure," I told her. "I'm already out."

"I'll put the top up," she said, and she did and we drove the rest of the way to Aunt Boo's in silence.

A yellow cab was pulling out of the Finemans' driveway as we approached.

"If that's Eddie, if Eddie's back, I'm not staying. I'll just drop you off and come back and get you later."

"Okay," my mom agreed with reluctance. "But Boo told me he's in New York at least until Thursday."

"I'm just warning you," I said but it turned out that it wasn't Eddie's taxi. It was Rosie's. She was still in the foyer, sitting at the bottom of one of the two spiral staircases under the crystal chandelier that had been shipped over from Paris in the thirties. Rosie was picking at the ties of her espadrilles with her free hand. She had a Bluetooth earbud attached to her ear, a *TUMI* overnighter parked at her feet and *ealuxe* shades pushed up on top of her head. She looked every inch the successful New York agent. She blinked at us under false lashes.

"Darling, I agree," she told the darling on the phone and rolled her eyes. "Ten a.m. is a savage hour to meet, but, you see, it is actually one p.m. my time and I do have to catch a flight at three." She smooched the air twice in our direction. "Oh, thank you *so, so much*. You are an angel. I cannot wait to meet you finally in person. No please. It is my pleasure. Okay. Fabuloso...ten...at the Ivy. Kiss, kiss. *Ciao*." She sighed with exaggerated exhaustion, stabbed her phone screen and undid the bows of her shoes. Then she pasted a bright smile back onto her face. "Aunti Di! Athena! Is my mother expecting you?" Summoned at the mention of her existence, Brenda appeared at the top of the staircase.

"Yes, your mother is expecting *them*. But where did *you* come from?" Boo asked her.

"Oh, *Gaaawwwd,*" Rose slumped against the Persian stair runner and kicked her shoes out of the way. "I've been in San Francisco all week." Then Rose remembered my address across the Bay and looked guiltily at me. "Oh, Tea, I was *going* to call you. I *was*. But I did not have one second to myself in the city." She clapped her hands suddenly like a kindergarten teacher. "But, never mind, since here you are in LA. I'll get to see you after all." She rose then and put a hand on each of my shoulders and air kissed both cheeks again with an insincerity that struck me dumb. My mother received the very same routine.

"Auntie Di! *You* look fabulous!" By then, Brenda had descended the long staircase and was waiting for some scrap of acknowledgment from Rosie. None came.

"Ahem," she held her hands forward and shrugged.

"Oh, Gaaaaawwwwd," Rose said again and gave her mother's cheek a wayward peck. "I just saw *you*, Brenda."

"Almost a month ago," Brenda clarified.

"Whatever, Mother. Please do not get all needy on me. I have all the needy people I can take right now. Which is why – to answer your original question – I'm in LA. Can I get a fucking drink, or what?"

"Let's all get a drink." Brenda briefly touched her cheek where Rose's lipstick stained her face before she opened her arms wide and herded us all toward the kitchen.

Bobby was whirling around the kitchen wearing spanking, new culinary whites and sporting a new Fu Man Chu.

"*Hola, chicas! Ay, que bueno! Cuatro chicas magnifica en mi cocina!*"

"Roberto, whatever that is in that pitcher, can you bring it out to the pool, Sweetie? We'll eat out there too. *Está bien?*" Brenda led the way and my mother and Rose followed her out. I held back. Bobby wiped his hands on the tea towel stuffed into his whites and gave me a strong hug and then held me at arms length and looked me up and down.

"Hey, Athena, lookin' good!"

"Hi, Bobby," I kissed his cheek. "What's with the *Español*? And who the hell is Roberto? Didn't you tell me you grew up in Van Nuys and didn't speak a single word of Spanish?" Bobby grinned and handed me a frosty wine glass.

"Yeah, yeah, I got a little side thing goin' here. Brenda's been letting me take some catering jobs...nothin' big...brunches and shit...up here in the Hills for her neighbors...whenever Eddie ain't home...which is like almost all the time." Roberto/Bobby gave me a significant look. "The ladies of B. Hills, it turns out, they love them some Spanish with their tattooed caterers. I'm takin' an online class. Here, taste this." He poured a pale concoction into the glass then spooned a piece of kiwi followed by a slender nectarine slice on top. The fruit slid seductively to the bottom.

"Wow, what is this?"

"White peach sangria. My own recipe. You can get it on my website."

"You have a website?"

"Fuckin' A." He winked. "Oh, and I'm writing a cookbook too." *Isn't everybody writing a goddamned book?* Roberto filled three more wine glasses and topped mine off before he deftly peeled an avocado. "Hey, you ever finish writing *your* book? The one you were writing about your real father? That guy your mom dumped? You got an agent yet for that, Athena?" I had a second before answering him to rue the day I had ever told anyone that I was writing a book.

"No. And, No." I downed the sangria and held my glass out, smiling a very false smile. "And now it would seem that circumstances are afoot that may require a sequel to my book before I can even finish the first one or even *try* to find an agent for it." Bobby followed my gaze out to the pool.

"Oh, you mean that shit that went down last night?" Not much got by the hired help at the Fineman household.

"Maybe," I said. "What did you hear last night?" Bobby re-filled my glass but held it back.

"You didn't hear this from me, right?" I crossed my heart.

"Your old man?" Bobby's scowl said everything. "The big doc fucked up!"

"Is that all you know?"

"Well, I also know this. Your mom gives me the word–I mean one fuckin' word – and I will personally kick that wetback mo-fo's fancy, Latino ass all the way back to Mexico."

"I'm sure she will not ask you to do that," I said. "But, then again, what the hell do I know? I thought everything was just peachy on the home front. My mother, it turns out, has been less than forthcoming."

"Hey," Bobby shook a warning finger. "Your mother is a saint. Doc Cervantes is the luckiest mother-fucker in LA." I waited until Bobby lowered his finger and I took another sip of my drink and put my glass on the tray.

"I'll take that out," I said. "You work on those famous tapas of yours." When I reached the French doors that led out to the pool Bobby hissed at me.

"She's a fuckin' saint, Athena! The big doc fucked up!"

Rule #89: The construction of adverbs by simply adding an "ly" to an adjective or a participle is all too easy. Don't be tempted to do it. Do you want it to be said that you write badly?

There was apparently just no limit to how affected Rose Fineman had become living and working for six years in New York. Affectations that she had begun to acquire early on as an under-grad at Smith she honed while in the MFA program at USC, and then perfected when she interned at William Morris (an old favor owed to her mother) in the New York city office. By the time Rose was hired at a little, boutique literary agency in the Village as an agent's assistant-slash-slave, the laid-back California girl who had practically been my cousin was unrecognizable.

"Oh, *grazie,* Bella." Rosie took the sangria I held out to her on Bobby/Roberto's be-flowered tray and gulped. "Fuck me, that's good!"

"Oh, yeah," I said already enjoying the benevolent effects of the generous portion of Grand Marnier that Bobby included in his killer recipe.

"Mamá," I said lowering the tray in my mother's direction. "Tía." I swiveled.

Once all three all had glasses in hand I reclined onto my own chaise lounge, balanced a third drink on my stomach, and surveyed the company.

"What did I miss?" I asked.

"Nothing," Boo said. "Rose was just telling us about her new LA client."

"Not *nothing,* Mother. This guy is the next Michael Chabon. He is so white-hot, Jocelyn sent me out here to court him. With an expense account that is covering brunch at the Ivy tomorrow. Do you know how rare that is these days?"

"You're courting him?" I asked disingenuously. "You haven't signed him yet?" Rose flared her nostrils large enough to put nickels inside.

"Everything but the paperwork," she said. "Just a formality."

"So, what's he write?" I asked around the big lump of white peach sucked up from the bottom of my glass.

"Honey, I *only* represent literary fiction now. Well, some commercial stuff, but..." The condescension in Rose's sentence was so heavy it felt like a blow. It silenced the rest of us. "So," she finally continued, "What's up with you, Tea?"

"Oh," I said. "I'm still at the *Trib*." Having downed about twelve ounces of sangria in under ten minutes I had begun to think that it was a good idea to make little farting noises with the bottom of the wine glass under my shirt. "I did do a great profile on Fremont's First Latina Rodeo Queen though." I enjoyed one of those stifled private laughs that make people look at each other nervously. My mother and Brenda did that and then they both looked at me to nod encouragement with concern on their faces.

"Are you still working on your book?" Rose went for the jugular. *I wonder where the pool man keeps the hydrochloric acid.*

"Yep," I said. "Still bangin' away...in between scintillating profiles on *reee-leeee* interesting people up there in the Bay Area." Rose touched her frosty sangria glass to her forehead, perhaps to indicate that I was giving her a headache, and I upended my own glass and poured the remaining drops of white peach sangria into my belly button.

"Well, I'd love to take a quick look at it for you, darlin'," she said. *Isn't there a limit to how much condescension one person can use in a single conversation?* "When you get it done. And when I have a moment to spare. You know?"

I hate you.

"Well, what's this white-hot client's name?" Brenda asked, because she is really into name-dropping and she was going to drop this one, whatever it was, before the next full moon, you could bet on it.

"Thadeus Burke," Rose said. I thought I heard wrong.

"What?" I said and sat up rigidly. "What did you say?"

"Thadeus Burke." Rose's spine stiffened. "Why, do you know who he is?"

I stared at her with my eyes bugging out. I felt almost sober.

"Rose, that's Burke!" Rose was back to rolling her wine glass across her forehead again and grimacing. Suddenly the light bulb went off.

"Oh, my god!" she said. "Holy shit! Thadeus Burke is *Burke?* That creepy guy you were engaged to at Davis for like a minute and a half?"

"Well, how many genius writers named Thadeus Burke can there be?"

"Holy shit," Rose repeated, this time with what we all recognized as genuine reverence. "I never knew his first name." Her face grew pale. "Holy shit," she repeated. "That means *I* fucked *Thadeus Burke!*"

Boo hoo. That's about how many tears I had cried over Rosie and Burke back in the day. Her admission of guilt didn't phase me. But our mothers were shocked, particularly Boo who always tried to give Rose the benefit of the doubt. I myself wouldn't want to be the person who has to keep track of who and how many people Rose has fucked or even just fucked over in the last ten years. It was little wonder to me that she hadn't figured out that Thadeus Burke, wunderkind, was my Burke.

Bobby/Roberto delivered a tea cart with tapas for twelve and he was lighting the gas heaters stationed around the poolside table. Rose jumped up to make a plate for me and held it out.

"You have to come to brunch with us tomorrow, Tea! Please say that you will! You ended on good terms with Burke, didn't you? With Thadeus, I mean. You and he are still friends?" I'll admit it. I did love that Rosie Fineman was begging me for something. My mother and Boo were still sitting motionless, both of them non-plussed that Rose had so cavalierly declared her sexual treachery.

"No can do," I said. "I'm going back to Oakland tomorrow. My flight is at three."

"Perfect," Rose said. "My flight to New York is at three fifteen. I'll get you to the airport in plenty of time. I promise. Oh, please, please, please!"

I might not have gone. I definitely would not have gone. Except for what happened next. My cell phone rang.

"Nikko! Hi!" I made my voice sound like velvet love. I struggled out of the chair and pointed at my phone and toward the house mouthing "I'm going to take this inside." Once in the house I lost the connection immediately. I waited almost twenty minutes for Nikko to try again but I guessed that he'd lost service and I plastered a big, fake smile on my face and re-joined the party.

"So, Brenda says you're dating someone?" My mother's voice betrayed her annoyance. She didn't like it one bit that Brenda knew something about me that she did not know. They had their own competitions. You can imagine how it killed her that Brenda had been the administrator of romantic first aid after each of my broken hearts. *Where were you when I really needed you, Mom?*

"Yeah," I said beaming.

"Alright," Boo said. "Spill. You promised." I sighed and tossed my hair back.

"Well, I did a piece on him last month. He's a very interesting guy."

"His name is Nikko?" My mother was asking.

"Yeah, Nikko Dimitriou." I saw her mouth make a little "oh" and she sat back in her chair like someone had pulled her string.

"Nikko Dimitriou?" Brenda asked leaning forward. "You mean that guy that did the World Peace Concert with Bono?" *People* magazine is my Aunt Boo's Bible.

"Yeah," I said. "The same." I started in on a half of an avocado with crabmeat and looked around the table in the ensuing silence at their stunned expressions. My mother especially looked pale in the flickering candle lights.

"Oh, Tea, Honey..." It was Rose who finally broke the prolonged silence. "I hope to God you didn't sleep with him." Something like true alarm flooded my very being. *If Rose Fineman has slept with Nikko, I will kill her painfully this very night.*

"Well, Rose, Honey," my sarcasm was aimed between her eyes. "I don't care to tell everybody who I have and who I have not fucked. Unlike some people at this table."

"Whom," Rose said and laughed. "Oh, Tea, tell me you didn't sleep with him."

"What are you getting at Rose?" I demanded.

"A guy like Nikko Dimitriou could never be interested in a woman like you! Are you kidding? He can have any woman he wants! What the hell would he be doing – no offense – with somebody like you? He's probably America's most eligible bachelor. Or one of, anyway."

I will admit. There was not one thing Rose said that I hadn't already thought to myself. I looked from Boo's stricken face to my mother's. They both shrugged. Just like when we were kids they were letting the two of us sort it out ourselves.

"Nikko isn't like that," I said quietly with as much conviction as I could muster. "Nikko's not like that." Once for her and once for me.

"Oh, Gawd," she said. "They are all like that. You are so naïve!"

"How do you know that?" I asked her hating how mewling and insecure I sounded.

"I live in New York! I'm a literary agent for fuck's sake! I've met a million of these kinds of guys. They use people up like tissues. And there's no end to how many people want to be used by them." I'll grant her this. This next part she said not only kindly, but with obvious sincerity. "The only time you get the time of day from one of them is if they need something from you. I've been there. If they think they can write a book and I can get it published for them...I'm the new best friend...but... if some Big gets a deal to them first? It's suddenly, 'Oh, yeah, who the fuck are you?'"

"What did you say?" My voice was in a register I didn't recognize.

"What? 'Who the fuck are you'?"

"No, 'your new best friend'". Why did you say *that*?"

"It's just how it is, Sweetheart." Rose sounded uncharacteristically sincere. "Guys like Nikko Dimitriou are a whole different ballgame. I'm telling you. This guy pals around with Bono? Trust me. He's got handlers and assistants who wipe his ass. He can have any supermodel he wants. What could he possibly want from Athena Cervantes at the *Oakland Tribune*? I mean aside from the obvious."

Finally Boo reached out and took Rosie's glass from her hand. "That's enough, Rose," she said. Rose glared at Brenda and grabbed the sangria pitcher from the cart. She re-filled the glass that her mother was still clutching and then she filled our glasses too. When her mother relinquished her glass without a struggle Rose leaned back in her chair as if the rebuke had never been uttered.

"I'm sorry, Tea," she said tiredly. "That's just how it is."

Later, it was arranged thus: Bobby/Roberto drove us home from the Finemans' in his big, black Escalade even though the Palisades are in the opposite direction from where he was headed back to the valley. Rose would drive my mom's car in the morning to our house and then we would cab together to the Ivy from there, and on to LAX after our meeting with Thadeus Burke.

"This is really nice of you, Bobby. It's so late." I checked my mother's sleeping form on Bobby's big, leather, backseat. She had a vaguely worried smile on her face.

"Not a thing," he said. "I would do anything for the doc. She saved my life, Athena. I would kill for her."

"Yeah," I said. "I think we covered that ground already tonight."

"I'm just sayin'," he said. "And, Athena?"

"Yeah?"

"All that shit that Rose said about your homeboy? Rose don't know everything. In fact, Athena, Rose don't know much."

"You heard her? Well..."

"No. I'm tellin' you straight up. I don't gotta say nuthin. You got a gun to my head? I don't see no fuckin' gun. And, I got no reason to lie or blow smoke up your ass, you know? How long I known you? Since you was a little kid, right? Since you was watchin' me make tamales over at your Abuela's place, over there at her place in Mar Vista, right?"

"I guess," I smiled at the sweet memory of a nervous, young Bobby learning how to make cornmeal masa and trying very hard to keep a civil tongue for my grandmother's sake.

"You are a lot like your mother, Athena. You don't mind my sayin' this, you are both really hot. No disrespect to the doc."

"I'm sure she'd be flattered."

"But the thing that's so cool is, you two don't act superior, you know? You are two of the hottest chicks I ever seen." Bobby paused for a thought. "For white chicks anyway. And, I been seein' some pretty hot chicks up here in B.Hills. All these movie dudes got hot, young wives. I seen Halle Berry one time. At a party I done for one of Brenda's neighbors. That is one smokin' hot chick. But, man, that bitch knows she's hot and she gonna let you know it too. And, man, you better give that bitch her due, you know? You and your mom? You ain't like that. You guys is cool. You ask me, homeboy is one smart dude if he sees that. Ain't too often a brother finds a smokin' hot chick who's smart and fuckin' nice too. I think Rose is just jealous. Always has been."

"That's what Miggs says," I admitted.

"Well? You know one person smarter than your brother? Huh? Besides yours truly, I mean." Bobby showed me all his teeth. I laughed.

"You tell homeboy I say he's one smart mother-fucker, but another thing? He fuck up and do anything to hurt you, Athena? You tell him he's gonna have Bobby Cisneros all up in his business and that ain't necessarily gonna be a good thing."

"*Rrrrroberrrrto* Cisneros," I said.

"Whatever," Bobby said and made a fist and a face.

"You gonna kick his wetback, mofo ass all the way back to Greece?" I smiled.

"Fuckin' A," Bobby grinned.

"I'll tell him. And, Bobby?"

"Yeah?"

"Thanks."

"Not a thing, Homegirl." Bobby steered the Escalade onto our street.

Rule #47: Use figures of speech sparingly. A metaphor is like a shot of liquor. One should do the trick. Two are like a reckless fender bender. Three are madness. And, four are a disaster of Biblical proportions.

Rose was drinking black coffee in the kitchen with my mother like the proverbial cat with canary feathers in its teeth. Unlike my mom who was a wreck, Rose looked none the worse for the previous night's heavy drinking.

I don't care what anybody says, it's true that women really dress for other women. Most of the men I've known, straight men anyway, could care less what a woman is wearing. (In my experience, they are much more interested in getting a woman's garments off.) I was primping for Rosie, yes, but also for Burke, whom, if the unvarnished truth be told, I was hoping to impress. *Thank you Baby Jesus for telling me to throw in my brand new True Religion jeans at the last minute.* Her highness was sporting the New York agent's uniform: a black pencil skirt with four inch do-me heels and a killer white shirt that nicely showed off her six thousand-dollar boob job.

"Oh, you look so cute, Hon," Rose kissed the air behind my ear. *Cute? What The Fuck? I look great and you know it. And, girlfriend? My boobs are real.*

"Ugh!" I said insincerely, and because Rose has always, always coveted my long, straight, blonde hair, I threw this out, "I desperately need a trim. I just haven't had time, you know?" *Roughly translated: I have a great, new boyfriend who takes up all my time with fantastically romantic adventures. And, we both know that I have great hair. You'd kill every member of your family with a serrated steak knife to have my hair.*

"Well," Rose said when the cab honked in the driveway, "our chariot awaits. Bye, Aunti Di. Kiss, kiss." My mother touched my cheek and gave me a weak good-bye hug.

"Can you call me later, Honey? When you get back to Oakland?"

"Sure thing," I promised. "The minute my flight lands."

The Ivy was crowded and Burke had already been seated.
"There he is," I pointed to one of the better tables.

"God, he looks so different," Rose said. But, to me Thadeus Burke looked exactly the same, only better dressed than he'd been at Davis. Rosie led the way and we presented ourselves to his table like ladies-in-waiting. We did everything but curtsy to the man that Rose assured me was destined for literary greatness. A man that both of us had slept with and one of us had been engaged to. Albeit, briefly.

"Burke," I interrupted his diligent perusal of the Ivy menu. "Do you remember me?" He dropped the menu and torqued his full water glass over onto his lap.

"Shit!" he sputtered, "Oh, shit!" A waiter immediately jumped forward and mopped the spill telling us all to be calm and sit down.

"Athena..." Burke rose as high as the table allowed and extended a damp hand forward.

"Don't get up," I told him. "I hope you don't mind. Rose invited me to join you." Burke flashed a quick look toward Rose and back to me. He did it once again and then he tilted his head as if he really just could not place her. She reached out her hand.

"Thadeus. We meet again."

"Again?" he said. "We've met?" Rose chuckled a low, throaty rumble deep in her augmented chest. "Please, may we sit and perhaps spark your memory?"

Burke nodded.

"Of course, please," he gestured. He seemed to be putting invisible puzzle pieces together while we took our seats. The waiter removed the soggy napkins. He refilled Burke's glass and promised to return.

"Wait, you're Rose Fineman from Writer's New Network?" Burke asked.

"The one and only," Rose said.

"And you know Athena? Do you represent Athena?"

"Oh, Lord, no!" Rose's dismissal of such an outrageous possibility scented the table in the same way a fresh turd in the butter dish would have. Burke blinked. I shrugged and grabbed a breadstick.

"How've you been, Burke?" I asked. "I hear you're writing some great stuff." His face relaxed into a smile then and I remembered what the attraction had been.

"We'll see," he said modestly. "I guess there's been some response. It's my first novel."

"Well, Rose says that every agent in New York is hot for you. Is that true?" Burke shrugged one shoulder and colored a bit.

"We'll see." This new humble Burke was unrecognizable. What had happened to suck all the swagger out of him, I wondered.

"Well, good luck," I said and I meant it somehow, feeling suddenly charitable toward the new Michael Chabon who had been a jerk to me in our former lives.

"And, you? Athena? Are you writing?"

"Well, yeah, I'm living in the Bay Area. I've got a beat on the *Oakland Trib* up there. Culture."

"Oh, yes," Rose chimed in with an actual snicker. "Athena just did a fabuloso profile on Fremont's first Latina Rodeo Queen." I ignored Rose and her snide comment and Burke did too.

"And, I'm still banging away on the "good, great novel" I started in Orloff's second term seminar. You know how that goes." Thadeus Burke nodded, his eyes growing round and wide with agreement.

"Did you use 'The Princess of Fire Island?'" Burke asked. "Is that your starting off point?"

"I can't believe you remember that title!" I said. "How the hell did you remember *that?*" I shook my head and laughed.

"You *are*, aren't you?" Burke looked genuinely pleased. He drummed a short beat on the wet table top. "Wow, I'm so glad." I wasn't completely sure that Burke wasn't making fun. I just stared at his handsome, smiling face. "That was a really moving piece. It changed my life," he said. His right hand touched his heart.

"You're joking," Rose and I spoke in harmony with identical sidelong glances.

"Not at all," Burke said. "It changed everything for me. How I write. What I write." His voice caught in his throat. "I'm really glad you're using it." Rose and I both watched as Thadeus Burke appeared to wipe a tear from the corner of his eye with his napkin. My iPhone vibrated in my purse.

"I'm going to take this outside," I said grabbing my bag. "Excuse me, please." Rose shooed me away and pulled her chair closer to the table. Burke started to rise until I waved him down. *When and how had Burke acquired such manners?*

"Nikko?" On the street in front of the Ivy it was nearly impossible to hear. Plus, I immediately heard very loud and equally bad disco music on Nikko's end.

"Athena, yes! It's me. Can you hear me?"

"Yeah, sort of. It's really hard to hear you."

"Sorry about that. We're in a club." *We? Naked jealousy was not my best feature.* "I tried to call you this morning but the connection failed. Listen, Athena, I had a thought after we hung up yesterday."

"What? What did you say?"

"I want you to come to Greece! Can you take some time off? Instead of flying back on Friday, I'll stay put and why don't you come here? We can take a few days and I can show you some of the islands. We'll take my dad's boat. He's docked in Athens but he's got to fly to Rome, so we can sail it back to Mytilini for him. Can you do it?" I knew from comprehensive Google searches that Mr.

Dimitriou's "boat" was a hundred-foot yacht with a full crew including a gourmet chef and a full-time masseuse. This was one of those moments in a woman's life when her sanity is revealed in the choices she makes.

"I can't, Nikko!" I yelled. "I've got to be in Napa all next week for a series on migrant workers in the wine country." I listened to disco for a good long thirty seconds.

"You sure? Someone else can't take over?" Well, in truth, someone or more likely everyone at the *Trib* would have jumped at the chance for that series, but I had fought for it and I couldn't let it go to just any other writer.

"I'm sorry," I said and, oh lord, I meant it.

"No worries. Another time. It was just a thought. Very last minute. We'll plan it next time."

"Are you sure? It's okay?"

"No worries," he said again.

I started worrying immediately. Had I just made a profoundly stupid decision? How many of those do I get? I started wondering who was in the disco with him. I started pondering a Worst Case Scenario.

By the time I approached Burke's table I looked like I had lost my best friend. My *new best friend*. Rose was alone.

"Where's Burke?" I asked.

"Ah, Tea," Rose said. "I'm wondering if I could ask you a huge favor?"

"Sure thing," I said.

"Could you...I mean would you...mind giving Thadeus and I the opportunity to talk business?" Rose held the back of my chair securely against the table and looked at me over her shoulder. It took me a beat to figure out that I was being dismissed.

"Oh, oh, sure thing," I said again.

"Fabuloso," Rose said. "I'll call you. *Ciao.*" She kissed the air and waggled her manicure over her shoulder and picked up her phone. I collided with Burke as he came out of the men's room wiping the edges of the wet stain on his pants.

"Oh, Burke, I'm glad I got to say good-bye."

"You're leaving?" he asked. "You can't stay for lunch?"

"No, you guys have business to discuss. I've got a plane to catch. I just wanted to stop by to say hello." We looked at each other the way old lovers do when they bump into each other after years incommunicado. "But, hey, I'll buy your book."

"You won't have to," he said. "I'll send you an advance review copy. Care of the *Tribune?*"

"That'd be great." I almost leaned in to kiss him goodbye. "Take care, Burke," I told him. "Good luck with everything."

"You too," he smiled. But it was not his best smile.

Rule #55: Mind the design of this enterprise you call a novel. This doesn't condemn you to a blueprint, however, one should have some idea of the whole and how the pieces of the whole come together. You cannot leave threads loosely hanging in a novel. Someone will notice.

I had six voice mails when I turned my phone back on in baggage claim at Oakland International. One from my mother. One from Rose. Four from the office. *Good lord, people. It's a one hour flight!*

"Honey, it's Mom...call me, okay? I want to talk to you about what Rose said last night. It's really important that we talk, okay? Call me. Love you."

"Tea, it's Rose. I'm in the air so don't bother calling me. I'll get you when I get in to Kennedy, but you are not going to believe this. I've got Thadeus Burke's manuscript. You've got to hear this, no, never mind. I'm going to scan a page and send it to you the sec-ond I get home. Check your email asap. Call me when you get it. Oh, and you'll never guess who called me. Billy! Your fa-ther. Weird, huh? Talk later. *Ciao.*"

I didn't call my mother back. Instead I downloaded my emails and caught up on work stuff while my cab struggled through rush hour traffic. A compact minivan was unloading on the curb in front of my apartment.

"What's all this?" I asked pointing to a small mountain of shoeboxes on the sidewalk.

"Are you Athena Cervantes?" I shook my head yes.

"Sign here."

"For what? What am I signing for?

"Delivery."

"Of what?" He looked at the tower of Nike boxes.

"My best guess? Shoes."

"But where did they come from?" The driver looked at the paperwork.

"Nike." He pulled an envelope from under the clip on his clipboard. "Here. Maybe there's something in here." A typed note folded over once solved the mystery.

A - I hope at least one of these fit. Whatever you don't want you can call "Give Something Back". They'll take them to a shelter.
  Love, Nikko

"Can you sign this, lady? I want to get over the bridge before six."

I signed the paperwork and opened one of the boxes. They were indeed Nikes. The model they call "Athena". I sat down right there on the curb, pulled off my boots and tried them on. I cuffed my jeans, opened up my apartment and spent fifteen minutes clearing the sidewalk. Then I changed into sweats and ran straight up the hill as if there were little wings attached to my new running shoes. I was panting when I got back and picked up my ringing phone.

"Athena? What's wrong?"

"Nothing, Mom. I was just taking a run. I just got back."

"You were supposed to call me," she said barely concealing how peeved she was.

"Sorry. I forgot."

"Well. Never mind. I've been thinking about what Rose said last night. About this man."

"Nikko?" I asked. My mother's voice sounded weird. Constrained somehow and unusual for her, very tense. She almost never got that way. Her interns called her "Doctor Mellow".

"Yes. I think you should listen to Rose." *What? What The Fuck? Rose practically told me that I was a piece of crap and that Nikko's interest in me couldn't possibly be more than carnal, and was, at best, transitory and carnal. You should have defended me last night! Who are you and what have you done with my mother who used to love me?*

"Mom? Are you serious? You really agree with her?" I felt a little sick putting that into words.

"I just think Rose probably knows what she's talking about. About men like this. She's had a lot more experience than you have." *Well, that could be the understatement of the decade.*

"Okay. Well, I will certainly consider your opinion very carefully."

"Athena, don't get pissy..."

"Mom, do you know what Bobby said last night when you were passed out in the backseat of his car? He said that Nikko was probably smart enough to recognize a quality woman when he sees one." *Paraphrasing here.* "He said that he thought Rosie is jealous of me." *There. Put that in your pipe and smoke it, Mother!*

"Well, Athena, Bobby Cisneros may not be the best one to judge character, you know?" *Jesus! I mean, Jesus!* I counted to ten before I responded. Then I counted to ten again once more before I hung up.

"You could be right, Mom. He thinks you are a fucking saint."

I won't say I was shattered. Rocked maybe. Before I could think about it I texted Nikko.

"thnx for the shoes - my feet have wings – they match the ones on my heart! XO – A"

I waited and watched my screen until it went dark. I waited another minute. I counted on my fingers. Seven in Oakland is four in the morning in Greece. Oh, fuck, I thought. Why the hell did I do that? *The wings on my heart? Nikko's going to think that I am such a dork!*

There's nothing that will not be improved by a hot shower, a tuna melt and a perfectly chilled bottle of Pinot Grigio. Also, I had a bunch of prep to do on my wine country piece so instead of staring at my iPhone screen and willing Nikko to text me back for the next three hours, I sat down to my computer to get some work done. At eleven an email from Rose popped up.

"Check it out!" was all she wrote in the subject line and nothing else but an attachment. An excerpt from Thadeus Burke's manuscript.

Burke
page 21

still young and inexperienced but there was a native skill to their lovemaking.

She was a natural born tease and Thomas both loved and hated this about her. She pushed his hand downward.

"Would I be taking untoward liberties?" he whispered.

"Oh, Tommy. For godsake. Take some liberties!" He fumbled with the snap on her jeans and even more so with the zipper.

"Have you ever done this before?" she asked, but her voice was kind.

"This?" He knew he sounded nervous.

"Undress a girl. Have you ever taken anyone's clothes off?" He wanted to lie, but the girl was adept at deciphering bullshit.

"No," he admitted. "I've never done this before."

"Aww," she said sweetly. "Why didn't you say so? I'll help you. I'll teach you." He sat back spellbound as the girl slowly stripped. The neighbor's plaintive cello practice floated in the open windows. It would form a lasting imprint. For years afterward, after the war, he would ask women to strip for him. He would play Yo-Yo Ma and instruct them so that he could conjure this girl. He would find women who looked like her. Straight pale hair that cascaded down their backs like blonde silk. Long legs. Muscular because she was a runner, but lean and feminine. Like a dancer. Like a ballerina. And their faces would be angelic like hers. Skin that made him think of ripe peaches and fresh cream. Eyes with pale irises that changed with her mood, green to gold. Flecks of

I called Rose in New York where it was almost two a.m. "What the hell, Rose? This is in Burke's manuscript?"
"It's you, isn't it, Tea? This is you."

"Shit!" I said.

"Wait, it gets better. On page seventy..."

"Rose! Stop! I don't want to hear." Rose was quiet for several seconds.

"Honey. This guy had it bad. Bad. Bad. Bad. Bad. Bad. All the romantic parts are about your relationship."

"Rosie. Promise me. You will not tell a soul." I didn't like her hesitation one bit.

"You should know, Athena. This excerpt is going in *The New Yorker.*"

"What?!"

"They're calling him this generation's James Salter."

"Do not tell a soul!" I begged.

"Okay," she said.

"On your mother's life."

"No problemo," she said and I wished immediately that I knew someone whose life she valued more than Brenda's. We both breathed and listened to a whole minute of three-thousand miles of dead air before I broke the silence.

"What did you say about Billy? What was in your message about Billy?"

"Oh, yeah. Too weird. Apparently, Billy was Googling me..." *Poor Billy. He's now one of those sad guys who sits at his computer all day long Googling people he hasn't seen in years.* "...and he found me on the New Writer's website. Get this. He wants me to look at his book."

"What? Billy wrote a book?" *Well, of course he has. Who the hell hasn't?* "What did you tell him?"

"What could I tell him, Tea? He's your father for fuck's sake."

"He's not my father. Mike's my father. I divorced Billy, remember?"

"Okay, chill. I told him I'd look at it. That's all. I tell practical-ly everybody that. It doesn't mean I will." *Note to self: good to know.* We observed another awkward silence.

"So, what do you hear from Mr. Wonderful?" she asked snidely. I looked at my iPhone that had no text messages and no missed calls.

"He sent me shoes," I said.

"Shoes?"

"Running shoes. Nike Athenas."

"How romantic," Rose rolled her "r" and oozed sarcasm.

"Okay, you must be exhausted." I put an end to it. "And, I've got to be in tomorrow early. Can I call you later in the week?"

"Just do it!" she said and laughed without mirth.

At two a.m. I remembered that Nikko had asked me to join him on his yacht in the Greek Isles. Jesus. How did I forget that? That would have shut Rose's pie hole. *Damn it! When was the last time somebody offered to fly you to Greece, eh Rosie?* I slept with my new running shoes on, holding my iPhone and praying for a text message, but when I woke up the next morning, there was still nothing. By the time I had coffee I had another full-blown case of insecurity bearing down on me like the swine flu.

THREE

"I would go to the war—I would kill and maybe die—because I was embarrassed not to."
                    - Tim O'Brien, *The Things They Carried*

I spent three days in the wine country talking to itinerant farm workers, earnest, humble enologists, and even a few winery owners. The span of wealth disparity up in wine country was mind-boggling, yet everyone I talked to had a near-obsession with the very same thing: producing a quality wine. Booze, good booze, was a sociologically unifying element in Napa.

During the days, conducting the interviews was a thankfully distracting enterprise. At night, I devoured Burke's novel after Rose FedEx-ed the galleys to me from New York. The wine and the interviews kept me from obsessing about my family drama, my own un-edited manuscript, and my romantic ambitions during the daylight hours. Burke's story kept me up very, very late three nights in a row, laughing out loud, sobbing, and most of all, thinking. And then sobbing some more.

By Friday's afternoon rush hour I was back in my cube at the *Trib* waiting for a call-back from an especially elusive source. Plenty mindful that Friday was the day Nikko was due back from

Greece, I was also hoping that I would get a call from him and I willed him to call me the second he landed at SFO.

I was busy plucking tiny brown leaves from my fern, "*if I remove every single withered leaf by 5:00 o'clock, Nikko will call me at 5:05*". I glanced toward the big-faced newsroom clock. The wholly unexpected sight of my brother's face bobbing along above the cubical partitions behind Security Ronald's bald head stopped my heart and sent a paralyzing chill down my spine. I literally froze in mid-motion. Miggs's appearance was wholly unprecedented. No member of my family had ever paid a visit to me in the *Tribune* building. *I thought you were in Hawaii opening up a shop. Oh, god! Something terrible has happened. Is it Mom? Dad?* Because that is how my mind works. Worst Case Scenario. Always.

Ronald swung into the cube's doorway with Miggs fast on his heels.

"Cervantes, you got somebody." I dropped a handful of brown fern leaves on the carpet. Ronald retreated and disappeared.

"Miggs, what's wrong?"

"Nothing. I was in the neighborhood," he said. He blinked, reached toward me and plucked the last brown leaf from the hanging plant smiling innocently. My desk phone rang loudly. I exhaled and looked at the number. I pointed to my headset and held up a finger while I plugged in.

"I have to take this...don't leave! Give me one sec," I said.

"No worries. Take your time." Miggs shrugged and backed out of my cube. My elusive Napa source started rapidly dictating the proportions of certain varietals in notable blends and I succumbed to the task of recording them as my brother slipped out of sight.

Once I had transcribed the acquired quotes into my desktop and checked them twice for accuracy, I went in search of my brother and the story of his unexpected appearance, *whatever it was going to be.* I found him in Howie's office chatting it up in a lively manner with my boss and one of his clones from Sports. Behold, the scene before me: a shocking study in contrasts. Miggs, young, lean, bearded, and heavily tattooed, wearing a vintage Nirvana t-shirt that had seen better days, holding sway over the two bald, fat, old farts in crumpled shirts and stained neckties. I could plainly see, even from a distance, that the two older men were completely enthralled, both of their big butts firmly planted on the edge of Howie's desk, jowly faces grinning and nodding like dashboard clown heads. Howie lept up when I approached.

"Hey, Cervantes," he accused, "you never told me that your brother was *Miguel* Cervantes." I gawked at Howie trying to imagine how in the world it could be that this neo-conservative, middle-aged, whiter-than-white, and straighter-than-straight, Northern Californian, whose major personal *and* professional preoccupation seemed to be the threat posed to our nation at large by "the damn wetbacks", how could he possibly know about – never mind care one whit about – my Mexi-Cali brother's celebrity on the pro surfing circuit? Fatty read my mind.

"I did sports in the South Bay before I moved up here," he explained. *I knew that!* "Back in the day, I covered the '99 Southern California Junior championships when your little *hermano* here took the title for the first time in Redondo." *That, I did not know.* Howard chucked Miggs on the shoulder in a manly way and dropped into an awkward, chubby crouch next to his desk, extending his hands out as if he were negotiating a gnarly sixteen-foot wave. I thought for a brief moment that I might actually be sick on the deck of Howie's imaginary surfboard. Instead, although already established as tardy, I made an unenthusiastic introduction.

"Dude, this is my little brother, the international surfing legend, Miguel Cervants. Ta Da!"

"Dude!" Howie yelled loudly, ignorant of my sarcasm and unconcerned about appearances. "That is so awesome!" Howie Falkenhorst gave Miggs a high five. Then the fat man got some air on his imaginary board. Lupe appeared. Snickering and rolling her eyes, she dumped a tall stack of stock photos from the research files onto the top of Howard's desk. The shots featured Miggs mostly accepting trophies. *Gosh, who knew the kid had gotten so much press?* Howie grabbed a handful of the photos without so much as a "thank you" for Lupe and thrust them at my brother.

"Would you, kind sir?" he asked. Howard Falkenhorst blushed, actually blushed red, handing my brother a pen. *Oh, the world is coming to an end!*

"Let me know when your fifteen minutes are over here," I told Miggs. "I'll be at my desk. I'm just going to shut down my computer." I left my brother to the demands of his fame shaking my own head in wonder. *So, the old man is a surfing groupie? Again, who knew? What other secrets could Fatty be keeping? Goes to show, doesn't it, that you just don't really know anything at all about people.* That last thought was unsettling. And it proved to be prescient. Sure enough, it had foretold two voice mails from my recently-revealed-to-be-enigmatic parents.

I listened to the first one. "Hi, Honey, it's me, Mom. I know you're avoiding me, and that's okay, but as soon as you get over your little snit, give me a call. It's very important that we talk. Please."

And, then, "Tea, it's Dad again. I've got to be at Cal on Monday and I have a dinner up there in the city next Sunday night. I was hoping that maybe we could get together after? Or, maybe on Monday? Leave a message for me if you can make it." There was a pause. "I love you, Honey."

Mike sounded so forlorn, so sad, I almost pressed redial, but before I could lift my finger Miggs sauntered back into my cube.

150

"So, other than attending to your fame, what *are* you doing here? I thought you were in Maui." I hadn't meant to, but I could tell by Miggs's face that I had made him feel defensive.

"We're open. The shop is up and running. It's all good. I'm on my way home. I had a connecting flight through SFO, so I decided to hop off and spend a night with my big sis. Is that not cool?"

"A little notice would have been nice," I sniffed. "I have a life, you know." Technically this had not been true for many years and we both knew it. But, note to family: *things are going to be different now with Nikko Dimitriou in the picture!* I sounded so pissy I was beginning to hate myself a little bit, but then, with sudden clarity, I suspected that Miggs, as my mother's double agent, could have easily arranged this little unannounced detour on a fact-finding mission for her.

"Oh, yeah, your so-called life," Miggs said. "The new squeeze. I heard about him." *Ha! Suspicions confirmed.* I opened my mouth to tell him as much and to give him a big, fat piece of my mind about boundary issues but my cell phone interrupted us. I again raised a finger. "Stay put!"

"Oh, Nikko! Hi!" My brother's eyebrows shot up at my honey-eyed tone. I stuck my tongue out and motioned that he was welcome to step away. He laughed, but this time he did not respectfully give me privacy for my call. He hovered.

Rule #18: If you were your character in a given situation, how would you feel? Honesty will lend credibility to an unbelievable scene.

Somehow, I succumbed to pressure from both Nikko and Miggs and within the hour all three of us were driving across the bridge to Marin to have dinner with Nikko's grandparents who had "a little place" up there. I let the people with the very long legs sit up front in Nikko's Prius as I unsuccessfully tried to eavesdrop from the rear seat while they traded manly tidbits of information about their lives. They were clearly hitting it off. At first, I was struck by my brother's apparent interviewing skills, but quite rapidly I started feeling more than a little jealous of the instant bromance that was obviously developing in the front seat. It was stunning how much common ground they found so quickly. I couldn't really participate in the conversation without unbuckling and leaning over the center console. I only heard about every third word but I could plainly hear the laughing. *Just what the hell is so damn funny anyway?* By the time we arrived at the gated property I was feeling, once again, like the perennial outsider. *Chill, Athena! For crying out loud. Miggs offered to sit in the back. You insisted on riding in back. Remember? You are such a martyr, but then, you did learn from the best.*

Rule #39: Always keep in mind what is most interesting about this story to your readers. You cannot do what's "fun" for you as a writer. These two things will likely be very different and the first one is much more important to the novel than the second one.

I guess I was expecting a big, burly Anthony Quinn type from *Zorba the Greek*. *(Oh, and by the way, Antonio Rodolfo Quinn Oaxaca-just for your information, is a man of Mexican-American heritage, not Greek, don't you know?)* Instead, Nikko's Pappou was as lean and broad shouldered as his grandson. My heart melted when he embraced Nikko warmly and kissed his cheeks.

"I am so happy to see you, Kookla," he said. Then he turned to me without any introduction. He faced me squarely. "Ah, this is your friend, Athena! You are so lovely." He bent down, took my chin in his hand, and adjusted his glasses to examine my face closely.

Unselfconsciously. His scrutiny made Miggs laugh. When the old man turned in my brother's direction, he stepped back and touched his creased forehead with two fingers, tapping as if, with effort, he could draw something from his memory. "I have forgotten your name, my son, since the last time we met. You must forgive this old man."

"This is Miguel. I told Yaya on the phone that he was coming," Nikko said. "Athena's brother from LA. You've not forgotten him, Pappou. You've never met Miguel before."

"Truly?" Nikko's grandfather stepped closer to Miggs. "We have never met? You seem so familiar." He glanced at Nikko. "Are you certain, Kookla?" Nikko shook his head. "Well, never mind. No matter. Perhaps we met in another life, eh? Or perhaps you remind me of one of Nikko's old friends from school." The old man clamped one withered hand onto Miggs's shoulder and with his other he lifted a glass from the table top. A crystal ice bucket sat sweating with four more jelly jar glasses at the ready. He put the first glass into Miggs's hand. "Do you like ouzo, Miguel?" Then, with his bare hand, he reached into the ice bucket, withdrew a handful of cubes and dropped them into Miggs's glass. He poured ouzo over the ice and winked. This simple gesture of such familiarity and intimacy inexplicably made my heart ache. An unwanted surge of profound jealousy made me turn away and bite down on my lip. *What is the matter with me?*

"Go inside, Kookla, and find your Yaya." It was amusing to see the old man order Nikko around as if he were still a boy, not the world's pre-eminent researcher in computerized cancer detection. Nikko didn't seem to mind. His grandfather began preparing the other glasses. "We make a toast when Nikko's grandmother is here!" Before her grandson could take one obedient step, Helena Dimitriou appeared in the open kitchen doorway. She was, to use the corniest phrase available, a vision. Anyone could see that this attractive woman had been stunning in her girlhood. She stepped from the doorframe with a lithe grace that completely belied her eighty-plus years. (Boo would have cast her in Ann Bancroft's role in *The Turning Point.*)

Immediately she made a direct beeline for me, ignoring the three men, as if she sensed my inexplicable desolation. Her silver hair was pulled into a wispy chignon and her makeup was spare. Her tailored, white slacks and simple, bright, white shirt were made of quality linen. They seemed to cast a soft glow all around her. She paused and looked deeply into my eyes before she embraced me. When she pulled back she gripped my elbows and smiled.

"Ah, at last! Here you are, my dear! We've been looking forward to meeting you. We are your biggest fans." I looked at Nikko and he just beamed. His grandfather handed me a jelly jar glass half full of smoky ouzo. In my shaking hand the ice cubes tinkled like the most delicate wind chimes. The old man's expressive eyes held mine like a tractor beam.

"My favorite of your stories, Athena dear, was the one about the little girl who's papa bought her a rodeo horse with money he earned picking in the fields. The little queen of the fields. Such a touching story."

"I loved the story you wrote about Nikko," Helena patted my arm.

"I told you," Nikko said. "You are a star." His grandfather distributed the other glasses to his family and then he raised his own.

"Welcome. Welcome Athena and Miguel to our humble home."

Well, okay, that may have been a stretch for people who had a twenty-four-seven security guard posted in a turret over their guest house, but I believe Nikko's Pappou used the term loosely if not metaphorically. *Can you meaningfully call your home "humble" if you have an unobstructed view of Mt. Tamalpais in one direction and a sweeping panorama of the Pacific Ocean in the other? I think not.*

In contrast with the grandeur of the property's larger grounds, clearly, out behind the main house, some effort had been exerted to re-create a truly humble Greek garden. Simple terra cotta pots full of lush, colorful geraniums hovered at every doorway and under every windowsill, and many more had been scattered on the stone patio. Wooden window shutters were painted in bright sky-blue to match the weathered wooden table, and beyond the low-slung rock wall grew a small olive grove surrounded by a vegetable garden and many grape vines. Nikko's Pappou tended the garden himself he told us with great pride, and soon he would be pressing his own olive oil on a very small scale. He promised to gift us with bottles of his first efforts.

Rule #6: Coincidences that get characters into trouble are interesting; coincidences that get them out of trouble are cheating.

Nikko's grandmother urged me into the kitchen instructing me to call her Yaya while I helped her with dinner. She had given the housekeeper/cook the night off.

"Nothing fancy," Helena confided. "Mousaka. But the potatoes and the peppers and tomatoes are all from Pappou's garden." I was instantly at ease with her, as comfy-cozy as I had been in my *Abuela's* kitchen as a little girl. Miggs and Nikko set the table outside and lit candles all around the patio while the sun set. We ate late, Greek style, and started dinner with a simple salad of fresh tomatoes, cucumbers from right there on the Dimitriou property, and big slabs of feta cheese under a drizzle of olive oil that Nikko had brought from Lesvos. I never felt more welcome in my life. *Maybe it was the ouzo.*

"None better," Pappou said tapping the slender bottle of olive oil. "In the whole world."

"Do you go back to Greece often?" Miggs asked in between bites. It was an innocent question, but the sudden way Nikko's Pappou put his hands together in front of his solar plexus and dropped his chin signaled that Mr. Dimitriou's answer was fraught with baggage.

"I bring gallons of the stuff," Nikko interrupted with a subtle shake of his head. He looked directly at Miggs while pouring more wine in his glass. My brother's question was never answered.

After dinner, while Nikko and I cleared the table and put the dishes into the kitchen sink for the housekeeper's morning arrival, Miggs entertained the senior Dimitrious with somewhat riotous stories about his business model and our family. The three of them sipped chummy glasses of grappa. Nikko pointed as I stood watching them through the lace-curtained window. He came up behind me and whispered earnestly, "Look how they seem so comfortable with Miguel." Then he asked hoarsely, his voice sounding tainted by emotion, "Do you think he likes them?" Nikko's proximity made me shiver and I could feel his warm breath in my ear. *You could so kiss me right now!* But, he didn't, seeming quite intent instead on the little domestic tableau in the garden.

"Miggs loves everyone," I said.

"It looks like they are really loving him too." An enigmatic smile appeared on Nikko's face while he continued to watch.

"It's a goddamn love-fest out there," I said wickedly under my breath. Thank Zeus, Nikko didn't seem to hear. *Jesus! What is wrong with me?*

Rule #56: Are you a novelist or a diarist? If the form of your story is principally a revelation of your private thoughts, insights and communications, take pains to give your reader the sense that you are being honest. Intimacy without honesty is masturbatory and nobody* really wants to see it.

*Obviously there are a few who do and will pay good money for that, but do you really want to be the Sovereign of the Voyeurs?

Just as Nikko and I joined the others again, a full moon grew up out of the olive grove and dimmed the lights from our flickering candles. Nikko yawned and on that cue his Yaya suggested that the three of us spend the night in Marin instead of driving all the way back into the city.

"Tomorrow is Saturday, yes?" she said. "You don't have to rise early for work, do you?" Miggs piped up that staying was an excellent idea since Papou had just challenged him to a game of backgammon. Nikko yawned again and apologized for his jet lag. Staying overnight was a done deal. Nikko went into the house to find a backgammon set. When he returned the conversation moved on to the coming dinner at the Fairmont Hotel where Nikko was to be feted by Stanford and the organizers of the National Science Awards. Nikko and his Yaya were negotiating the transportation details when he turned abruptly to me.

"Athena, this is such a horrible thing to do so late. Please forgive me, but would you please come on Sunday? You really should be there." He smiled. "We should have members of the press, right? Miggs, you should come too."

"Oh, my god," I sputtered, "I couldn't."

"Why ever not, my dear? You should be there. You wrote such a great story about Nikko!" His grandmother leaned in and squeezed my hand. *And why not? Why can't you go? Really?*

"Well, I...I... honestly," I confessed, "I don't really have anything I could wear to a formal event." Miggs also declined on the grounds that he had pressing business in Los Angeles. Helena told him that she understood, but then she rose from her chair and reached out to me.

"Come," she said. "Come with me."

Helena Dimitriou and I were almost exactly the same size and build. In the master bedroom she pulled one exquisite gown after another from her huge closet until there were a dozen draped across the big bed.

"Choose, my dear," she said eyeing me closely. "Which one do you like? They will all fit, I am sure."

"Really?" I asked shyly. "I don't think I've borrowed a dress... ever! And these! These are..." Helena picked up a gown that slit up the side and plunged to the waist in the back and was the color of emeralds.

"This one I think." She held it out. "It's been many, many years since I wore this one. Perhaps it's a style better suited to someone your age, Athena. I would really love to give it to you."

"Oh, I couldn't accept it!" I blurted.

"Nonsense!" She took the dress off the hanger and handed it over. "Truthfully I should have donated some of these dresses decades ago, but I guess I've been saving them for a reason." We shared a moment, our eyes locking before I took the dress and held it up. "Put it on, dear. I'll be right back." When she came back into the room she found me staring into the long, antique mirror.

"Put these on, too," she said. "These are perfect with that dress."

"Are these real?" I whispered, my nose just inches away from a pair of exquisite pendant emerald earrings. She laughed and told me again to put them on. I obeyed and she drew my hair back and turned me toward the mirror.

"Just the thing!" she said. "For the National Science Awards. You will sit with us. You will sit at the family's table."

Rule #15: When attempting to write about romance, bear in mind that the pleasure of reading a romantic story is only available to the reader when they can recognize and sympathize with the idea that a particular connection between two characters is interesting, worthy, believable and involving. Proceed accordingly.

Early the next morning Nikko made the briefest, tousled appearance at breakfast, coming down only long enough to give me the details for Sunday's event and lend me his Prius for the weekend. He kissed my cheek and hugged Miggs warmly goodbye before going back to bed.

On the way to SFO Miggs explained that the two of them had been up very late "bonding". Well into the wee hours, he told me, Nikko had confided three generations worth of Dimitriou family history.

"Sissy, we are not the only ones with crazy parents."

"Crazy how?" I asked but I was not at all anxious to hear the answer if it would make me less in love with Nikko Dimitriou or his family.

"So, didn't you think it's kind of weird that Nikko is getting some big award and his parents are not gonna be there for it?" Miggs asked.

"Well, they live in Greece, right?"

"They do but they are actually *in* Toronto right now. They actually *live* in Toronto for a good part of the year. They actually *could* come to this shindig on Sunday, but the deal is, his old man will not set foot in the U.S. No way. No how. Not gonna happen. Nikko could be elected president. The parentos are not coming in for the inauguration. And, get this...You remember that weird little second last night when I asked Pappou how often he goes to Greece? Turns out...never! Nikko's pops will not – on principle – step one foot in this country, and his grandpop will not go back to Greece. This has been going on for thirty years! More than that. And we thought our parents had problems."

"Did he say why?"

"Yeah, for Nikko's dad he said it's about something that Richard Nixon did back in the day, and for Pappou it's all about shit that the Greeks did with the Nazis in the nineteen forties...old shit...*really, really* old shit, but these two guys are some kind of stubborn. The whole family only sees each other together in Canada!"

"That's sad," I said.

"Sucks for Nikko," Miggs added.

When I dropped Miggs off at departures, even in the immediate wake of Nikko's sad family tale of stubbornness and secrecy, I made my brother swear on my life that he would tell our mother *NOTHING* about my love life.

I had to buy shoes for Sunday and also get a mani-pedi so it was Saturday evening before I logged on to pick up email.

To: acervantes@oaklandtribune.com
From: rfineman@newwriters.net
Subject: please call your little friend: (310-455-1122)
t-that little putz, Thadeus is playing so hard to get. (Btw - Sez he doesn't remember f-ing me @ Davis. Who does the little shit think he's kidding? C'mon! I am so not NOT memorable. U Rn't mad about that, R U?) So, did you finish his book? Wowza, huh? It's *Love*

Story meets *Apocalypse Now!* He's a world class putz for stringing me along, but, fucking A, Tea, the boy can write. When U call, put a good word in for your homey – puhleeeez doll face. If – no , make that WHEN – I sign him, I think there's a chance Jocelyn will make me a partner!!!!! Squeee!!!!
Tons of love. Rose

Rule #23: Discipline is essential when undertaking the task of composing a novel because of the length of the work. You will find discipline to be imperative because you need to sustain and cultivate your initial inspiration. Start by putting your butt in the chair in front of your computer for several hours each day no matter what comes out.

With mixed emotions, I sent a guilt-induced text to Burke. He called me back immediately.

"Athena, I'm really glad to hear from you. I've been thinking of calling you." There was a long, pregnant pause. "I know that Rose Fineman gave you the galleys of my manuscript." There was *another* long, pregnant pause. Longer than the first one.

"She did. Yes, she did give it to me."

"Did you...did you read it?"

"Yep. Yes, I did."

Again. Maximum pause.

"So, did you...what did you think?"I was mean. I let him sweat a second more before I exhaled.

"Oh, Burke. I loved it. It's wonderful. It's heartbreaking. It tore me up. You must have done a lot of research." Burke laughed but there was no mirth in his laughter.

"I guess you could say that," he said. "I guess you could call it research."

Holy shit!

"Wait, were you *there?* You went to Iraq?" *So that's why Burke dropped out of sight after Davis! He enlisted! Holy Hell!*

"Yeah. I went. I was there. It was a stupid thing to do, but...I had my reasons at the time."

You know those conversations that you find yourself in when suddenly you wish you could not be in them anymore? That was this one. But I had to ask.

"How much of what you wrote in your book really happened?" I watched the numerals change on the digital clock. "You don't have to tell me," I whispered.

"All of it," he said. His voice was barely audible. "It isn't a memoir, Athena. It's fiction. But, I think it's fiction the same way your story about the Fire Island Princess was fiction. You know what I'm talking about, don't you?"

"Well, I hardly think...I mean...there's no comparison...oh, Christ, Burke! I'm sorry. I'm really sorry."

"Hey, no worries. I made it back. I'm back anyway." My mind was racing. I didn't know what I could possibly say. So I talked about his book.

"I didn't know that about Rod Serling. I didn't know he was in World War II. Did you really enlist so you could experience war? So you'd have something to write about that mattered? Like Tom?"

"Something like that," Burke said. "It wasn't the most intelligent decision I've ever made." I waited. He waited. We waited together without saying anything.

"Your love scenes were really sweet. I liked them," I said finally. When he laughed, his laugh sounded genuinely amused.

"Well...I revealed an awful lot about our relationship in that book." He hesitated. "I honestly don't think very many people could figure out that it's you, though. That you were my character, Kira. Me...of course they'll know that the fucked up protagonist is me. I'm Tom and everyone will know it. Or, I guess it's more accurate to say that Tom is me." Burke laughed again, this time a deep-throated, self deprecating laugh. I remembered how he could always make me laugh too. And cry sometimes. Neither of us knew how to go on talking about Kira and Tom.

"So, anyway," I said, "I promised Rose that I would give you a nudge. She's still sort of waiting to hear from you."

"Oh, yeah, I'm sorry, Athena. I should have told you this. I sold my book last year."

"What? You already have an agent?"

"I don't need an agent. I sold my book directly to an indie imprint."

"I'm confused. Why does Rose, and everyone else, think you're unsigned? That you're still up for grabs?"

"That's part of my publisher's marketing plan. It's part of the scheme. To make me even more desirable."

"Huh?"

"Hype. It will get me better reviews. It sells books. It gets buzz."

"Oh." *I sound dumb. I am dumb.*

"It isn't unethical to withhold that information." I thought Burke sounded just a tad bit defensive.

"No. I'm sure it isn't. Technically." Against my own better judgment I started to feel some sympathy for Rose (and all the other agents who were still hoping to sign Thadeus Burke, the wunderkind).

"Publishing is dog eat dog now, Athena. It's the rodeo. All bets are off. You've got to do whatever you can to make a splash." Was this really Burke talking? "That's what my publisher says anyway." Just then he sounded a little sad. Or maybe it was just unconvinced. I was remembering our long talks and meaningless promises about never selling out. I didn't know what he was thinking, nor did I ask him.

"So what about *your* book? Let's talk about your book." he said. "You almost done?"

"I am taking another pass…it needs to be trimmed some. And it needs editing. It needs a lot of editing."

"Would you like another set of eyes on it? I could…"

"Burke, it's over twelve hundred pages. I couldn't ask you to put that kind of time in…"

"Twelve hundred?" I pictured him wincing.

"Over." A lot more dead air bounced between us while I waited for Burke to politely withdraw his offer.

"Maybe what you've got is enough for a trilogy." He had injected a forced hopefulness into his voice. "Maybe I could help, you know, make some suggestions for how to break it up. Series are all the rage just now, they say." I thought about it for no more than five seconds. Of all the human beings on the planet, Thadeus Burke was the single person I knew I could trust to be completely honest. I knew in fact that Burke could be brutally honest. And would be.

"I'm going to upload the file into Dropbox and send you the link right now. If you get sick of it at any point, just quit. I won't hold it against you."

"Deal. I'll look it over. There's something you can do for me too."

"Okay.....?"

"Just don't tell Rose I've sold my book. Not just yet. The publisher wants to milk the ambiguity for a little while longer. They're building up the hype so that the pub date gets maximum PR. Also, they don't want what's left of publishing to put a whammy on us."

"They can do that?"

"Well, they can still freeze you out of any chance you'll get a review in the traditional publications. People are still holding on where they can. They can make sure you don't get reviewed in the old bigs."

"Does that matter?"

"Less and less. More than a few agents have gone commando and opened up their own shops. Remember Rhoda Weiner?"

"Sure. Patty Orloff's agent?"

"Well, Rhoda is one of the principles in the imprint that's publishing my book. It's Rhoda and two other agents. They got sick of being unable to sell anything besides celebrity memoir bullshit so they're going behind the backs of the industry and setting up their own little shop. She's pretty genius when it comes to marketing." A note of ambivalence had crept into his voice again. "I guess," he said. "That's what she says anyway."

"Wow. Congratulations on that. She's huge." I did feel bad for Rose then. She was going to crap herself when she heard that Patty's agent, *THE* Rhoda Weiner, had gone commando and was publishing Thadeus Burke under her very own indie imprint. Rose Fineman couldn't get Rhoda Weiner's coffee.

"Thanks," Burke said. "But mums the word, okay? Tell no one."

"Yeah, sure. No worries." It seemed after his announcement that our conversation was over. "Okay, so I'm going to send you my book, and you let me know what you think. Whenever. When you get the time. And, really, if you get bored at any time...just you know..." I was prattling.

"What's the title?" Burke interrupted my perseveration.

"*Wooden Nickels,*" I told him.

"Nice. I like the title," he said. "I'll be in touch. Load it right now."

And so I did.

Rule #12: Consider taking on a teacher. It is tempting to show your work in progress to an adviser to get advice, or even just as an antidote to the lonely world of writing fiction and the self-

doubt that generally inhabits that world. But, be aware that not every teacher can reinforce your productivity. Some even set themselves up to discourage their students rather than encourage them. No teacher can tell you whether or not you have talent or if you will "make it".

The Fairmont Hotel in downtown San Francisco is spectacular. I hadn't walked through a hotel lobby in an evening gown and heels since my high school prom which, I'll admit, I attended ostensibly to cover the event on behalf of the school newspaper, wearing a thrift store, hand-me-down ensemble, dateless. *Not the same thing.* The evening in the Fairmont found the men mostly in tuxedos and the women heavily be-jeweled. I got my fair share of appreciative looks, starting with the parking valet who relieved me from behind the wheel of Nikko's Prius. It felt good to be admired.

One of the three officious, young women manning the reception table ran a finger down the list of the invited.

"I only show one Cervantes," she said primly. "You're clearly not Dr. Miguel Cervantes, are you?"

"Dr. Miguel Cervantes from UCLA?" I instantly started to sweat and followed her finger on the guest list. The girl and her two cohorts looked at me in the same way one might look at the most ignoble of party crashers.

"I'm sorry..." the girl began with the bitterly imperial tone of a Stanford undergraduate, and not a bit sorry.

"You're at the family's table." Nikko swooped in to appear suddenly at my side. He leaned down to plant a chaste kiss on my cheek. The three Stanford girls gaped. "Ms. Cervantes is sitting at the family table," he told the girl in front of us. The one with the finger. She nodded with an unattractive display of her silver amalgam fillings. I mouthed the words "family table" and favored all three of them with my best false smile while I slipped my hand through Nikko's arm. We turned and walked no more than ten yards into the pre-party before we bumped smack into Mike.

"Dad!" I stiffened. He was holding a glass of amber liquid and also holding forth among a circle of young men, all in tuxedos, all of them unabashedly adoring my dad. The circle parted when they recognized Nikko.

"Tea! I didn't expect to see you here." Mike leaned forward across the circle with some hesitation, but managed to kiss the exact spot on my cheek where Nikko had just left his kiss. "Dr. Dimitriou," Mike said extending a handshake.

"Dr. Cervantes," Nikko bowed in a courtly manner and shook Mike's hand. All the young doctors in the circle introduced themselves to Nikko while Mike and I looked at each other quizzically over all the handshaking.

"I'm honored that you're here, sir," Nikko smiled at Mike. Then he looked around the circle of younger doctors. "All of you. Thank you so much for coming. It means a lot." Then he put an arm around me and beamed. "May I introduce you all to Athena Cervantes from the *Tribune*." Nikko gestured toward Mike, "... and also, obviously, Dr. Cervantes's daughter." It was my turn to shake hands and collect names. When the introductions were over Mike cleared his throat.

"So, how are you...? How do you two...?" His puzzlement made him uncharacteristically inarticulate.

"Your daughter wrote a very flattering piece about me a few weeks back for her paper. She was kind enough to accept my invitation tonight. Hardly a fair way to say thank-you...some rubber chicken and a lot of boring speeches. Nevertheless..." He smiled at me and the circle of docs laughed politely. One of them made a joke about talking shop and asked Nikko a question that was completely over my head. I excused myself, slipped out of the circle, and Mike followed me to a waiter carrying champagne. We each grabbed a glass of Moet and Chandon and Mike surrendered his bourbon glass to the waiter's tray.

"You didn't call me back," he said sounding more sad than mad.

"Yeah...I've been pretty busy," I had been busy but that wasn't why I hadn't returned Mike's call. Mike looked over where Nikko had replaced him in the circle of young doctors.

"I guess so," he said. We both drained our glasses.

"You look spiffy, Dad." I straightened his bow tie.

"And, you....wow. You look...amazing. That's a pretty snazzy dress you're wearing."

"It's vintage," I told him. "Borrowed." I said. "From Nikko's grandmother."

"Oh." Mike's eyebrows moved toward each other as he no doubt contemplated the kind of relationship that involved sharing formal-wear garments, or maybe he was just then remembering the severe grandma dresses that had been favored by Abuela.

"So I guess this is the event you said you were coming up here for in your message, huh?"

"Yep." He looked over at Nikko again. "So, are you...? Is this...?"

"You aren't communicating with Mom much these days, are you?"

"Your mother knows about this? That you know Nikko Dimitriou? That you know his *abuela*?" I was gratified that Nikko's name held such reverence for my dad and also that my mother hadn't broadcast my business, but it was also kind of unnerving how little they were talking to each other.

"Yeah, I told Mom." I stopped a passing waiter and exchanged my empty glass for a new one. "She thinks he's too good for me," I said flatly. Mike scowled.

"I'm sure that's not true," he said defending her.

"Oh, it is," I said. "She said so in no uncertain terms."

"What?" Mike looked and sounded incredulous.

"Yes, she said that someone like Nikko Dimitriou couldn't possibly be interested in someone like me. That's a direct quote. According to Mom, he can have any woman he wants. So, obviously…"

"Athena…" Mike started to make excuses for her, I could feel them coming, but Nikko joined us and then immediately a member of the wait staff appeared and his little bell sounded to move us all into the dining room.

"Can we meet tomorrow?" Mike asked. "I can cancel my meeting at Cal."

"Sorry, Dad, I've got work tomorrow. I'll call you though." Mike and Nikko said polite goodbyes, and Mike congratulated Nikko again on the fabulous award he was getting, and later I saw Mike slip out of the ballroom when the speeches were in full swing. He looked forlorn and I felt for him. I was glad though that he didn't come over to the family table to get introduced. It just made things easier for me.

Rule #8: After you read over your rough draft, be not tempted to judge. Your task at this juncture is an analytical one. Do not decide, for example, whether or not your work is "publishable". How the hell would you know? Many novels previously published and heartily enjoyed might be completely "un-publishable" in today's market. This decision is not yours so put it out of your head and just get to work making it better.

I figured that no matter what their deal was, my parents would convene pretty damn fast after I bumped into Mike while on Nikko Dimitriou's arm wearing Helena Dimitriou's borrowed gown. I figured right. My mother sent two emails, one text and then she called me, all before noon on Monday. You can run, but you cannot hide.

"What's up, Mom? Can I presume you spoke with Dad?" I called her back from the safety of my cubicle in the *Tribune* building.

"I'm not pleased that you misrepresented my statements to your father," she said. I let a long, long time pass. Too long for her. "Athena? Are you there?"

"I'm here."

"Can we talk?"

"Aren't we doing that now?"

"No. I mean really talk. I've got some things I'd like to say. I want to clear some things up."

"Well, I'm actually pretty clear, Mother. I don't need to hear anymore about how little you think of me."

"Athena, please..."

"Please what, Mom? Please come to my senses and realize that Nikko Dimitriou is just too damn good for somebody as flawed and inferior as I am? Is that what you want to make clear? Because I think you've already done that. I'm clear. Crystal." Nobody ever said I couldn't bust out the melodrama when I needed to.

"Okay. I know I hurt you. I want to make it up to you. And maybe explain some things. This is kind of a hard time for me. I'm maybe not communicating the way I should be."

"Mother..."

"Honey...Tea...just think about helping me out a bit okay? Maybe we could meet up in Morro Bay next weekend. Just a girls' weekend. You drive down. I'll drive up. We'll take some walks. Maybe rent those kayaks and paddle over to the dunes. Just have some quality time alone. And if you decide you don't want to talk, we won't. I just really need to see you." I was trying to find the catch. "Tea? How does that sound?"

"I'm not sure. Let me think about it, 'k? I'll call you by Wednesday. Let me see how my week's going."

"Sure. I'll call you Wednesday." I hung up without saying goodbye and I tried to dig into my story about a young Iraq war vet who'd come home missing a leg. One of the many, many victims of IEDs in Iraq. I re-read the notes I'd made about Ricky Titus. They made me think about Burke and his book and his character, Tom. Maybe, I thought, I ought to re-read Burke's manuscript before I try to write my piece about the ravages of war. Ricky Titus's story felt momentous. He was running a non-profit for underprivileged kids, hooking them up with free tutoring services in the East Bay. He was also hitting the gym hard doing mad hours of physical therapy so that he could master his prosthetic leg in time to walk his little sister down the aisle at her wedding and dance the father-daughter dance that their missing father wasn't going to be around for. People like Ricky Titus made me feel like a self-indulgent slacker. (People like Thadeus Burke made me feel like one too.) By day's end I wrapped up my story and decided to drive over to Ricky's digs in the warehouse he worked out of to get his approval. I was getting into my car when a Fed Ex truck pulled up and blocked my exit.

"You wouldn't be Athena Cervantes now, would you?" The driver hopped out with a small box and a signing device.

"Who wants to know?" I asked stupidly. The driver shook his head and pointed to the big "FED EX" on his van.

"Right," I said. "How did you know who I am...?"

"Easy. The sender said, 'You're going to recognize her because she will be the most beautiful girl you've ever seen.'"

"Seriously?" I felt myself blush.

"I recognize you from your picture in the *Trib*. Sign here."

"Oh, you are bad," I scolded, but he was a cutie-pie, and true or not, I enjoyed the idea that someone thought I was beautiful.

The box contained a tiny, silver evil eye on a long chain. The engraved card read, "Athena, thank you so much for attending the NSA event with my family. Your presence at our table meant more to me than you will ever know. Please pass on my regards to Dr. Cervantes as well and thank him for the great honor of his presence. Please wear this "evil eye". The Greeks believe it will ward off evil and keep you safe from harm. Not a very scientific theory, but very, VERY Greek. Hope to see you soon. Love, Nikko" The delivery, the gift, and Nikko's note pushed all thoughts of my mom out of my head. I drove over to see Ricky Titus with a light heart. Feeling beautiful.

Rule #22: As you proceed, take a moment to reflect: Why must you write THIS particular story? What's the belief burning within you that your story feeds off of? That's the heart of it!

Wednesday morning was crazy. The governor's people called to say that he was paying a last minute, unannounced visit to Ricky Titus's offices to lay some serious grant money on them and Howie sent me over to cover it with a photographer. Back to the East Bay warehouse we went. In the midst of all the hoopla, I got a text from Nikko:

"Are you free tonight? I'd like to see you. I have a business prop." I texted back, "Sure. Where? When?" In the commotion around Ricky Titus and his kids, I barely had time to contemplate the possibilities.

We convened at "Alexi's". Nikko got there before me. He was drinking Vodka on the rocks with Alexi and there were very serious expressions on their faces as I approached.

"Gentlemen," I said. "Whattup?" They both rose from the table and bowed in that way that some European men do. We all kissed each other on cheeks.

172

"You vill excuse me, friends, I must do tings in da kitchen now." Alexi bowed again and left us. Nikko seemed nervous. Then without preamble he rocked my world. He rocked my world *and* he offered me a job. Not just a job. A POSITION with Naxxos International, the family owned conglomerate. He said he wanted me to take over the in-house public relations for Naxxos North America. My starting salary would immediately roughly quintuple my income. Over night.

"Nikko, I don't know anything about PR. I'm a newspaper hack." I was probably whining.

"We think you'd be perfect," he smiled.

"We?" *Who was "we"?*

"Pappou and Yaya. They sit on the Naxxos board. They've been reading your writing in the *Trib* for years. They both agreed that your sensibilities regarding the human element far outweigh your relative inexperience in public relations."

"Yikes," was my response.

"Is that a yes?" he asked. "You'll have to be in Toronto for at least six months. And some of that time you'll be expected to be in Greece too. You'll have to leave almost immediately. After, we can see about moving you back to the states." I sat for a full minute completely dumbstruck. Nikko barely moved. He stared at the little, silver evil eye around my neck. Finally he touched my hand. "You will really like Toronto," he said softly.

Rule #24: Make sure that your characters voice strong opinions. Passive and malleable might seem likable characteristics to you in the real world, but it's poison in works of fiction.

The minute I got home, as promised, I got in touch and agreed to meet my mother in Morro Bay after work on Friday. Whatever her agenda was, I now had my own. I had to avoid Rose's multiple text messages and voice mails. No word from Burke about *Wooden Nickels. No worries, Burke-O, I'm going over to the dark side. Forget that silly novel. I'm going to write public relations!*

We almost made it through dinner. My mom noticed that I was a little on edge. "Tense," she said.

"It was the traffic," I said. "And the fog. It was foggy all the way down the 101."

"Right." I guess she decided to accept the lie. Morro Bay was cloudless. "So, you had dinner with Dad?"

"We didn't eat together. We were at different tables."

"He mentioned that you were at...a different table. He said you looked lovely." I stabbed my asparagus, raised it to eye level, and stared at it as if it might reveal the secrets of the universe.

On her own plate, my mother arranged and re-arranged the elements of her dinner artfully. The restaurant was mid-week-almost-empty except for us, and the only sounds were coming out of the kitchen.

"And Miggs?" She finally actually took a tiny bite of her own asparagus. I let her chew. "I heard you had a visit from your brother," she said.

"Yeah." I quickly took a bite and smiled at her around a mouthful of potato. My mother signaled the server for what was, in her case, an unusual second glass of wine.

"Athena?" She pointed to my glass, which was still full. I wanted to stay sober in case I had to abort our little mother-daughter tryst and would have to drive back to the Bay Area. I shook my head and the server gave me the kind of sympathetic look that indicated that she, also, had a mother.

"So, what did you and your brother do?" My mother asked sweetly. But I heard the edge in her voice as hard as she tried to camouflage it.

"Nothing."

"Nothing?" She stroked the stem of her wine glass with two fingers. I swallowed and wiped my mouth.

"Well, we didn't talk about you and Dad, if that's what you want to know." She tried to look all-innocent. I put my fork on the table. "In fact, you are a hundred percent right about that, Mom. What's going on between you and Dad is private and none of our business. Miggs and I are both out of the middle of it. Truly." I leaned in and looked her right in the eye. She made a little face. "And you know what else, Mom? I think I owe you and Dad an apology." She was full-on frowning. "What happens in a marriage, or in any adult relationship between two people, is a private matter. Miggs and I shouldn't have been so intrusive. I'm sorry. So, so sorry." I think that's when she saw it coming.

"Okay, thanks for that, Honey," she said carefully. She lowered her own fork with uninterrupted eye contact. We silently dared each other to look away. She caved.

"And you? What's happening with you? How's your book? How's work?"

"Ah, funny you should ask." I reached for my wine glass. I downed it. *Fuck it.* "As a matter of fact, I've finished my book."

"Oh, Honey! That's wonderful." I have to give her this much. She truly did look and sound genuinely pleased for me on that score.

"No biggie," I said. "Remember Burke? He's reading it. He's got it now. But it really isn't important what he thinks. The book is no longer important."

"Well, Athena, he's just one opinion. What if Rose...?" She caught herself before suggesting the unthinkable. I cut her off at the pass.

"I'm going to quit my job, Mom." She sat back and waited for what came next because my mom is really good at predicting human behavior. She didn't look one bit happy.

"I'm going to Toronto at the end of the month. For at least six months. I'm taking a job with Nikko's family company, Naxxos." She slammed her hand down on the table. Her face colored red and her lips trembled. She appeared to be struggling for control. She wasn't successful.

"I forbid it!" she all but shrieked.

"Mother!" I said. "Get a grip! I am thirty years old!" Our server had gone in to get the chef and the sous chef who were all standing by the bar now watching us as if we were performing dinner theatre for the exclusive entertainment of the kitchen help.

"I will not let you do this, Athena," she wailed. "You will ruin your life! You don't know this boy! You don't know anything about him! You can't move to a foreign country with him."

"You can't stop me, Mom." *Had Nikko said anything about moving to Toronto himself?*

"Athena," She looked steely. Her voice was raspy. "If you do this, I will never speak to you again." In that moment, I did not recognize my mother.

"You cannot be serious!" But I wasn't at all sure. Then she went a step too far.

"Abuela would be so ashamed of you." I didn't even blink. I stared at her. Calmly I picked up my purse from under my chair. I made it all the way to the French doors of the hotel's dining room. I turned around and marched back with tears brimming in my eyes. She was still sitting there, unmoving. At the table I waited until she finally stood up.

"Abuela would NOT be ashamed of me. Abuela would be proud of me. No matter what. And you know what else, Mom? There is not one thing any of us could have done to make her dis-

176

own us. Not one thing. So who do you *really* think Abuela would be ashamed of?"

After our little drama in the dining room, I tearfully took another room on the other side of the Inn and gave the desk clerk twenty bucks to forget I did it in case my mother made an inquiry. I hid my car across the road and snuck back to the Inn in the dark. I expected my cell phone to ring immediately and in this I was not disappointed. The caller, however, was not my mother, which was a surprise given her expected state of mind.

Rule #26: In terms of plot progression you must discount the first thing that comes to mind. And then also the second, third, fourth and fifth. Get those out of the way and allow yourself to be surprised.

"Rose Fineman is no fool!" It was after midnight in New York.

"What's up, Rose?"

"Something is hinky with our little friend, Burke..." She let the end of her sentence hang out there in the void for a second or two, and I didn't volunteer what I knew. "Have you talked to him yet? As you promised me? And, if not, why not? I thought we were besties, Athena. I'm not feeling the love."

"Rose, I have a job. A J – O – B, you know? I did put in a call to him..." *This was the truth at least.* "I suspect Burke is busy too." *Maybe also true. Who could say?* "I'll just speak for myself though and tell you that I did what I could and you can't expect him to be at your beck and call."

"Yeah, right...." We played chicken for a full long minute. "Also, your father is being a real pain in the ass."

Two can play the stupid game.

"What has Mike done to you, Rosie?"

"Not Mike. Your *real* fa-*thurrrr....Billlleeee." Always the
bitch!*

"I'm not really going to be of much help to you with either
of those things tonight, Rose."

"You don't have to be a bitch," she said and hung up. *Now
that's funny!*

Immediately I felt guilty about talking to Burke and knowing what I knew that Rose didn't yet know, so I gave him a call.
Also, if the truth has to be told here, the real reason I called him
was because I wanted to know if he'd made any progress with
Wooden Nickels.

"Hi, Burke," I said. "I got a call from Rose. She really needs to
know what you've decided about her agency."

"Yeah," he sighed. "I know. I should call her. It's not easy.
I've been on the receiving end of rejection for so long now. I always
thought that it would be fun to tell agents to fuck off." He sighed
again. "It's not fun at all."

"Well, maybe it's because it's Rose. You kind of have some
history with her, you know?"

"A history? I don't have a history with your friend. That's
not it. I've had to say no to a whole bunch of agents. They've all
been hard."

"Well, now you're kicking them to the curb in flocks." *What
did he say about "no history with Rose"?*

"Listen, Athena, forget everything we thought we knew
about publishing fiction back in grad school. I told you. Everything's changed. Traditional publishing is crumbling. Especially for
unknown novelists. The agents know it," Burke said. "They can't
sell a novel if you are an unknown. Since that stupid James Salter
piece was published in the New Yorker I've had phone calls from
every single agent I got rejected by. Those mother fuckers are a

bunch of sheep, and they'll go right the fuck off a cliff behind one bastard who suddenly thinks he's found the next T.C. Boyle and has the balls to risk his reputation to say so."

"Hey, speaking of T.C. Boyle...hey, hey, hey." Burke must have been grimacing. I certainly was. "Have you had time to read any part of *Wooden Nickels* yet?" I didn't like his response one bit, which was total, un-ambivalent silence followed by an exhalation that could have blown a hundred birthday candles out. "That bad, Burke?"

"There's nothing wrong with the writing. I love the writing. I do. I love your writing, Athena."

"Tell me straight, Burke. What *don't* you love?"

"Well... the story."

"Huh?"

"And the voice. Your narrator is pretty much a whiny bitch."

"Hey, can't you just say what you really think?" My voice betrayed the panic I felt and hot tears were already spilling onto my cheeks. I was really glad we were on the phone so he couldn't see them.

"Athena, I don't know whose story this is, but it isn't yours and it shows. If I know anything at all about writing, you've got to write your own story."

"I don't want to write a fucking memoir, Burke." There was too much venom in my voice.

"I'm not talking about a memoir, Athena. I'm talking about *story*. You've got to tell your story from inside of it and you didn't do that. You wrote this story from outside of it." I was quiet. He waited for me. Too much time went by, but maybe it was only a minute. *Holy shit! He's absolutely right.*

"Should I scrap it?" I whispered at last. The thought of abandoning six years and twelve hundred pages of blood sweat and tears was at once excruciating and...oddly... weirdly... liberating.

"I would," Burke said as kindly as he possibly could. "Unless you can figure out a way to go back in and tell the story from inside."

"No," I said feeling heartsick, weak, and just a little exhilarated. "It isn't really my story to tell." I blew my nose. "You're going to have to call Rose," I told him. I didn't say goodbye. I tore the bedspread off the bed, found the mini-bar, flipped open my laptop, and signed into the hotel's WiFi. I Googled Naxxos International. My new Plan B.

Rule #31: When stuck at a certain point in the story, make a list of what would NOT happen next. A lot of the time it's the stuff that you think won't be possible that can get you unstuck.

Without needing a wake-up call I got up before the sun to go back to Berkeley. My mother's car was already gone. I drove twice around the hotel parking lot in the dark to be sure.

Halfway home I got a text message from Burke. "Call me asap. Please." *Oh, sure, why not, Burke? So we can talk a bunch more about how much my book sucked? I'll do that right away.* I knew that I should be grateful for Burke's candor. And I knew that he was right about *Wooden Nickels*. I just wanted to dwell in the pool of his rejection and nurse my hurt feelings a little longer. I threw my phone in the back seat so I wouldn't be tempted to read any more messages while I drove, and naturally, as soon as I did that, I got about a dozen more. My phone sounded like a pin ball machine but it was out of reach.

The *Tribune* building is in downtown Oakland and I had to drive practically right past it to get to my place in Berkeley so I decided to stop in and submit my official resignation letter. I swung into the parking lot and checked my texts. All of them were from Burke exhorting me to return his calls. I didn't.

Ronald from Security was manning the front door. He opened it for me. The place already seemed like foreign territory.

"Hey, Ronald, how's it goin'?"

"It's goin'," he said. Then, "Hey, I heard a rumor that we're not going to have Athena Cervantes to kick around too much longer. Any truth to it?"

"Geez. Howie must be psychic. Was he passing out champagne?"

Ronald chuckled.

"Naw, just the opposite. I heard they're worried you're going to the competition."

"Really? You heard somebody use the word 'worried'?"

"Yeah. Actually, they used the word 'panic'."

"Oh, c'mon...?" Ronald made a little cross on his heart with his chubby hand.

"This is a direct quote. I heard it myself. 'Don't panic. She hasn't submitted a resignation letter. YET.'"

"Isn't that interesting?"

"But, is it true?" he asked. "You get a job at the *Chron*?"

"No. I'm not going to the competition. I'm going to Toronto." Ronald's light bulb went off instantly.

"Ooo--oooh," he nodded. "That dude...the America's Most Eligible Geek guy..." Ronald is way too smart to be manning the doors of the *Tribune* building.

Rule #32: You have to come up with the end of your novel before you figure out the middle. Really. It's the ending of a story that comes hardest. Get your ending working for you up front.

Because it was a Saturday, only two reporters were up in the pressroom, one to man the AP wire and another who had no life. They both just looked up and nodded when they saw me. Only when I sat down and fired up my desktop did I get an inkling of what I'd be missing about my job. It wasn't much. My very first order of business was the back up file of my novel, which I had recently learned to keep on my work computer "just in case of an accident". I opened the *"Wooden Nickels"* file and watched the cursor blink on the title page for a good minute and a half. Then, without a shred of remorse, I hit "select all" and "delete" and then hit it again. I looked up at my two coworkers, a little in shock that they didn't seem to notice that I'd just deleted six years of my life with two keystrokes. Neither one even glanced over. Apparently they hadn't felt the shudder in the universal force field. But let's get real. That was just my back up. Still, it was a good symbolic start, I thought. I opened a new doc and typed up a resignation letter effective immediately. I gave no reason. After I put the letter into inter-office mail I systematically opened all my desk drawers and threw away the contents. I got another text. Burke again. "Important tht u call me!!! Asap!!!! Urgent!!!!"

"What do you want, Burke?" I tried to sound bored but I really, in that moment, had no enmity towards him. My purest feeling toward Burke just then was one part envy and one part admiration and a tiny inkling of gratitude. He paid no mind anyway.

"Athena!" he said. "Jesus!"

I tilted my desk chair back and put my feet up. "You are taking the name of the Lord in vain, my friend."

"Cut the crap, Athena. I have news. Huge, hopefully happy news for you."

"Yeah?"

"I was feeling really bad about our conversation last night. About what I said about your book..."

"Forget it. You were a hundred percent correct-a-mundo. The book sucks and I appreciate the candor. So thanks. You did me a huge favor. I'm in your debt."

"Not quite yet. But you might be. I called Rhoda. I told her about you and about your profiles for the *Trib.* She asked me to send her a compilation, which I did at six this morning. I took the liberty of putting a bunch together off the internet and I titled it 'The First Latina Rodeo Queen of Fremont, California'. I was up all night long doing it."

I was completely nonplussed. Burke continued. "Are you sitting down? She wants to publish this stuff as an anthology. A collection of these profiles you do. She wants to publish you. Your work at the *Trib.*" I couldn't speak. "Athena? Athena? Are you there? What do you say?"

"Holy shit!" I whispered.

"Okay!" Burke said. "She'll call you tomorrow, then. The *Trib* owns those stories and they will have to be in on the negotiations to buy them, but she says it won't be a big problem. I told her you have a work-in-progress called *The Princess of Fire Island*, too. She said that Orloff gave her a copy of that story a million years ago and she *still* fucking remembered it." I couldn't speak. "Did you hear me? She remembered it. She said the anthology will drive the sales of '*Princess*'. She knows her shit about publishing, Athena."

"Holy shit!" I said again.

"Okay," Burke laughed again. "She knows her holy shit too. By the way, I turned down seven figures to go with Rhoda. She's the real deal, Athena." This was the Burke I used to know and love! "You can tell Rose now. And, Athena? You and me? We're not in Davis anymore, Toto!"

"Holy shit," I repeated like a Tourette's patient. I heard Burke chuckling before he hung up.

My very first instinct was to call home. I wanted to tell my mom. But, I remembered that she wasn't ever talking to me again. I just looked down and stared at the contents of my trash can and watched teardrops fall onto the Double Bubble.

Rule #14: It is far better to show your work to a teacher, if you must, than to a friend, colleague, or (horrors!) a relative. You will not believe what a friend or colleague says, no matter praise or criticism, and then you will spend needless time ruminating upon their opinion. You will look for hidden meanings in the doubt expressed by relatives, and they in turn will look for inferences about you, or worse, themselves, that will make you both crazy. The only legitimate eyes are strange eyes and even they can be corrupt. Reveal with caution.

Rhoda's advice was all business.

"You can write. There's no doubt about that. I'm in agreement with Thadeus about your longer work though."

"Yes," I told her. "I agree one hundred percent. I'm so sorry he even gave that to you. I deleted the manuscript yesterday as a matter of fact."

"You did *what?!* Are you completely out of your mind? Never, ever, ever and I mean never, delete anything again."

"But..."

"Look, you're going to have a long and lustrous career, my dear. I'm going to see to that. You are going to buy me a beach house out on Montauk. So, listen: I want you to save everything you write from now on. Every word. Save your grocery lists. You'll have some fallow periods and in between the gems, we'll push the crap. Nobody is hot always and forever. We'll need some fillers. You can publish some dogs, but you cannot NOT publish, *capisce*, chickie? Please tell me you have a back up."

"You," I said. "You're my back up. You have the whole file."

"Oh, for fuck's sake," my new publisher said. "You're absolutely right. I keep forgetting. Just between you and me, Athena, I hate technology. But, remember, always, always have a back up."

Thanks to Security Ronald I had back up.

Rule #34: Let's talk "twists and turns" that keep your reader guessing. What is your hero good at? What are they comfortable with? Throw the polar opposite at them. Now, how do they deal with that?

Monday morning at the *Tribune* office was a real eye opener. Ronald gave me a head's up on my way in.

"They think you're going over to the *Chron*," he whispered when I handed him a blackberry Danish from Nabalom's.

"Where'd they get that idea?" Ronald just shrugged and chewed.

The pressroom grew quiet when I walked in. Or as quiet as any pressroom ever gets.

"Nice goin', Lois Lane." Our music critic gave me a high five as I passed his desk. I gave him a quizzical look. My waste basket had not been emptied from Saturday's purge of my desk drawers. The top of the desk was a wasteland save for a single business-sized envelope. I stared at the return address. People started to gather. The old-timer who had been nominated for Pulitzers several times sat down on the corner of my desk and pointed down.

"Go ahead. It's kind of a thrill the first time." He grinned. "Maybe *every* time."

Dear Ms. Cervantes:

The jury members of the Columbia School of Journalism are pleased to announce its nomination of your entry, *The First Latina Rodeo Queen of Fremont California* to the Pulitzer Prize Committee in the category for a distinguished example of feature writing, giving prime consideration for quality of writing, originality and concision.

Deliberations are scheduled for April 10th-13th at Columbia University in New York City and the winners will be notified by electronic mail and U.S. Post following selection.

The committee would like to extend its sincere congratulations for this nomination and best wishes for your entry in this important category. Good luck.

Sincerely,

Neil Hickman, Committee Chair, Features; News

"Is this for real?" The letter was shaking in my trembling hand.

"Baby," the old timer said. "This is as real as it gets." He bent toward my ear. "Tell Ronald to keep an eye on your car." Then he stood up and bent over to filch a tear-stained, unwrapped package of Double Bubble from my trashcan. "Do you mind?" he asked. He pocketed the gum and strolled away before I could say anything else. The others offered congratulations on the nomination and semi-sincere wishes of good luck for winning, but like I said before, it's dog eat dog among writers. Howie was notably missing from the group but he sent me an email a couple hours later.

To: acervantes@OaklandTribune.com
From: HRF@OaklandTribune.com
a-
nice work. We need to discuss a few things asap.
HRF

I avoided him until lunch and then I ducked out and went to my car to get some space. In the parking lot I read and re-read the letter from the Pulitzer committee a dozen times. *Who can I call?*

I pulled up Burke's number but I didn't call. Instead I added it to my favorites. I thought about calling Rhoda to tell somebody, anybody, about the Pulitzer nom, but I was afraid she would think I was weird. I certainly did not want to make the impression that I was going to be one of those needy, insecure, embarrassingly self-promoting clients before I even was one.

And. And, the one I really wanted to call, I realized, was my mother. I tapped her name. Her number went to voice mail without ringing. The same thing happened when I called my dad's number and then Miggs's too.

"Lovely," I whispered out loud to myself. "Just grand." The loneliness was unbearable. It was the kind of loneliness you only experience in your car, behind the wheel after making some scary, possibly stupid, definitely life-altering decisions.

I was literally hiding out from my fat, nasty boss in a parking lot while my family were all off somewhere *together,* like "*Together*" was some mythical geographic destination. In my head, it was. It was just down the road from Unavailable. And I could feel in my bones that they were all there together having a gay old time not caring at all about my Pulitzer nomination, or my anthology, or Rhoda Weiner, or my fabulous new job offer from Nikko Dimitriou, or anything else about me. I tried, in succession, each of their cell numbers again. Nope. They were all still in Unavailable. Not taking my calls.

A quick rummage in my center console turned up nothing reasonable with which I could blow my nose, but in horror I found the small, white box containing Helena Dimitriou's borrowed emerald earrings. Borrowed and *NOT RETURNED!*

"Oh, shit!"

A quick rap on my passenger side window interrupted my pity party. Howie's red face was peering in through the glass. *Super!* I unlocked the passenger side door. The car rocked like a canoe when he got in. He spent a full minute trying to arrange his fat self in some semblance of comfort and wheezing like an asthma patient.

"Geez, these suckers are small. How do you stand it? Why don't you get something new? Bigger, for crissakes?" His big, fat head met the rooftop and he did indeed look massively uncomfortable. For an instant, while he thrashed around like an oversized teenager, I could see the awkward high school linebacker he had been back in the day.

"My parents gave me this car when I graduated from high school. We go way back. History. I can't bring myself to part with it." I didn't bother to point out that on the measly salary I was paid by the *Tribune,* I could barely survive. A monthly car payment was out of the question. Neither did I say that with my new job I would definitely be upgrading my transportation.

"Yeah, well, ya' wanna go get a Starbucks? I'm buyin'. Fancy." The Starbucks in Jack London Square was considered a *Tribune* satellite office by most staff.

"Fancy? Are we celebrating?" I tucked the box with Helena's earrings into my purse and started the car.

Howard gave up on the impossibility of attaching his seat belt and pointed toward the street. "Just don't kill me in this rattle trap."

I ordered a decaf, nonfat, no whip mocha – venti, and we found a corner with a big, overstuffed chair for my editor and a lean, mean wooden one for me.

"What will it take?" Howie barked. I looked over my coffee cup rim and blinked.

"Beg pardon," I responded. "Take?"

"Don't give me that shit, Cervantes. You know. How much are they offering?"

"Offering? They? Who?" I asked. I was completely in the dark. Howie's demeanor was that of a nervous hostage negotiator and a bad one. He was sweating bullets in spite of the grande frappucino he clutched with two hands between his knees. He stared a hole in my face. I set my coffee down on the table and threw up my hands.

"No shit, Howard. I got nothin' here. I don't know what you're asking me."

He ran his hand over his balding brow.

"Fuck, you're really gonna do this, aren't you, Cervantes? You're gonna break my goddamned balls." I sat back.

"Howard," I said without mirth. "I promise you. I have absolutely no interest in your balls. Breaking them or otherwise. Trust me. None." He set the frap down and punched his palm.

"Whatever it is...fifty percent more. Not another penny, so don't even try with me."

"Uh huh," I said. "I wouldn't dream of it." I looked around. *Beam me up, Scottie!*

"So...?"

"So...? What?"

"So, what was the *Chron's* offer?"

"Huh?" I suddenly recalled Ronald's comment about my impending defection over to the *San Francisco Chronicle.* Howard had already moved on.

"Those bastards over there are snakes in the grass. Every time one of our people gets a nom, they swoop in like carrion birds." Howard made his hand into a swooping bird. I cringed when the fly-by came perilously close to landing on his crotch. My cell phone rang in my purse. I peeked in. It was a blocked number. I took my phone out.

"Yeah, Cervantes," I answered giving Howie the "one minute" signal. He didn't even pretend that he wasn't leaning toward my phone.

"Athena?" It was Helena Dimitriou. She sounded funny. Not funny 'haha'.

"Mrs. Dimitriou? Yaya. What's wrong?" She only breathed a huge, alarming sigh into the phone. The kind people do in the movies when they're going to lower the boom.

"Dear, I imagine you're working today, but I have… something of an emergency here." She paused. "I need your help."

"An emergency?" I asked. "You're not calling about your earrings?"

"My earrings?" she asked. "Oh, heavens no! No, this is…well, can you come?"

"I'll be right there!" I told her. "I'm on my way! Howard, I…"

"Go," he said. "I heard." He waggled a meaty forefinger in my face. "Family first at the *Trib*, Cervantes. You KNOW that's true! Not like those cold bastards at the *Chron*! Take the rest of the day for your family emergency and we'll nail down that salary increase tomorrow."

"Howard…" I started. He held up a hand and took his cell phone out to call somebody from the newsroom to pick him up.

"Go! I'll get Lupe to pick me up," he said loudly. He didn't have to say it again. "The Tribune is all about family, Cervantes!" he yelled at my back.

Rule #3: Is your novel an epic? If so, you are obliged to characterize your protagonist and his group (usually his nationality) as different from other groups in particular ways. You must flesh out a realistic "group identity".

Maybe you saw this one coming. I didn't see it coming.

But I'll tell you that about a billion different scenarios ran through my head on that crossing over the Golden Gate Bridge.

One I couldn't imagine, and didn't, was my mother's Mini parked in the Dimitriou's driveway. I knocked frantically on their front door.

Helena answered looking as if she'd just gotten out of bed. She was wearing a pretty silk caftan and matching teal slippers and her hair had been pulled back and clipped into a simple pony-tail. She hadn't even bothered to apply lipstick. I practically fell into her arms.

"Is that my mother's car?" I asked pointing stupidly as she closed the doors. We both skipped any niceties.

"Yes. Your mother is here. Come, Athena," Helena pulled me through the house by the hand. The only useful word to describe the air around this elegant woman just then is "grim". It is a perfect word.

Indeed, my mother was outside in their courtyard, sitting at the little, painted, wooden table, pale face raised to the sun. She did not, however, look as if she were happily sunning herself at a side-walk café in Greece. She looked crumpled and desperate and some-how just a shell of herself. I felt a strange mixture of pity and anger and then suddenly...terror. She sensed my presence and looked up through the French doors and then rose slowly to her feet as if her executioner had arrived. That would be my role. It took her forever to shuffle in her bare feet the short distance to the house.

"Mother, what have you done?" My voice was a frantic tone I had never heard myself use before. She didn't answer. "Mom?" Like Helena, my mother was also wearing some kind of dressing gown. A garment the likes of which I had never seen her wear. Something she had borrowed from Yaya. Her slipper-less feet looked bluish and veiny and there was no trace at all of any make up on her weary face. Her hair, which always fell softly to her shoulders, looked as if it hadn't been washed or brushed in days. She had aged ten years since our dinner in Morro Bay. When her eyes met mine I almost moved toward her, but I checked the impulse and stepped aside to allow her to enter the room. The perfect word for the air around my mother is "tragic". She looked absolutely tragic.

"Sit down, Dear." Helena guided me to the sofa and she sat down beside me holding on to my hand. "Diana, I think you had better begin. I think this may take some time. Should I leave you two alone?"

"No!" We both barked the word so loud that a dog in the canyon somewhere down the hill started to howl. Helena got up and closed the French doors before she sat beside me again.

"Fine. I'll stay. As long as you need me."

My mother relaxed one iota. She closed her eyes and whispered, "Thank you, Helena. Thank you."

Helena nodded and squeezed my hand.

"Your mother has a lot to tell you."

Rule #36: Your readers will admire your hero or heroine more for trying than they will for actual success. Write about the struggle, not the accomplishment.

And then Diana Ward-Byrne-McGuire-Cervantes started to spill the beans. It was a monumental, toxic spill.

She started with this:

"First, I want to tell you, Tea, how much I love you, and that I would never really stop talking to you. No matter what." I snorted derisively and Yaya gave my hand a quick, gentle pat. I don't know if my mother caught that but she continued without commenting.

"I am so, so sorry about what I said to you on Friday. I'm so sorry that I threatened that. I've been sick ever since. And ashamed." She took a huge intake of air and coughed and brushed away a few tears. "Let me go back to the beginning. I want to tell you everything. I don't want there to be any more secrets." She waited for me to nod. "I'm going to start at the beginning." Her eyes were the color of a crater lake. A melted glacier. "First...my parents...your grandparents..." She blinked several times. "...they aren't dead."

"What?" I asked. "What do you mean?"

She shook her head.

"Well, I don't know for sure. I haven't heard anything from them or about them in a very long time." She looked at me directly. She spoke very deliberately. "They could be dead. I don't know. We haven't had any contact since I was quite young." *You could find out. You could Google them for crying out loud.*

"Your grandparents told me, when I was eighteen-years old, that as far as I was concerned, they were dead. To me." Her posture straightened and her eyes welled with tears. She studied her hands in her lap. "They said they never wanted to see me again or talk to me again. It...um. It's a terrible thing to do your child and I swore that I would never say or do that to mine..." She looked up, shaking her head. "And, yet..." Her gesture was neither an excuse nor an apology. She seemed to be truly in awe of the ironic circumstances we had found ourselves in somehow.

"But why?" I asked. "Why did they do that?" She looked at Helena who nodded.

"They were opposed to my choices...to some of my choices."

"Well, well..." I whispered meanly. Helena squeezed my hand softly again. Mom pretended not to hear and re-launched into a breathless soliloquy that made her chin tremble.

"I was arrested at a demonstration at UCLA when I was a sophomore. My brother had just been killed in Viet Nam. He was a Navy pilot. I think my parents thought, well they felt...that my anti-war activity dishonored my brother. It hurt them." She was staring again at her hands in her lap. Down in the canyon, the neighbor's dog was still at it, though we could barely hear him through the closed doors.

"I felt that it dishonored him...Michael...my brother's name was Michael...I felt it was a dishonor to him to support the war." It was a whisper. "Mike. We all missed him, but..." The dog stopped barking as if on cue and not one of us even breathed. "We had very different ways of missing him, my parents and I."

"So," she shook her head as if she were shaking off that period of her history. "I got some loans. I stayed in school. I met a boy. A man..." She smiled a faint smile. "I need a tissue," she told us and she got up and left the room. Helena looked at me and stroked my hair.

"Beautiful girl," she said very softly, and we returned to waiting in silence.

"I'm sorry," my mother said when she returned. She put a box of tissues on the table next to her chair. She had washed her face. Or maybe just thrown some cold water on it. Then she talked again. Her recitation was in a strange, staccato monotone, as if she were reading a script. One she had been practicing.

"It was near the end of the war. The lottery had been put into place and my boyfriend had a very low lottery number. Which meant that he would be one of the very first to be drafted." Her voice was weaker. "No one was coming home from Viet Nam without great injury by then. Either injured or in a body bag." There was still a trace of bitterness in her soliloquy. "We left the country immediately after the numbers were drawn. We went to Canada. I drove the car. I smuggled him across the border. In the trunk. It was very dangerous." She leaned forward and looked at me sternly. "Do you understand what I'm telling you, Tea? I believed that in order to save his life, I had to quit school and make sure he got out of the country. I gave up everything that I had left. I felt it was a tremendous sacrifice. I was committed in my opposition to that war. We both were. We were absolutely committed. I know it must be hard for your generation to imagine how it was back then. This war...the war that we are in now, in Iraq, it hardly seems like war at all." I nodded but she might as well have been speaking in tongues for all the relevance I felt that this information had to the matters immediately at hand. It was like hearing an unbelievable history lesson. An odd, fragmentary picture of old Jerald Franklin terHorst flitted through my head.

"At first we stayed with friends of friends up there. There had been a few sweeps in our neighborhood. The Canadian author- ities were cracking down on American draft evaders. The FBI was everywhere. They were searching for deserters. We were moving constantly. I wanted to stay but it was decided...my...we...we decid- ed that I had to go back to the states. I got a ride with an American minister and his wife who had been helping the anti-war commu- nity in Canada. They drove me all the way to LA and then they turned right around and went back to Oregon. They were very kind. They were nice people. Anyway, I know it's hard for you to understand how slow communication was then. You kids have had cell phones practically your whole lives. We had only letters then. Long distance phone calls were very expensive. Out of the question for poor students, and anyway we were always afraid that the phone lines could be tapped. We were afraid that our mail could be intercepted by the FBI. I know this must sound melodramatic to you now, but it's important for you to know what was at stake. We both could have been sent to prison."

I looked at Helena to see if she were as lost as I was but she was only looking at my mother with compassion. My mother was returning her gaze with a look that was completely indecipherable.

"I got a letter more than a year later from him. It was a risk for him to even write a letter. He had somehow obtained a falsified Canadian passport by then and he had gone to Europe with another American. He was somewhere in Greece. He couldn't give me an address. I had no way to write back. But I waited. I did wait." A flash of some emotion, maybe anger, crossed her face. She swallowed and then, as if she had reminded herself, she said, "I'm very thirsty. Can I get some water?"

Helena said, "I'll be right back." She disappeared and the room became a no-talk zone. My mother bit her nails, something I'd never seen her do before. Helena returned shortly followed by the housekeeper carrying a tray with three big tumblers of cold water and wheels of lemon. My mother let the housekeeper leave the room before she cleared her throat and resumed her story.

"I was a senior in college when I got a letter with a return address. An address that I could write back to. So I did. I wrote for more than two years. Jimmy Carter was elected president in nineteen seventy-six and on the day of his inauguration he signed the amnesty declaration that finally gave all American draft dodgers living abroad the freedom to return home without criminal charges. I had been thinking that whole time that if that ever happened, that it would change everything. I was certain that Peter would come home. I thought all of them – all the ex-pats – would come home.

By then I had already met Boo and I had already written *Webster's Peace*. It was a catharsis but I should never have written it. It was Peter's story not mine. I had no idea that Billy would steal it when I wrote it. I wasn't involved with Billy romantically then. He was just a classmate and I knew that Boo kind of had a thing for him. I didn't know that Billy had an agent and was trying to sell my script as his own. Had I known, I would have tried to stop him." My mother looked at Helena. "I would have, Helena."

"I know that, Dear." Nikko's yaya nodded.

My mother cried for a moment and then she was staring outside through the French doors into the beautiful, little Greek garden. "I don't know why I wrote what I wrote...it wasn't my story to tell. I stole the story from Peter and then Billy stole it from me." She repeated it again.

"Mom," I said. "I know that Billy ripped you off. I've known that for a long time. Boo told me. But you're saying now that *Webster's Peace* was a true story? About the guy you went to Canada with?" She nodded.

"Yes," she confirmed. "It was his story. Yes. It's true for the most part. Anyway, after President Carter gave the ex-pats amnesty, I went that following summer to Greece and I fully expected, I really believed, that when I returned, I would not be coming back alone. I thought I would bring Peter back, but I was wrong. He refused to return. I came home alone." She laughed an odd little laugh. "Well, no, that's not true. When I came back from Europe I was pregnant. With you, Tea. I came back with you. Inside me." Her hands went to her abdomen the way a woman's hands will do when she remembers being pregnant. For a moment I thought I missed something. Something didn't add up. Helena was gripping my hand tightly and tears were streaming down her cheeks too.

"Wait, say that again, Mom. You got pregnant in Europe?" Her face was ashen. She sucked in her bottom lip and nodded once. I felt sucker-punched.

"Oh, my god!"

"Let me finish, Tea. There's a lot more to tell you."

"More? What more? Are you telling me that Billy's not my father?" She shook her head.

"Wait, I'm confused. Billy is my father?"

"No. Billy is not your father." I sat staring at her for many minutes, blinking like a stunned gecko.

While I watched my mother raise the crystal goblet to her lips and drink her entire glass of water, ancient suspicions and unexplained intuitions clicked into a coherent reality in the back of my mind like tumblers turning in a lock. When I finally found my voice again there was a note of hysteria in it. "Does Billy know this? Has he known this all along? When did Billy know?" *That would explain an awful lot!* She shook her head again and set the empty glass down.

"Billy does not know."

"Jesus Christ, Mother!" All three of us were silent for a long minute, pondering (I'm just guessing here on their part) what the implications of my mother's confession would have on Billy Byrne-McGuire.

"Let me finish, Tea. I have to tell you everything. Then I'll answer your questions." I snuck another quick peek at Helena but she was stoic. She didn't look at me but she reached around my shoulders and pulled me into the crook of her arm. I didn't resist and let myself be held.

"So... I had been gone for two months. All summer. In my absence Boo and Billy had..." She didn't need to finish the sentence. "But it was over. Whatever they had had, it burned out really fast. I didn't realize that she was still in love with him until much later. I guess I didn't want to realize that. Anyway..."

Most of the rest of the story I had learned from Boo the night of Rosie's eighteenth birthday party, except the Billy/Boo part. That part she had seen fit to withhold. She had begun her version with Billy's reputation as a terrible womanizer. Both versions agreed that he came on strong when Mom got back from Europe. When he sold her script without her name on it he came up with the brilliant idea that they should get married. It was a way that he could have everything. The girl. The success. The money. So they went to Vegas. Obviously, he got me, unwittingly, in that bargain too.

"Poor Billy," I said. "You've got to tell him, Mom." I thought for a minute about all the times Billy Byrne-McGuire had come up short as a father. I thought about all the Byrne cousins and the McGuire cousins and the rest of Billy's huge Irish extended family in New York and how I'd never felt a part of the clan and always blamed my estrangement on my parents' early divorce.

"No wonder!" I said out loud. Then, "So, wait, my real father doesn't know he has a daughter, does he? Do you know where he is? Do you know how he would react?"

"Tea," she said. "I know this is really hard for you. It's unbearable for me. I've got to tell you everything though. Please. Let me finish first?" I tucked myself back into Helena's embrace and told her to go ahead. I think I was in shock just then.

"Well, you know a bit about our divorce. The circumstances and everything. But, you don't know some other things that you should know." My mother exchanged a look with Helena.

"I don't know how much you remember about the years after I left Billy. It was pretty hard. It was just you and me and by then, the movie had been made and I'd gone back to school to get my PhD so we lived pretty close to the bone. You and I. *Webster's Peace* won the Oscar and after that Billy gave us the means to survive, but not by much. I don't think he wanted to give me anything but he was always afraid that I would tell everyone that he hadn't written *Webster's Peace*. It would have been really easy to prove, so he..."

"That's extortion in some states, Mom." I showed no mercy.

"Yeah," she said. "Yeah, it is."

"But why didn't you ever tell?"

"You mean reveal that Billy hadn't really written that script? It was a devil's bargain, Tea. What I did was wrong on so many levels. I don't know...I guess eventually I felt I owed him that much. I don't know."

"You let him have *Webster's* and you made him think that your illegitimate kid...your bastard...was his kid. Alright, what's the rest?" I felt disgust then, and I didn't even try to keep that from showing.

"So, I was interning at UCLA after I defended my dissertation, and that's how I met your dad." My eyes narrowed at the word. "Mike," she clarified. "I fell for him, but at first the *abuelos* were dead set against him marrying a woman who had a child from a previous marriage. They were Catholic so they didn't believe in divorce. They weren't keen on the idea of Mike getting saddled with somebody else's kid."

"They actually said that?"

"At first. Before they'd met us. They didn't like the idea. It wasn't us they didn't like. But after he told me that..."

I interrupted. My anger abruptly shifted to Mike. "Wait. He told you that they said that? Why the hell would he tell you that?" She just shrugged.

"Don't know. People do stupid things."

"Obviously," I said. "Go on."

"Well, Mike had some issues with them maybe. You know he was their only child. A Mexican family. The Catholic thing. We loved each other, but he was going back and forth. I hadn't let him get too close to you. I was afraid you'd get hurt if ... "

"Thanks, so much," I said sarcastically. She winced.

"So while I was finishing up my internship, I was offered a post doc at Harvard. I was going to take it but Mike got upset. He wanted me to stay in LA. He didn't want to get married, but he didn't want me to go to Boston either. I was hurt by that. So we fought about it and then...do you remember the summer that Billy took you back to New York and took you to Fire Island?" *Do I remember? I am THE PRINCESS of Fire Island for god's sake!*

"Yes, of course. It was the highlight of my life."

"Well, I let him take you. You were tiny. Only five. You kind of wanted to go, but I knew it would be too much for you. But I let you go with him because I decided to go back to Europe while you were with Billy in New York. I wanted Mike to miss me. To miss us."

"You did what?" I sat up straight. "Are you kidding me? Did you see him? The same guy? My... my... my... *father*?" Those words were unbelievably hard to say.

"I know," she said. "I had to find out if there was anything still there. I guess I went for closure. Before I put any pressure on Mike. Before I made a decision to give up Harvard. Or. Before I made a commitment to Mike."

"Oh, closure. Well, la dee dah. Did you get it?" Her features froze. She stood up.

"I got...what I got...I got your brother." A full half minute of nausea passed before I stood upright squaring off. I almost wanted to slap her. Slap her silly. In that instant I was so appalled on my brother's behalf I could not think straight. I was a hundred percent rage. I felt that weird combination of extraordinary energy and utter weakness.

"You did what?" I believe that my voice was quite shrill. Helena tugged on my hand. I looked down and I collapsed next to her on the edge of the couch, my knees weak.

"Fuck." I said. "Mother, what have you done? What have you done to us? To all of us?" I couldn't even cry yet at that point. The shock of her confession was too great.

The room was quiet and it had grown dark outside. I think that my mother and Helena were both waiting for the obvious to dawn on me, but it took a while.

I was panting. Furious. Then finally the obvious did dawn.

"Christ, Mother! Oh my god, Mom...is Nikko's father..." I couldn't bring myself to say the words.

"Is Nikko my...our...oh, my dear god." I looked at Helena. I touched her hand.

"Yaya..." I said and very oddly, she smiled.

"I think I knew," she said. "I think I knew the moment I met you. When you and Miguel came for dinner. I think I knew then." She stroked my face.

"But...?" I turned to my mother. I thought about Miggs. "Oh, my God, Mom! Does Miggs know any of this?" She nodded one time.

"I drove back to LA after we had dinner on Friday in Morro Bay. I told them both, Mike and Miggs. I told them everything on Saturday. Then yesterday I came here to tell Nick and Helena."

"Papou!" I said. "Where is he?" Helena smiled.

"Resting. Papou is resting, my dear. Now we should rest also."

Helena dismissed my mother who left the room quickly like a guilty specter. Then she led me to a guest room on the other side of the house and at the door she grasped my hands.

"Does Nikko know this, Yaya? Does he know any of this?" She hugged me tenderly.

"He's coming tomorrow, my dear. He's bringing your father."

Rule #86: When boredom with the subject of your novel sets in (as it inevitably does from time to time when writing a lengthy novel), it is only a symptom and it can mean any number of things. Sometimes boredom comes when you are confused about how things take place in your book, so you can't see your way forward to the next step. In this case, remember that the action, whether slight or complex, is the organizational spine of the book. The plot is a piece of logic. Logic draws conclusions from premises. If you don't know your premises, you will draw illogical conclusions from them, get confused, and then get bored.

It took an hour of pacing before I could even think about lying down in the bed. I should have cried myself to sleep but I couldn't lie down. When I did, finally, I fell instantly asleep, or maybe unconscious, like a head injury victim who had been stunned by the blows of a blunt object.

Papou woke me up the next morning by knocking on my door. From my room's windows I could see that the sun wasn't yet visible behind Mt. Tamalpais but the whole eastern sky was streaked beautifully with orange and purple.

"Would you like to take a walk with me, Kookla?" he whispered behind the door.

"I'll get dressed," I whispered back. I did so as quickly as I could, back into my rumpled clothes from the day before. My limbs could barely pull my clothes on. It felt as if it had been weeks since I drove to Marin.

Papou smiled broadly when I kissed his cheek at the kitchen door. It felt natural to address him affectionately.

"Good morning, Papou."

"Yes," he said, and I knew exactly what his embrace meant. "We have lost much time. Let's not waste a minute more. Come." We walked first up the gently sloping driveway to the main road and up again. A hundred yards from the gate Papou looked up and waved into the security camera mounted on a telephone pole.

"They're going to have a very interesting day today," he said pointing toward the guesthouse garage and presumably whomever it was in the small tower manning the cameras. Then, with a professorial demeanor he looked at me directly for the first time. "You'll get used to the security, Athena. At times, you'll even be grateful for it. You won't like the intrusions into your privacy, though. The worst of those seem to be an American phenomenon. Nikko and Peter agree that things are not so bad in Canada or even in Greece for that matter. There, nobody cares very much that you are a Naxxos heir. You'll remember to tell me your thoughts when you get there, yes?" I nodded, but the notion of being one of the heirs of a multi-national conglomerate was not yet a reality, just more of the unbelievable events of the last twenty-four hours.

We walked at a surprisingly brisk pace, considering Nick Dimitriou's age and the incline of the hill. At the summit, he paused and led me down a short path to a slat bench set off the road in a small clearing. Sitting, we could look down on miles of the winding coastal road and the wide expanse of the Pacific Ocean. Behind us the sun was now perched on top of Mt. Tam like a glowing pom-pom on a giant clown's hat and I could feel how warm the day would become. In front of us, at the base of the mountain, the ocean was a flat, gunmetal color under what had become a vast, pale, blue sky.

"None of us will forget this day, my dear," Nick said, his voice full of emotion. He took my hand. "I'm glad we're starting it out to-gether." I knew I should say something profound, but nothing came to me, so I just squeezed Nick's hand in return. "I'm very angry at your mother. I won't try to pretend any different. But I do under-stand too." Big Nick's profile as he gazed out at the Pacific was striking. I looked for a similarity to my brother's handsome face. He sighed. "I have a lot of understanding for the things she's done." He shook his head. He sighed again.

"I think I see a little bit of my brother in your profile," I told him. Nick beamed for just a second and then a barely visible flicker of emotion pulled his glance back to the sea.

"He does look like a Dimitriou, doesn't he?" I squeezed his hand again. "Anyway, you...you are the image of your grandmother when she was your age." He squared his shoulders in a gesture that told me he had more to say. "We both saw the likeness, of course. The night you came here for dinner. We didn't speak of it though until after the Stanford affair. That was the night we pieced the puzzle together. So, you see, we were not entirely shocked when your mother showed up on Sunday afternoon. We hadn't said anything to Nikko except to agree that you should be offered a position with the company. We wanted to wait to let him know that we knew who you were until he was ready to tell us. We weren't sure that your mother would come forward on her own. When she did, of course we phoned them immediately in Toronto. And, of course, Nikko had known all along." *Of course! Nikko has known all along!* Papou shook his head and raised my hand up to kiss it in a gesture that tweaked my heart. He sighed deeply. "So...my son returns at last to the U.S.... after more than thirty years, Athena. It's been a long time. He's coming for you and for Miguel."

"Does Peter...does my father...look like you, Papou?" I asked. I don't really know why, but suddenly appearances and similarities seemed important. Crucial. He repeated that quirky sequence, a big sigh followed by a shake of his head, the squaring of his broad shoulders, and then a smile that looked somewhat sad spread across his face.

"Well, you'll see for yourself in..." He looked at his watch. "In less than an hour if they had a tail wind." Nick stood and held out a hand. "Let's get some good, Greek coffee, Kookla. Before everyone starts arriving."

Rule #87: Sometimes boredom is a mask for fear. As your first draft takes shape, it might not be turning out the way you thought it was going to. You don't think it's any "good". Well, of course it isn't. It's a first draft after all. But maybe you are afraid that it isn't telling the story you wanted it to tell. It begins to diverge from the story you intended. Now you are lost.

You don't know anymore what the results are going to be in terms of plot (what the hell is happening?), and you no longer know the fates of the characters as you originally intended (who the hell ARE you and what have you done with my main character?). What to do? Know this: A novel, especially a "first novel", is your baby and it's normal to have fear while you are expecting your baby. Also know that when your baby arrives, you will love it and you almost certainly will be proud of it. Keep writing through your boredom.

By the time we arrived back at the house, a new rental car had been added to the growing fleet in the driveway, and Miggs and Mike were already in the courtyard garden off the kitchen drinking coffee with Helena at the little, blue table and speaking in somber tones. My mother had apparently not yet shown her face. I stood for a moment watching my brother and my dad wondering what their reactions to my mother's confession had been. From the way they appeared in the garden together with Helena, it seemed that nothing was different. I allowed myself to speculate for a moment how this incredible news would change them and their relationship while Papou paused to pour us each a mug of thick black coffee. He said something to the housekeeper in Greek and bent to look into the oven at the source of the pungent smell of cinnamon. He reached from behind to hand me the heavy mug and whispered, "I'm right behind you, Kookla." I stepped through the French doors.

Mike rose to his feet just a second later than Miggs who, it is accurate to say, sprung from his chair like a jack-in-the-box.

"Sissy!" He grabbed me tight and whispered into my hair. "Do you believe this shit? Fuck me!" When Miggs released me after a long embrace, Mike stepped forward and put his arms around me.

"You okay, Honey?" He bent down, his face inches from mine. We studied each other. "Are you alright?" I smiled weakly. He looked grave.

"Are *you guys* okay?" My composure was clearly not the response either my brother or my dad had expected. They had been obviously making some speculations of their own about my reactions. They flanked me protectively as if I was a mental patient who had not recognized a critical piece of reality before they turned together to face Nick Dimitriou. Helena stepped forward and grabbed onto Nick's big forearm before she introduced him to Mike.

"Dr. Cervantes, this is my husband." She patted Nick's bicep. "Nicholas, this is..." she paused one second. "This is the children's father, Dr. Miguel Cervantes." Mike reached out a hand but Nick ignored it and pulled him into a bear hug instead. Miggs gave me a sidelong glance and raised his eyebrows while the two men held each other for a long moment. When they pulled apart they both had to wipe their eyes.

"I'm so glad you came, Miguel. For Diana's sake," Nicholas Dimitriou said sincerely, his hands still on Mike's shoulders. Then he turned slowly to Miggs. My brother went so easily into our grandfather's embrace, it seemed the most natural thing in the world.

"Hey, Papou!" Miggs said. "This is cool! I didn't expect to see you again so soon!" My mother coughed from the kitchen doorway. She had a wan smile on her face and she actually looked rested. No one moved toward her and she did not advance toward any one of us. The moment was, to say the least, awkward. Helena spoke first.

"Good morning, Diana. Did you sleep well, my dear?"

"I took an Ambien," she admitted with a shrug. "Two, actually." She looked at Mike. She was the picture of contrition. "I wasn't expecting you two to be here," she told him.

"We flew up yesterday and stayed in the city last night. We thought about it for a while and decided you might need some back-up today." My mom nodded and shrugged again.

"Thanks. I need something," she said flatly.

"Coffee. You need some coffee. And let's see what's baking for breakfast." Helena herded us all back inside the kitchen and made sure everyone ate at least a bite of a cinnamon roll. Miggs ate two and finished mine. No one said anything of any substance. We reorganized in the large family room to wait for Nikko and Peter to arrive. Miggs and I sat closely together in the middle of the over-stuffed sofa, looking, I am certain, just like two naughty kids who were waiting to face the music. As mad as I was at her, I was happy to see Mike pull my mom onto the love seat next to him. Helena sat in the queen's chair directly across from them and I noticed that she looked as nervous as anyone. Nick paced back and forth behind the sofa where Miggs and I were sitting. Helena broke the strained silence speaking directly to Mike.

"You know, Dr. Cervantes, Peter hasn't been back here in the states for more than thirty five years." *Is that why you're so nervous?*

Mike interrupted her explanation.

"Please, call me Mike, and I would like your permission to use Helena. May I?"

"Of course," she smiled. After a long quiet moment she resumed. "You must think us a very odd family, dependent as we are to see one another on the hospitality of the Canadians." Mike shook the suggestion of the family's oddity off. "Well, we are," she said. Her tone had become decidedly accusatory and Nick stopped pacing behind us. "And we are also a stubborn group and short-sighted among our other flaws. I hope by the end of today you don't see the worst of us." Behind me Nick made a gentle snort. Kind of like a "pfffft" sound. It dawned on me then why Mike had come. He hadn't wanted my mom to be alone in a room with so many people who could be very, very mad at her. And, maybe just a little bit, he also didn't want to be alone in LA while all the rest of us were together, whatever was going to happen, when Nikko brought Peter to meet Miggs and me. He didn't want to be an outsider. I felt a sudden rush of love for Mike.

"Dad," I think my voice was at first barely audible. "Thanks for coming. I have to tell you something before Nikko gets here with his dad." I stared down at my hands in my lap. They were shaking but I had to tell him the truth. "I've always been afraid – because Miggs was your biological child," I shot my mother a quick look. I choked up. "...well, because I thought that he was - that you couldn't love me as much as you love him. I know it's crazy, but, I think I've been angry at you about that."

"Oh, Honey!" Mike shook his head.

"What?!" Miggs elbowed me. "God, Sissy!!" I turned to him and let two fat tears roll to my chin and then fall into my lap.

"Baby brother, it wasn't just that you were...that I thought you were... Dad's *real* kid...and I was just adopted...that was part of it...but mostly it was because you were so golden. Everything you did was just perfect. Everybody instantly loves you. You're successful in everything you do. I always felt like such a loser next to my little brother. You're our golden boy. I felt... compared to you...how could Dad love me as much?" I was crying in earnest by then.

"Are you nuts?" Miggs shoved me again. "You're the golden one! Phi beta kappa...a double major, and then grad school. I'm the loser! I couldn't even hang at San Diego State!"

"Big deal," I said. "Who cares about degrees? You're a champion! You've got how many businesses? You own a house!"

"You are a writer! I can't even spell!"

"Hey!" Mike stopped us. "Hey, I think I heard a car door."

Nikko was the first through the door. He was carrying a couple of overnight bags and he set them down just inside. We all stood up in unison. We were the world's oddest standing reception committee.

What can I say? Imagine seeing your father, your biological father, for the very first time. Peter Dimitriou was looking around the room. He seemed overwhelmed. His eyes landed finally on my mom. Mike's arm was around her shoulders. Everyone was staring at Peter. He ran a hand through his hair and then he stepped toward Mike. He held out a hand.

"Dr. Cervantes...Miguel, I hope you'll forgive my intrusion. I had to come." I would have recognized his voice I think anywhere. My two fathers shook hands solemnly. Then Mike touched my mom's shoulder and pushed her toward Peter one inch. She hesitated but then she reached out and put her hand on her heart and bowed her head.

"Peter, I am so very sorry. I...I..."

"Shhh," he said. "We all have things to regret, Di. And I have a few confessions of my own. Some things you'll need to hear." Then he worked his way around the room hugging Helena and Big Nick first and then, at last, standing squarely in front of me and Miggs. He looked at us. Back and forth. He looked us over.

"Could I hold you?" he asked shyly and we both hugged him between us. He sobbed and we sobbed and then he drew back and looked from one of us to the other. "You are so beautiful. Both of you!" he wept. Of course we were crying too, and clichés be damned, there wasn't a dry eye in the house by then. Nikko disappeared and came back with a box of tissues and a chair from the dining room. He placed it closely next to Helena's and then beckoned his grandfather.

"Papou, sit. Please. You'll need a seat." When Nick sat down everyone else did too and only Peter was still standing. He ran his hand through his hair again in the exact same way that Miggs does and then he removed his jacket and folded it across the arm of the couch next to Nikko. Nikko gave Peter's jacket a tender pat and he grinned up.

"Go on, Dad," he said. "It's going to be okay."

"Where do I begin?" Peter asked no one in particular. He looked around the room and took a deep breath. "Diana knows this part. And Nikko does. But I'll start at the beginning for the rest of you." Peter Dimitriou paced the floor.

"I met Andreas Stavros right after Diana left Toronto. He was working for Uncle Alex in the port and we spent all day together scraping boat hulls in dry dock. Andreas was in love with a Quaker girl named Kathryn who had come with him to Canada just as Diana had come with me, and besides that, we had politics in common. Both of us were conscientious objectors to Viet Nam, and of course we were both Greek. We were like brothers from the beginning." Peter looked at Nikko. His eyes were glistening. "Andy was the best man I ever knew." Nikko smiled. "It was Andy's idea to sail a boat to Greece. We both had family there that we knew would take us in, and we knew if we made it that far we'd be able to sit out the war on the islands. It took us almost a year to put together enough money to buy her and get her sea-worthy. It was Andy who named our little boat '*Webster's Peace*'," He looked around the room. "... from the dictionary's first definition, 'an absence of war'." Peter's voice changed when he resumed his story. It was little more than a harsh whisper. "It was a miracle, a goddamn miracle, that we made it to Europe. Because we had to avoid the major shipping lanes and the military ships, it took us twice as long as we calculated. We were almost completely out of stores when we arrived in Piraeus and we had been blown off-course and almost capsized and drowned three - maybe four - times." He ran his hand through his hair again.

"But Andreas was a great sailor and we did make it." He looked at Nikko who nodded. "We still had to go on to Chios and by the time we reached port there, Kathryn, Nikko's mother, had sent word from Toronto that she was pregnant. Andy wanted to return immediately. I knew that if we tried to return there was a great chance we could be apprehended. And a greater chance that we would never make it. But if we did make it, we would have been sent back to America and probably jailed. Andreas and I quarreled badly. I believed that if I refused to go back he would have no choice but to stay in Greece. I was wrong. I misjudged him. He sailed *Webster's Peace* alone. Nothing was ever found of our boat. Or..." Peter's voice broke. Only Miggs repeated the obvious.

"Dude," he said, his voice full of wonder. "Just like the movie!" Peter nodded and took a big breath. He seemed to collect himself before pressing on.

"Yes," he said. His voice was thick. He stared down at the floor. "Just like the movie. And that is how Nikko..." Peter paused. "How your brother... discovered the truth that we are all just now discussing. He saw the film. He saw the film on an Air Canada flight to Athens. Ironically." Peter's smile was rueful and apologetic. "Nikko is a great researcher. He pieced the puzzle together very quickly after that. And then he found Athena." When Peter looked at me something shifted into place in my chest. I felt my heart leap into place as if it had always been a little off kilter.

"Peter!" My mother broke in. "I'm so very sorry. I never should have...I never intended...that script never should have been written, much less sold." Peter raised his eyes ever so slowly to meet hers. Tears spilled onto her cheeks. "It never should have been written..." she said, but Peter held up his hand and shook his head. He turned back to those of us sitting on the couch.

"No, Di, you wrote a great script. It was a great movie. I never minded. Please believe me. The film honors Andy's memory. I'm glad you wrote it." Peter looked kindly at my mother who took one deep breath and then nodded.

"Thank you for that, Peter," she whispered. Mike's arm pulled her close. Peter smiled.

"This is no excuse, but when your mother came to Greece the first time, I was still...what do you kids say? On a bummer? We had been writing to each other quite a while by then. I had at some point confided this story to her in my letters but, somehow, when she arrived in person..." Peter and my mother exchanged a look. "Well, I was not very nice to her. When she left Greece, I let her believe that I wasn't returning to the states out of principle. I told her..." He looked just then at Papou and Yaya and his face was full of grief and regret. "I told you all," he said, his voice resolute now, "I claimed that President Carter's amnesty only to the draft dodgers and not the deserters was the reason I would remain an ex-patriot."

Yaya sat forward on her chair. Her face was earnest. She knew he had to tell us everything then.

"And the real reason?"

"The real reason, Mama, was that I was ashamed. Because I felt like a coward." Peter's voice was anguished.

"That was an illegal war!" Papou shouted. "An unjust war! Fought for ill-gotten gains. Fought for U.S. Rubber's filthy investments, not for U.S. security!"

"I know, Dad," Peter said kindly. "I know. But I deserted my friend." He looked at Nikko. "I deserted your father," he said. Nikko nodded once. The room was quiet for no less than two whole minutes, which is a long time in a room like that. Finally Peter continued.

"I spent the next six years starting Naxxos. I worked all the time. I think it's fair to say, I had no life." He allowed himself a rueful smile. "And then, when Diana came back to Greece the second time I was just too dug in. I'd been telling myself my own lie for so long, hiding out from the truth for so many years..." He said to my mother directly, "It was the biggest mistake of my life, Di. I should have come back with you."

"I could have stayed in Greece," she said, but nobody believed that she believed that. "I should have told you about the kids," she said and, oh boy, that had a ring of some truth. She looked around the room. "I should have told you all..." The room was quiet again in another round of absolute silence and stillness until the reality of all that had been related and the meaning of it all finally dawned on Miggs. He jumped to his feet and spun around pointing two finger guns at Nikko and me.

"Fuck yeah," he yelled happily. "You're Andy's kid! You dudes aren't *really bros!* You could marry my sister if you want, Dude!"

I patted the couch next to me and Miggs sat down again slowly, joy plastered all over his silly face. It was my turn for a sudden happy realization and it hit me like a wave. The question of his own paternity, of who was his real, biological father had been of little consequence to my brother. The worst part of my mother's confession for Miggs was his concern on my behalf. The whole affair was most distressing to him because he thought that Nikko and I would be committing incest.

"You're so good, Bud," I told him. "You were worried about us, huh?"

"Well, yeah," he said. "All that other crap? What's the big deal? A couple of people told a few whoppers. No real harm done, right?" He gestured around the room in a grand sweeping motion. "And look! We get some cool new peeps in the fam. It's all good, right?" He leaned toward Nikko. "But, dude, you just can't marry your sister, you know?" Nikko leaned across me and ruffled Miggs's

214

hair. I loved them both so much in that instant I thought my heart would burst.

"Kathryn and Nikko visited me eventually in Greece and they stayed on." Peter addressed Nikko, "Nikko, you *are my son!*" Nikko grinned and gave him a thumbs-up. "So that's it." Peter said. "That's everything. I think everyone knows the truth about everything now."

"Not everything." The room's participants turned as one to Helena.

A big collective "Oh, shit!" wasn't spoken out loud. But we were all thinking it.

"Mama?" Peter said.

"Helena?" Nick croaked. "You do not have to say anything, my darling." The room was suddenly close and so still, not a mote of dust stirred. "I know everything," he said softly.

"Whoa!" Miggs blurted. I could feel his whole body go tense next to me.

"No. No, Nicholas. You don't know everything. What do you think you know?" Helena looked at Peter. Then back at Nick. Tears were making her eyes glisten and her lips were trembling.

"Panagiotis," Nick said, his voice a hoarse whisper. Helena's mouth fell open and I thought, *Whoa, Boy! What now?*

The bottom line is that history does repeat. But do we ever learn from history? Probably not so much. Nick looked pained when he addressed Peter as if the rest of us were not there, as if the rest of us were invisible.

"You should have been told the truth years ago. Decades ago, my son." Nick straightened his shoulders. "Panagiotis Mousalimas - your father – your *real* father was a Greek Commando. He died in the mountains of Macedonia in 1944 at the hands of traitors to Greece. He was a hero killed by Nazi cowards. He was my best friend. And he was a man of principle. A loyal Greek. Like your Andreas, he was the best man I ever knew. His death is the reason I have never returned to my homeland. When Panagiotis was betrayed, I made two vows. I would raise his son as my own, and I would never set foot again on the land that took his life. I have kept my vows to this day. Today however, I know this one thing: a vow that a man makes in anger and in grief should not condemn his entire life. Such a vow must be broken. It does nothing to honor the dead." Nick looked at Helena. "Such a vow dishonors the living."

"Papa?" Peter's face was a study in disbelief.

"All these years, Nicholas..." Helena was in shock. "...all these years you have known. You never told me..."

"What was there to tell, my dear? That I knew you loved my friend before you loved me? Why was that important? Did you think I was that bad at math? Peter was a premature infant who weighed almost nine pounds? I truly thought, my love, until today, that we had simply agreed silently not to discuss it." Helena smiled weakly at him.

"I have loved no one as I love you, Nicholas," she said. Papou smiled at her, the smile of a man who has loved a woman for a long time. The smile of a hero in a classical Greek drama.

Rule #88: For the novice writer of lengthy fiction, boredom can be a sign that their ability to execute their own work is far less sophisticated than their taste in the work of others, and this is a real drag. To discover that what you put on the page in your first draft is something you would disdain utterly if you were asked to review it is disconcerting in a way that can take the wind from beneath your writerly wings. If you insist on applying opprobrious terms to your faulty first efforts, you will feel sadness and shame. Your first draft will do the only thing it can do. It will die an early and ignoble death and it will be seen by no other eyes than your own very critical ones.

Okay, so that's the story. My story. It is, I grant you, convoluted and unbelievable. Shakespearean in its twists and turns, but now I know. This cliché about writing is absolutely the gods' truth.

Truth is stranger than any fiction could ever be.

Rule #98: It is tempting when approaching your denouement to try to tie things up with a rash list of exposition. This is the shortest route to annoying your reader. Put yourself in their shoes. They've invested a good bit of time and energy into these characters. Just because you've grown bored with them and the story has gone cold for you, you owe the reader more. More story.

What's left? Well, of course there was fallout. Major fallout from that day up in Marin.

First the Finemans. As you might well expect, Boo was not delighted that the jig was up after thirty plus long years. I for one would have loved to be a fly on the wall when, just days after he learned that he was not my biological father, Boo fessed up and told Billy Byrne-McGuire that Rosie was actually *his* child, not Eddie's. Because she couldn't really fire any of us, before she was kicked out of Chez Fineman, she dispatched Bobby C. and all of his relatives who were then still under her employ. Understandably, Eddie Fineman, upon learning the whole truth, moved Brenda out and the nanny in. He then re-hired everybody else back (everyone except Bobby C.) after Boo's purge. It isn't easy to find good help in LA.

Fineman Creative Artists is no more. The last I heard Brenda was in New York now working as Rose's assistant. Rose is trying to represent Billy's twelve-hundred page (a coincidence?) memoir to the "bigs". (Best of luck with that, Billy.) Billy took the news about the switcheroo in paternity quite well, Rose told me. *Why wouldn't he? His real kid is a New York agent who "loves his work".*

Ultimately Rose confessed that maybe she hadn't actually slept with Burke at Davis, maybe it had been some look-a-like. She didn't really know, but whatever. (*Your real father, Rosie, is Billy Byrne McGuire. Oh, the irony!*)

Joshie quit school (again), disappeared for a while, and through some guys that work for Miggs in the Hermosa Beach shop, we heard that he's soon to be one of the co-stars in a reality TV show called "Rehab" with a twelve-step guru who goes by the name, Billy the Kid. But I don't want to know. I really don't.

Miggs continues to split his time between LA and Maui. He's got a pretty serious "squeeze" who teaches Math at UCLA. In his spare time, with Naxxos backing, he's started a completely cool non-profit in both places, too. It's a unique surfing school for autistic kids. All the instructors are on the pro surfing circuit. Miggs says the idea came to him in a dream. "Dude, it was tough enough just to be ADHD, I can't imagine how rough it is to be one of those little fuckers." You should see the little fuckers in the ocean. I wish you could see them with my younger brother and his posse. He's such a good man. They are all good men. Cowabunga, dudes!

Perhaps not at all surprisingly, all the parentos have established quite the unique little friendship. Mike and Peter play backgammon online, Peter from either Greece or Toronto, wherever he and Kathryn are, and Mike from LA when he and Mom are not traveling. Kathryn and my mom Skype a couple times a week, both of them heavily involved with the new Peace movement, and both of them on the Board of Directors for Ricky Titus's non-profit agency in Oakland, and both of them absolutely still convinced that they can make this old world a better place (for their grandchildren, they say). Mike and Mom are better than ever. For them, the crisis really was an opportunity.

After sixty-plus years, Papou has finally returned to Greece. ("You wouldn't recognize the place!") And, if not forgotten, he has finally declared the war over with the Germanotsoliades who betrayed Panagiotis Mousalimas.

My new big brother, Nikko, America's Most Eligible Geek, now runs the Naxxos Foundation full-time which involves his favorite thing: figuring out how to give away scads of money to worthy people. His job necessitates a lot of travel in between Canada, California and Greece, so Bobby C. runs *"Alexi's"* as a full partner in Oakland so that Alexi can accompany Nikko whenever he wants to. They talk about marriage every once in a while but they say they won't do it until it's legal for everybody everywhere. (By the way, the Roberto Cisneros show, *"Hot Bobby"*, premieres in a month on the Food Network and in a certain "full circle" kind of way, the first episode was shot on location in my parents' kitchen in the Pacific Palisades. They cut a deal which involves handmade tamales – Abuela's recipe - once a month, shipped down overnight from the Bay Area – for life.)

Rule #100: If you pay any attention to anyone else when writing your first awesome novel, or if you let their rules dominate your story, you will never get anywhere. Write your own rules.

And now that brings us to me.

I am a writer.

Immediately after the epochal two days in Marin featuring my mother's disclosure and my introduction to my *real* father, I flew to New York to meet with my new publisher, Rhoda Weiner. We recognized each other instantly.

"Silver bracelet girl!" she said rising from behind an impressive oak desk. The Hudson River shimmered behind her.

"Southwest flight from Oakland!" I answered. Rhoda sat back and took her reading glasses off. "Tell me everything." She pointed a red-lacquered nail at the chair in front of her desk, she put her glasses back on and sat forward. It took a while. She took notes and did a lot of nodding.

"Okay, whew! So let me go over the basic facts. You fell in love with Mr. Perfect...Mr. I-give-girls-silver-charm-bracelets-at -the-drop-of-a-hat, who also happens to be America's Most Eligible medical tech genius, who has a heart of pure gold, and is also an heir to a vast international shipping fortune..." She looked up. I nodded. "But...he turned out to be your brother, but not your *real* brother, because he was adopted by *your* real father after his *real* father drowned at sea." I nodded again. Rhoda's pencil moved down the page of notes. "So... you actually *could* get married because you aren't related by blood, but that's not going to happen because he doesn't love you in the same way because he's in love with a Russian national named Alexi and, small but significant factoid – gay!" She peered over her glasses. I shrugged. " – And then you find out that the boy you loved in grad school, who also happens to be our Thadeus, who was a real weirdo, isn't all that weird when you factor in that he was raised in foster care by wolves who let him emancipate at age fifteen, and he's been carrying a torch all these long, lonely years, for you...have I got it correct so far?" I nodded. "To top all of this off you also had severe mommy issues because you and everyone else thought that your mother was a perfect human being whose perfection you could never live up to, but she turned out to have some massively ugly skeletons in her closet, including the fact that the guy that you *thought* was your father wasn't your father at all. He's Rose Fineman's real father." Rhoda turned the page. "Do I know Rose Fineman?"

"Probably not," I said.

"Do we like Rose Fineman?" Rhoda squinted.

"Probably not," I gestured maybe – maybe not.

"Ok, so anyway, your *real* father is your new brother's father, but not his *real* father, but he *is* your other brother's real father. I think I'm repeating myself." Rhoda looked triumphant. "Now, other than the previous generation's shenanigans – we'll get to that eventually – did I leave anything out? Is that everything?"

"Well, World War II and Viet Nam and Iraq..." I said.

"Oh, Pssssst!" Rhoda dismissed all three wars with a flip of her wrist. She threw her notes and her pencil onto the desk and adjusted her Rolex and tapped its face.

"We've got to wrap things up for now. I have another meeting. I'll be brief." She smiled. "Athena, this is a great fucking story but nobody's going to believe a single word of it. You'll have to call it fiction. Get crackin' on it right away. The anthology will launch in three months. I want a first draft of your novel in my hand before that."

My anthology, *The First Latina Rodeo Queen of Fremont, California* has been on the New York Times best seller list now for twenty-five months. The eponymous article nabbed me a Pulitzer before Rhoda published it. Maximizing the hype.

I learned from that first book that it actually *is* okay to write somebody else's story. (Just maybe not your mother's. Really anybody's story but your mother's.)

Burke's book, his first awesome novel, was everything they said it was going to be. Some even say it is our generation's quintessential anti-war volume. It is also still on the *New York Times'*

Best Seller List for fiction and soon to be a major motion picture. They are casting now. (*Mena Suvari for Kira, c'mon!*)

We decided to hold off on the wedding until after the baby comes and after the movie premieres, and before Burke's second book gets released. It will be a private affair. Just the family. Minimum hype.

Peripheral Characters:

Patricia Olivia Orloff's *99 Rules For Writing Your First Awesome Novel* was published last year by Rhoda Weiner's publishing imprint, Ambiguity Press. It's still an amazon.com sensation. Look for it.

Howie Falkenhorst will marry the Tribune newsroom clerk, my old *amiga*, Lupe, (*I know, right?! Did not see that coming.*) It will be a small, private ceremony in Baja, Mexico this month at the home of the bride's parents.

Nadia Pusenkoff is now a permanent sub in the strings section of the San Francisco Symphony. She has a green card. When not playing for Maestro, Nadia can be seen fiddling for the international gypsy punk band, *Quel Bordel*, all over the continental U.S. She teaches violin to a couple of Ricky Titus's kids in Oakland when she's in town.

Sadly, Jerald Franklin terHorst passed away on March 31, 2010 of congestive heart failure *(a broken heart?)* at the age of 87. Mr. terHorst's final book, *The Flying White House,* currently ranks 520,194 on amazon.com.

America's Most Eligible

America is still at war and sadly, tragically, the future looks extremely bright, as bright as ever, for the U.S. Military Industrial Complex.

Security Ronald works for Google.

And that's pretty much the end. For now anyway.

CPSIA information can be obtained
at www.ICGtesting.com
Printed in the USA
FSOW03n0140190515
7184FS

9 780983 154457